DAD'S NUKE

MARC LAIDLAW

DAD'S NUKE

A Critic's Choice paperback
from Lorevan Publishing, Inc.
New York, New York

Reprinted by arrangement with Donald I. Fine, Inc.

ISBN: 1-55547-147-1

First Critic's Choice edition: 1987

From LOREVAN PUBLISHING, INC.

Critic's Choice Paperbacks
31 E. 28th St.
New York, New York 10016

Manufactured in the United States of America

FOR
GERALDINE
On All Fool's Day,
1985

From:
FAMILY HEAD—THE JOHNSONS
For Intra-Family Use Only
Re: *F.N.S. May 1998 Fuel Demand Forecast*

June 18, 1998

FAMILY MEMBERS:

The Family/Neighbor Solidarity (FNS) Fuel Demand Committee, consisting of parents in the Laurel Woods and Cobblestone Hill residential compounds, recently released its biennial May 1998 gas demand projections. The end results are very similar to the Johnson family's own forecasts.

An overall fuel demand growth rate of 1.5 percent is forecast for the 1999 through 2020 period. The Johnson family forecasts a 1.3 percent rate over the 1999 through 2020 period. FNS's baseline forecast, by way of contrast, projects a 0.7 percent growth rate. Many of the underlying assumptions of the FNS and Johnson forecasts are similar.

- The only significant increases above 1998 levels are projected in the educational and entertainment areas. In these areas, cogeneration is expected to have slight potential for new load. Positive growth results from the introduction of nuclear technology in some nontraditional uses such as procreation. Much of the remaining increase is a recovery of load from the recession and unfavorable oil/gas price ratios.

- Residential demand is not projected to grow because increases in number of family members are offset by conservation.

- Electric generation growth is also stagnant since nuclear power is projected to replace baseload oil and gas units, this load being only partially replaced by combined-cycle units. The Johnson's use of natural gas is expected to decrease until 2010 due to the installation of garage-based nuclear units. After 2010, extension of service lives allows generation load to recover, but not to earlier levels.

All the forecasts discussed show the importance of nuclear purchasing, new nuclear generation technologies to recover lost electric generation load, a favorable oil-to-gas price ratio achieved through rate design to recover neighborhood boiler load, cogeneration supply absorption, and new applications for fuel. Even so, total Johnson load in 2020 will barely exceed 1998 levels, despite projected enhanced recovery of sales. There is great potential for profit, however, in the sale of excess nuclear-generated energy to the Cartel.

WM. D. "DAD" JOHNSON

WDJ (x3397):pjj
cc: C.R. Johnson
    V.L. Johnson
    P.J. Johnson
    N.J. Johnson
    L.B. Johnson (1 & 2)
    S.T. Johnson
    W.D. Johnson, Jr.

THE BEST DEFENSE

IT WAS A DAY ripe for the picking. Skin would tan and hair would bleach, for the fog had burned away early that morning and might not come back again—ever. That was how Dad felt. From the summit of Cobblestone Hill, looking down Arch Street between the orderly diagram of lawns and sidewalks and kicked kickballs and regular dogs sitting like ornaments and kids of various sizes and shapes (though all styled alike) and especially the pleasingly similar houses, he could see the ocean. Green and gray, glassy, it seemed to come right up to the hillside and stop at the westernmost of the lawns. The fact that its upper limit, the horizon, was an almost perfectly straight line was to him a source of real satisfaction. The few fluffy, shimmery clouds kept above that line, as if the sea were off-limits, and there weren't enough of the fleecy things to pose any kind of threat; they weren't about to band together and form a fog bank. They were independent, like Dad. Floaters. Just hanging out, waiting to see what they could get away with. Maybe they were goners, but not Dad. Today he knew for sure that he could get away with anything. By the time the sun had set, Dad would have made some kind of conquest. Yep. He had high hopes. He could already hear the snickers of the victory parade, though it might be a parade of one or two and it would only lead across the street between Jock Smith's house and Dad's house. And it might be more like a sprint than a leisurely parade. Smith would be pissed at Dad. That was as certain as the death of those clouds in the heat of the day.

Damn those clouds anyway. There were more of them now. Dad didn't want to stand around and watch his morning get spoiled, so he went back inside.

Sensing his resident's I.D.-implant, the gates opened automatically for him, a series of micro-thin tungsten-alloy lamellas sliding into the juniper bushes one after the other until he came to the welcome mat. At the door, even Dad had to prove who he was by means of voice-pattern recognitions—a coy good morning conversation with the sentry-comp—and a discreet minty tongue print. Fingerprints could be altered, but no one was going to mess around surgically with his tongue just to break into the Johnson house; Dad didn't have much worth stealing, when you got right down to it, except for his state-of-the-art security and defense systems. It looked like Wolfie had been at the kids' tongue touch-pad, lower on the wall—not that the twins minded.

Wow! The smell of breakfast came at him like some kind of burglar-repellent through the opening door, borne on a current of soiled diapers, dog musk, unrecycled trash. He almost turned and went back out, but then his nose got past the smells that were fixtures and singled out the transitory odor of bacon and buttered toast and scrambled eggs. That, he thought, is more like it.

"Get it while it's hot," called Connie Johnson, more widely known as Mom, from the kitchen. "Bill, is that you?"

"No," he said softly, "it's Jock Smith come right through your intruder-ionizing perimeter and over your welcome mat, hoping for a look at tender little Stephanie in her bath, or maybe a roll in the shag with Lyndon Baines and Lady Bird, one at either end."

10

She couldn't hear him, of course, even as he crept toward the kitchen through the livingroom's tumble of toys and clothes and broken Etch-A-Sketches. For Jock to have secretly penetrated Dad's defenses and seduced the twins into illicit gymnastics, he would have to be smarter and even more depraved than he looked. This was Dad's worst fear, which he fed daily on a diet of rumor and suspicion. He had considered sending his highly developed fantasies of Smith's obscene proclivities—signed "Anonymous" —to the *Leaf and Cobble Neighborhood News,* but a nagging fear of incrimination had dissuaded him. There was something of a romance between his own Nancy June and the carbuncular Arnold Smith, the Romeo-and-Juliet aspects of which had not escaped him. Eventually he counted upon Nancy to spy upon the elder Smith in his own household.

His first sight of the breakfast table, hard-won considering the obstacles of grape juice puddles and teflex street-skates, hardly seemed worth it. A battle had been fought there with forks and knives and bared teeth. He felt like a scavenger loping into no man's land, nothing left but a few half-eaten remains, and Wolfie was already getting to those. The children, except for Steph and William D. Jr. in facing highchairs, had been and gone; thus the unaccustomed silence.

But Connie, dear heart, had at least saved something for him. She tore the cover from the insta-serve and handed him the steaming plate.

"That's my girl," he said.

She gave him a Sungleam smile, one she had picked up from the pictures of model housewives he had liked so much on the boxes of Sungleam appliances. How quickly they learn, he thought now. After seven kids and another on the way, she's finally getting the hang of it.

"Were you rototilling?" she asked. He didn't think she knew what the word meant, but she liked it and kept repeating it. Everytime he got off work, she asked if he'd been rototilling.

"No, nothing like that," he said. "Just checking on our neighbors. I don't see that Smith has anything to get excited about,

11

judging from his front yard. Same old muzzles under the eaves. His paint's peeling though." He laughed aloud at that. "Weatherproof, my ass. I told him when he put it on last year there's no such thing as weatherproof. Weather gets through no matter what you do."

"The launcher is in his backyard," Connie said.

"Huh?"

She turned away to the sink, ran blue water from the disposal tap, and watched the silver insta-serve trays dissolve in her hands beneath the flow. "I had coffee with Doris the other day and—"

He choked on a little ball of scrambled egg. "Coffee with Doris Smith? In her house? You go over there alone?"

"Sometimes. When Jock's on work," she said. "I saw it in the back—"

"You don't take the kids over there, do you? Stephanie or the twins?"

"What does it matter? Of course I take them." She turned off the water, dried her hands, and yelled at Wolfie to get off the table. "I knew you'd get all worked up about it; honestly, I wasn't going to say anything, but I thought you might want to know about the launcher."

Dad's imagination was too vivid to let him speak for a moment. He saw Jock Smith coming off work, pulling his hands from the sensi-gloves, peeling the psycho-pad from his brow and eyes and spotting helpless little William D. Jr. sitting on a counter somewhere or eating dice in a corner; saw the slow, wicked smile on the swarthy cratered face; saw him come toward the stupid-faced baby with a decidedly lecherous look in his dilated pupils.

"It was covered with a tarp," Connie said, "but I don't know. It looked pretty big to me."

"It's kit-built," Dad said, and slammed his hand down on the countertop. Wm. D. Jr. made a startled noise and something dribbled from the highchair onto the synoleum. "Nothing that Jock Smith put together from a kit is going to change the balance of power in my neighborhood."

Connie didn't say anything. Her head was in the wall unit, like

12

something to be baked. She came out with a child's chartreuse tennis shoe.

"How did this get in here?"

"I'm telling you, Connie, I'm not afraid of any kit. It's got to have a weak point. The missile itself may be a tough piece of hardware, but I'll bet the console's fragile. No one ever thinks to protect the controls. You might be surprised to hear—"

"I wouldn't be surprised by anything you told me, Bill. All I know is that Doris said the missiles were in the garage in several pieces because they were too big to fit any other way, and that launcher was enormous. You could tell that even under the tarp."

"Tarps make anything look enormous to you," he said, the definitive quality of his statement putting an end to the conversation.

Connie sighed and unstrapped Stephanie from her chair. She leashed the toddler to the counter, watched for a moment as she weaved slightly from her breakfast soporifics, then took a mop to the varicolored mess under Wm. D. Jr.'s chair.

Wm. D. Sr. was upset for a number of reasons. Those clouds had come in all right, and it looked like something worse than afternoon fog. It looked like rain.

"A kit!" he said, and slammed his hand, and the insta-serve platter, and everything down in the middle of the kitchen table. Junior screamed, blanching, and shuddered so hard that his high-chair shook.

"Don't scare him, Bill," said Connie. "It makes him wet."

Dad listened to the liquid raining on the kitchen floor, then looked at his youngest son—the squashed, mongoloid features. He began to smile as an idea took root.

That fogbank of gloom didn't stand a chance. It might take some doing, but Dad had his secret weapon.

When he came downstairs an hour later, snapping his infrascan binoculars into the case, Connie was still in the kitchen.

"I'm making my famous oriental fried noodles," she said.

"Oh?"

"I don't know what it is about potlucks, Bill. They're a little scary. Maybe it's because no one dares bring insta-serves. I know a few of the girls are good cooks, Doris for instance, and they can make what they buy at the supermarket taste like real food. But there are some women—oh my. I think when they get inside the super they panic and buy whatever's near the door, so they can get away. And then when they cook. . . I don't think they know what smoke means; they can't taste the difference between bread pudding and burnt pudding. And they don't know how to season. Do you remember Mrs. Baker's lemon-frosted Bundt cake with the hot green chili stuffing? The best I can ever think of to say at these things is that it tastes just like insta-serves, but that's usually a lie. It's a good thing Elaine Wesson can cook; I'd hate to think of Virgil marrying someone who couldn't."

Dad stared at her for a good long time. This was her equivalent of rototilling. What the hell was she talking about?

She gave the dish a final toss, the better to mix the crispy noodles with the creamed corn and garbanzo beans.

"You sure that's the right recipe?" Dad asked. "I don't remember it looking like that when your sorority mother made it."

"That was twelve years ago, Bill. Recipes change."

Twelve years was a long time, he thought. Time enough to raise a twenty-three-year-old son—Virgil Lamarck—and a string of others. Number eight, Erica Valentine Johnson, was due in two weeks, though you wouldn't have guessed it by looking at Connie. These days it was hard to tell anything much by looking at her; each morning she arranged her expression by shifting the mortice joints of her high, inlaid cheekbones, after a night of sleeping on her belly had crumpled her face. At the moment she looked aloof, pleased with herself. It was an easy pregnancy, as they all were now. Erica Valentine Johnson was halfway across the neighborhood, fleshing out nicely in the time-bake oven, in line with Dad's innovative specifications.

Connie checked the kitchen clock, put a lid on the casserole, and yelled at the thunder upstairs, where their children were supposed to be getting ready.

The twins came down first and hurried to swing from Dad's hands and legs.

He said, "I took a look over ol' Smith's roof and didn't see anything more dangerous than a robin's nest over there." He shook the twins from him and handed P.J. the binoculars as he hit the bottom of the stairs. "Run these back up to my office, would you, Peej?"

P.J., almost eighteen now, twitched a wan lip and almost said something to his father—some typically rebellious, late-adolescent thing—but then he seemed to think twice and suppress it. So, he was coming out of *that* phase; and about time. Dad winked at Connie as P.J., doing what he was told for a change, ran back upstairs.

"Well," she said, "you believe what you like about the launcher, Bill. You'll see it soon enough. It's lying down probably."

"That just shows what you know about missile launchers," he said. He rubbed his hands together and beamed down at Wm. D. Jr. "Come on, let's keep this show moving. I'm, uh, anxious to congratulate Jock."

As usual, they seemed to advance in slow motion in spite of the frenzy of activity in the house: the twins vibrated rapidly from wall to wall; tall, thin Virgil waded with dignity through the sea of smaller bodies, a sweater about his shoulders, untouched by the chaos and also contributing nothing to their progress; Nancy June screamed at the other children, except for Wm. D. Jr., because she didn't want to clean up his mess. P.J. was upstairs until almost the last minute fetching things for his father: a windbreaker, a pinochle deck, antacid mints.

"Are we all ready?" Dad called.

There was general agreement from those able to give it. Connie slipped Stephanie's leash around her wrist and picked up the casserole and then Junior; no one could keep Wolfie from following them out the front door. When they were outside, Connie gasped.

"This is the first sun I've felt in a week," she said. "It feels like a blessing. You know, Bill, after all the work I do, I'm going to enjoy myself. It's been so long since I've seen any of the other wives, except Doris. I was thinking . . . I might even get drunk, if that's what it takes. Nobody's going to spoil my afternoon, I'm determined. I am going to have fun."

Dad smiled, feeling a little sorry for her. Good luck, he thought.

With a twin seemingly surgically affixed to either hand, he took his first step across the safety of his front lawn and led his family into the street.

Bring on the bombs, Smith, he thought. Bring 'em on. Built 'em with your own hands, did you? Well, it looks it, old boy, it looks it.

The Smith's house looked much like the Johnson's—almost too much, he found himself thinking, which was a disturbing way of looking at it when he could appreciate the symmetry of repetition in every other house along the streets of Cobblestone Hill. Of course, Smith's paint was peeling; it was tan, like the paint on the other houses, but it was of cheaper grade. And Smith had never managed to disguise his artillery nearly so neatly as Dad had done. Here and there, among the flowers in their beds, one could see the obviously fake lawn-lamps with their vari-directional nozzles for swift sprinkling of explosive pellets. Underslung like wasps' nests beneath the second-story eaves, cameras and laser barrels winked at the Johnsons as they came up the brick-lined walkway to the practically naked front door. There was nothing to stop you from getting to the door, no alloy plates. Smith had tried installing them last summer, and had nearly ruined the front of his house in the attempt.

Dad laughed, remembering the whole affair.

By the time they reached the front door, he could see that it was unlocked. That didn't surprise him. Pretending that he was an uninvited assassin, he slipped over the threshold, whispering at the twins to be silent, and they glided down the hall toward the sound of voices at the back of the house.

Dad stopped and let the kids slip past him. "You all go on out there now, act normal, mix with 'em."

"Sure, dad," said P.J.

"Why wouldn't we?" said Virgil.

As Connie squeezed past him, he said, "Here, hon, let me help you with Junior."

She handed the baby to him gratefully, but the leash slipped down her arm and she almost lost Stephanie. "Oh, no, she's waking up." The toddler strained down the hall, pulling her mother along, almost snapping the leash. "Nancy, did you bring her pills like I asked you?"

Dad watched them turn the corner at the end of the hall, then he whinnied gently, so as not to frighten Junior, and walked quietly toward the livingroom. It was dark, silent, clean of toys, but light streamed from the bar in the next room, and the patio beyond. He heard the Smiths and their guests welcoming the incomplete Johnson family into the backyard, and P.J. said loudly, "Holy cow! Is that it?"

Dad was a little unnerved by that, as P.J. was a hard one to impress. But then it was probably still under the tarp, and things under tarps looked impressive to teenagers.

He walked quietly to the division of the bar and livingroom, hoping for a quick look through the back window at the patio, the better to map things out; but Smith had adjusted his Levelor blinds so that while plenty of light came in from above, there was no view. He was standing there, unsure of his next move, Junior drooling on his shoulder, when he heard a soft squeak of deck shoes and that voice—that hateful voice—the voice that could belong to none other than Jock Smith himself.

Dad turned around slowly, with a painful smile, and found himself facing a silhouette.

"Hiya, Bill," said Smith, coming forward into the light with his hand held out as if to snatch Junior away. Smith looked so normal that for a moment Dad wondered why he disliked him so much. That's part of his danger, he reminded himself. Such a normal-looking character, insidious. The kind who'd sneak up on your wife, or she upon him, and at the last instant—as he entered her, for instance—he would molt: in one shuddering shrug all that normalcy would slough away around his feet, revealing some un-imaginable fiend.

He was all surface, Jock Smith. Dad prided himself on the fact that he was normal to the marrow. Normal height, blood type, shoe size, aspirations, income, everything. That was why he would triumph.

"Hey, Jock, old boy," he said, and slapped Jock's shoulder, jiggling his highball glass so that it slopped.

'Glad you could make it, would you like a drink?" Jock's voice was high, a little manic. "I guess so if you're looking for the bar. I moved everything out onto the patio where we could get at it. Come on out, Bill, I want you to see my baby."

Smith turned and walked back the way he had come, and as Bill followed, hanging behind a few feet, he mumbled for Junior's ears only, "His baby, did you hear that? His baby is a ground-to-air missile. It makes you wonder about his kids."

"What was that?" Jock said, rounding on him suddenly in the hall.

"Oh, nothing, just talking to Junior here, baby talk like he understands. Goo-goo, Junior. Goo-goo ga-ga."

"Well, Bill Johnson," said a woman's voice, "I do believe that's the cleverest thing I've ever heard you say."

Dad smiled so hard that his eyes closed, and when he opened them, reluctantly, it was to see Doris Smith giving him that kooky grin she had. Crooked teeth, which Jock had apparently never offered to have fixed, made her mouth look like a kid's drawing of "Mommy."

He shoved past her, calling for Connie at the top of his voice, and stumbled right out through the sliding glass door and onto the crowded patio. In his haste to avoid conversation with Doris, he was completely unprepared for his first sight of the thing beneath the tarp.

"Holy shit!" he said, and almost dropped Wm. D. Jr.

The object, of which only the lower parts—truck tires and hydraulic legs—were visible, took up virtually all of Smith's back-yard, excluding the cement patio where the guests were standing, staring. Seeing their slack-jawed expressions, Dad knew that he had blown it. With all his plans of coming in coolly, surveying the kit, and shrugging it off, he had relaxed his guard for an instant and given Smith the pleasure of seeing him caught by surprise, like every other dumb animal at the potluck. Dad swore it would never happen again, and that he would make up for it this very afternoon.

"It's something, isn't it?" said Marv Coolidge, Dad's gullible co-worker. Marv limped toward him and offered him a drink.

"It's something, all right," Dad said, recovering his composure now. Out of the corner of his eye he caught Smith watching him, so he smiled and raised his glass in a sardonic toast. "Nice work, Jock."

Smith's head bobbed. He stood with one arm on an electronic cabinet and console, the whole set-up in the shade under a big yellow lawn umbrella. Dad could hear a fan whirring in the cabinet; there were vents all along the back and a ventilation grill on top, and wires running everywhere. It was a vulnerable-looking system, considering the size of the launcher.

Dad thought he was ready to look at the launcher again. He wasn't going to freak out this time. After all, it was under a tarp; there was no telling how big it really was.

But it wasn't a tarp, it was a parachute, and covered or not, it took up the whole lawn, reaching from corner to corner; the swing set and jungle gym had been forced back into the banana plants. The undercarriage alone looked like it could have supported a house.

"I told you it was lying down," Connie said in his ear.

"Lying down?" he said, tearing his eyes from the thing. "And I told you, you don't know the first thing about ground-to-air missile launchers. Something that big doesn't lie down—"

"Oh, but it does, Bill."

He turned around. Doris again. Smith's cockamamie wife looked cross-eyed; no doubt she'd had a few too many. That was why she thought a launcher could lie down.

"It lifts up for launching," she said. "You'll see, Bill." She turned toward her husband. "Jock, don't you think it's about time?"

"Well, I guess," he said, obviously relishing the suspense. Everyone was gesturing at the thing, some were trying to lift the parachute for glimpses.

Smith called his kids together and directed them to take the edges of the parachute. Nancy June helped Arnold with his share. Dad moved back from the unveiling, into the shade of the yellow umbrella, and set Wm. D. Jr. down on top of the control cabinet, next to the console keyboard. Junior laughed at the breeze that came up from the vents.

"Thataboy," Dad said.

Everyone else said, "Hey!"

Dad took a slow, restrained look at the now naked giant.

The launcher itself was insignificant by comparison to what lay upon it: a long tapered cylinder, two meters in diameter at the fat end, with a white body, a red payload cap, and three thin silver fins running a quarter of its length.

"Watcha got in there, Jocko?" somebody wanted to know, a dip from Smith's office, no doubt. "That's not a nuke warhead, is it?"

"Nah," Smith said. "Didn't want to waste explosives on a demonstration."

"A demo?" Marv said. "You're gonna show us this thing in action? Well, come on, Jock, hop to it."

Doris sidled toward Dad and said, "Now you can see it really stand up."

He flinched from her voice and unpleasant memories. That nutty smile, those goofy eyes, her laughter cutting him in bed.

"You're sweet, Doris," he said, covering Junior's ears. "Really sweet."

"I'm so glad you care, Bill."

What had he ever seen in her? It must have been the thrill of his first affair. She went away to gloat with the other wives as her old man sauntered over to the console and pulled up a lawn chair.

"Speech!" someone yelled. "Let's make this a real inauguration."

"God, no," Dad said.

Jock looked at him, uncomprehending, then turned back to the crowd of admirers.

"Thanks, thank you, everybody." They quieted, beaming at him, drinks in hand; the biggest smiles went along with the biggest glasses. "We, uh, we stand on the brink of a new age in community defense."

"Hear, hear!"

"My missile may be the first in this neighborhood, but it will almost certainly not be the last. I hope that we can all build our solidarity and protect our independence as a residential compound by solid investments in affordable defensive technology. When those planes come circling overhead and the ships come in from the West to soil our pure beaches, why neighbors, we've got to be ready to blast them out of the sky and sink them under the waves."

"You tell it, Jock!"

"When those subverts come knocking at our walls for free handouts or building permits, we've got to show 'em the barrels of our guns before we show 'em the door. What I'm talking about is protecting our investments, ladies and gentlemen, making our homes safe for our children and our children's children and so forth. We must make our part of America, no matter how small, the strongest part. Let us join together in friendship and trust, with a true community spirit, and keep the others out."

Dad found the applause unbelievable. First of all, it was practically the same speech Dad had given at the last Compound meeting. Secondly, all the talk about defense against external threats was just so much bullshit: the real threat came from within the community, from men like Smith himself. Dad knew that this was Smith's real game. That missile wasn't intended for any low-flying bomber or off-course Jap shrimp-boat: it was meant to fly the width of Arch Street, from Smith's house to Dad's house, and the explosion would be just big enough to reduce the latter from a two-story manor to a subsurface crater without more than superficial damage to the paint on Smith's house. That was Smith's whole idea.

Dad stood aside as Jock came back to his lawn chair and started running routines on the console keyboard. He gave Junior a salted peanut to play with.

"Don't lean on that, Bill, please," Jock said.

Dad stood back from the cabinet, spreading his arms and his smile. "You want me to take Junior down? He's put on weight."

Jock just chuckled, shaking his head. Dad could see him feeling sorry for the little retard. Wait a few minutes, he thought.

Dad heard a buzz and turned to look at the launcher. It was standing up, like Doris had said. The missile lifted its red bulbous nose to the sky, the fuel nozzles tipped toward the lawn sprinklers. P.J. pulled Wolfie away. The heads of spectators fell back as the missile stood taller and taller. It rose until its payload shell was higher than the orange tree, higher even than the rooster weathervane on Smith's roof.

Dad swallowed. You wouldn't even have to put explosives in that thing to ruin a house: just drop it from a height and it would make quite an impression wherever it hit.

"Arnold," Jock said, "you want to turn on your shield?"

"Sure, Dad," Arnold said, running onto the grass. He had something like a remote control box in his hand, and he went to every corner of the lawn checking little bulb-studded stakes against some meter on the box. Dad heard him explaining to one of the other kids that this was a prototype model wave-field shield of his own design, something he'd come up with in school, whose practical aspects for the community should be obvious: it would make regular walls obsolete. That Arnold was a clever kid.

"Get back on the cement," Arnold said. "If you're caught in the shield it'll chop you in half."

Everyone stepped back. Arnold flipped a toggle. The air in the yard seemed to catch and hold, forming a flat screen, then a box that enclosed the grassy area. It rolled a bit, as if the vertical hold were out of synch, but Arnold adjusted it until it held steady.

Arnold had found an audience in Nancy June, and he went on regaling her with descriptions of his invention while she nodded politely. "The best thing about this shield is that it powers itself with the energy of the blast. It's exactly as strong as it has to be."

Most of the crowd was more interested in the missile than the shield, however. Its head poked over the top of the shimmering walls, raring to go.

All this, in a way, Dad had been counting on. He had suspected that a simple unveiling of the long-touted missile would not be enough, that a launching was inevitable. But as he had expected all along, it would be possible to steal the show. The sheer size of the thing, that had thrown him for a second; but with tiny things, like the chips in the control system, he was on familiar ground. He patted Junior on the head, beamed happily down at Jock Smith as the other's fingers roamed over the keyboard, inputting final coordinates and configurations.

"Okay," Smith said, "there's going to be a little light and noise. We'll see it go straight into the ocean."

He made the last entry with his pinky.

Light and noise was the least of it. Sight failed, eardrums temporarily ceased to thrum, people staggered sideways. Dad held onto Junior, laughing at the top of his lungs, aware that his youngest son was bawling and, no doubt, other things.

It was as he had hoped. If the sound of a raised voice was enough to trigger Junior's discharge, the effect of this blast must have been enormous.

He scooped up the child, felt the spatter of warm urine tossed back by the fan in the console, smelled ozone, and caught a whiff of burning. But the missile, inside the transparent cage that held its fires and fumes imprisoned, was making quite a stink itself, and Junior's little mess, like Dad's disappearance, was hardly noticed.

Swiftly down the hall with Wolfie at his heels, out the front door, across the street, through the sliding panels, a quick lick of mint, then up the stairs and into his office: Dad had the blinds thrown up and the binoculars pulled out in half a second, his triumphant hoots of laughter echoing out the window and onto the street where now he heard shouting, even screams, though they were not as loud as Junior whining in the lounge chair. People ran over Smith's lawn, looking not toward the sea but to the south, their eyes and fingers still aimed high, but then quite suddenly dropping straight down and catching Dad in the window. Doris yelled . . .

He ducked from the window, ran down the hall into Virgil's room, and raised his binoculars to examine the southern view. There were the hills of Laurel Woods, green in early summer, the thin black walls around them, and there the emerald expanse of the golf course on rolling mounds and cliffs above the sea. Many a day he had strolled through there, teaching Virgil the sport, taking springy steps on the soft grass, wading into the shallow pond after balls caught in the sand trap below the pine and eucalyptus grove.

And now into his memories, soaring down at a dreamy angle, came a flashing arrow of white and silver, the tiniest blur of red at its tip. The pennants at the sixteenth hole, the sand trap, flapped in the sea breeze. There were no clouds, no threat of fog. There was only the sleek missile sliding in across the blue.

Then the explosion of earth, green and brown flying everywhere, a few little men running, the edge of the cliff sheared into the sea.

Hole in one.

Dad stood up, tucking the binoculars back in their case. Downstairs he heard the steel panels sliding shut, protecting his family as they ran into the house. He was safe and secure. No one could even get to his door to knock upon it. Just let them try. They all knew what kind of defenses he had put into his home, his castle.

Connie came to the doorway, panting, weeping. "What have you done to us, Bill? What have you done?"

"There, there," he said, putting a strong arm around her. "My nose is clean. It's Junior they'll be wanting."

2

HOME
MOVIES

DEAR DAD:

The time has come to tell you what I

No, that wasn't it at all.
Peter John Johnson cleared the screen he was working on and tried again.

Dear Dad:

The thing is, Dad, that you are an asshole—an unmitigated, uncompromising asshole. If you could hear half the things the people in Cobblestone Hill say about you, you would probably sh

Footsteps sounded on the stairs, approaching the door to the study. P.J. cleared the screen again and turned on a recording that no voice-recognition computer could transform into readable prose. Wm. D. Johnson spoke intermittently, between snorts and pauses:

"Now I'm sure really—uh, I do feel godawful about the—well, damn, the golf course getting wrecked up, sure. Who'd have thought it would land there, of all places? I didn't think it would get off the ground once, uh, the-the-the—oh, the hell with it. I didn't do anything and my kid didn't do anything. It's a mistake anyone could make. That suspicious bastard Smith is making a big deal out of—"

The footsteps, heavy and easily identifiable, stopped in the hall, and P.J. heard the door swing open, brushing the shag. He swiftly went on with his transcription, which read:

GENTLEMEN OF THE WHELK LODGE COUNCIL:

I offer my heartfelt apologies for any inconvenience that may have resulted from the accident that occurred last week, and which Mr. Jock Smith claims was deliberate sabotage to himself and the Laurel Woods golf course. Also, allow me to convey herein the apologies of my son, William D. Johnson, Jr., who is unable to express his own dismay at this unfortunate turn of events. I am sure you can understand the displeasure of a father who, after months of patient endeavor, discovers at an inopportune moment the inability of his own flesh and blood to absorb and retain the basic lessons of sanitary propriety. Yet he is young, and there is still hope for

"How's it going, kiddo?" said Dad, putting a hand on his shoulder.

Oh, P.J. thought, my friends aren't allowed to see me; I'm low on Vitamin K because you've always got me in here typing up your stupid memos; I'd be afraid to go outside anyway because Mr. Smith is crazy and he'd like to get ahold of one of us; and I wish I could pull your half of my genes out of my cells and go on without them so that maybe I could get something done besides coming up with ways of killing myself.

"Okay," P.J. said, shrugging. "I think I've come up with a good apology."

The hand dropped from his shoulder.

"Good, good, glad to hear it. Don't worry, though; they'll never call me on the carpet. I've been a Whelk too long. More likely they'll be putting me on the Council."

Dad seemed nervous. He cleared his throat, coughed into his fist. "Hey, I see your typing is improving. That's damn good; it's really important. You've got to get in there and build those skills right into the old reflexes, the muscle and marrow, right smack into the DNA, so that you don't have to think about it. You've got to have perfect accuracy, Peej. Keep your wrists straight, don't let 'em hang like that. Well . . . I guess it's okay if they hang."

"I know, dad."

Dad warmed to his pep talk. "You've got to have perfect accuracy and you've got to type at least 110 words a minute, not counting glossary strings. You've got to have it all down, kid, and you have to get it while you're young. Then . . . *then* you can really go somewhere. When you've got all that you'll be able to slip into the gloves and really move. The sooner you go, the farther you'll go faster. By the time you're ready for a job, boy, you've got to be flying."

"You wanted this letter out by three o'clock, Dad."

"Oh, did I? Did I say that? Well, say, Peej, store what you've got and let it cool for awhile. I, uh, your mother and I want to have a word with you."

Oh great, he thought.

He stored the screenload, stood up, and looked at Dad standing profiled in the doorway, the increasingly bloated yet flaccid belly blocking any possibility of escape. When Dad saw that he was coming, he turned away and went down the hall toward his office. Dad held the door open for him.

"Hi, Mom," P.J. said.

She sat on the black leather accessory footstool that accompanied Dad's lounge chair. Her smile was compressed, and there was something in her eyes—some emotion or concern—that overpowered the anger she'd been holding there all week since the potluck disaster. She looked nervous, intense.

Dad sat down in his lounger, almost hidden from view behind the desk console. His dark eyes fixed on P.J. as he said, "Have a seat, son."

"Thanks." P.J. pulled up a chair at the corner of the desk, so that he could see both of them. His mother reached out and patted his knee.

"Peter," she said.

"Son," Dad said at the same time.

They looked at each other, and Dad deferred to her with a little nod. By the time she looked back at him, he felt claustrophobic, despite her reassuring smile.

"Peter, we love you very much," she said. "You're very special to both of us."

"I love you, too, Mom," he said with a quaver in his voice that wasn't there when he finally said, "And Dad."

"And we've always had your best interest at heart, that you be happy with us, that you be glad to be part of the family."

"Sure, Mom," he said, his throat suddenly dry. "I'm glad."

She smiled and sat up; she had been leaning ever closer to him, as had Dad. Dad was now hunched forward like Rodin's *Thinker*, peering up at P.J. through bushy eyebrows, his hand over his mouth as if suppressing a burp. Seeing P.J. look at him, he nodded and tipped his head back to Mom.

"Planning our family to be the right sort of family was something we took very seriously when we were younger," she said, "and now we're seeing the—uh, results of all that. Each of you is very special, and you all have a place here that no one else has, and it's that unity of difference that makes us such a special family. If it were any different, it wouldn't be the same."

P.J. had to agree with that.

"I know what you mean, Mom. Our personalities and everything, the way we interact, they all balance out. If one of us were gone, we wouldn't be so balanced."

"We wouldn't be a unit," Dad said forcefully, and then settled down again.

P.J. went on cautiously, to show them that he was following:

"Virgil is sort of the scholarly type with all his Greek poetry and stuff, and he'll grow up to be a real model citizen, and Nancy is kind of more rambunctious but in a healthy way, and we need both these kinds of people in our family. And you're real support-ive and nurturing and Dad is, well, Dad. And the twins are like some kind of fountainhead, I guess, just pure energy. It's harder to tell with Stephanie and Junior, they're still so little, but I guess Junior being retarded and kind of ugly also balances things out because we're all pretty perfect, mentally and physically. And me . . ."

"Yes," Mom said. "You. P.J., uh, what we meant to tell you, is." She took a breath, looked away, then summoned up some strength and looked him in the eyes. "P.J., you're gay."

That's not true, he thought. Maybe I was happy a week ago, but it's been bleak since then. He couldn't just say that, though. They wouldn't understand. So he smiled as best he could.

"That's the way we arranged it," she said after an awkward minute. "Genetically, we did what we could. There was some use of infantile conditioning, sublims in your bassinet, just to make sure it would be expressed. But we were sure all along that we wanted you to be gay. Studies show it's best for a large family; it balances things out, smooths the edges, rounds the corners."

"What?" P.J. said. "I—you genetailored me to be happy? Well I hate to tell you, but I don't think it worked very well."

Awkwardness crackled through the air. Dad cleared his throat, tried on an ill-fitting smile, exchanged it for a solemn pucker. Mom sighed.

"You wouldn't know that use of the word, would you?" she said. "It's nothing you hear around here. What your father and I are trying to say is, you are homosexual, Peter. Attracted to your own sex in a sexual way."

Dad sat up suddenly, as if he couldn't take any more pussyfoot-ing. "You're a queer, Peter. A fag. A fruit."

P.J.'s mouth worked incompletely: "I'm a . . . I'm a . . ."

"A *homo*, P.J., you got that?" Dad roared the word, then

fell back in his chair, drained, pressing the heel of his hand to his brow. "I'm sorry. I didn't want to make this any harder on you."

"Oh, dear," said Mom. "Dear Peter. We hope you understand, and that you'll accept yourself for what you are."

"A mincing little queen," Dad mumbled, staring into a corner of the room.

"Your father's had a little trouble getting used to the idea," Mom said.

P.J. rose slowly from his chair, his face on fire, feeling worse than he would have if his hair had stood on end and exploded into wisps of smoke. He could find no words to express what he felt. He had stumbled—no, been pushed—into a yawning pit, and as far as he could tell it had no bottom.

"You can go back to that memo now," Dad said. "That's all we had to say."

P.J. felt the rush of tears, but he couldn't believe they were coming from his eyes. Not him, not him.

"Don't take it so hard," Dad said. "It's not like you're missing out on anything."

"Bill!" said Mom.

P.J. shook his head, his voice trapped in the swiftly closing vise of his throat: "How could you?" he shouted at them. "How could you have done this to me?"

"Jesus Christ," said Dad. "The doc said we had to."

P.J. flung himself out of the room, nearly fell down the stairs, and ran for the door. He was hardly outside when he remembered where he was, and what woke him was the first warning *pung!* of gunfire against the receding tungsten plates.

Across the street, in a second-story window, he saw Mr. Smith with a handheld rifle trained on him.

"Go on," P.J. shouted. "Put me out of my misery."

And with a final scream, imagining his body riddled with bullets that were less hot than his shame, he fell in a heap to the lawn.

The sprinklers when they went on were a cool balm.

From the
LEAF AND COBBLE ONLINE TV GUIDE
Screen 451, Monday, Daytime Programming:
10:00 AM

NETWORK LISTINGS:

02 General Education: Today the General takes viewers to the Jap
    /Arab border in Central Pennsylvania.
05 Cleaning Your Automat Kitchen
09 Whiling Away the Time: Using an electronic level to check door-
    jambs; what to do with those old kitchen drawers; pills to purge
    melancholy, and how to order them.
13 Doctor at Large: Gratuitous surgery—good for the neighborhood.

LOCAL LISTINGS:

01 PIEducation
27 The Ricky Stephenson Show: "Impressions of My Parents in the
    Shower."
58 Danny and Lucille: "Christmas in July."
96 Billy Drew's Video Extravaganza: "The Longest Glitch."

Screen 477, Monday, Evening Programming:
8:00 PM

NETWORK LISTINGS:

02 Family Network Satellite News (Local Events)
05 Family Network Satellite News (National, Global)
09 Will You Be My Neighbor?
13 Special: "Hoeing Your Own Row."

LOCAL LISTINGS:

46 The Van Patten Family Hour: "Goodbye Crewel World"—Mrs.
    V.P. gives up knitting after Muffin eats her eighth half-finished
    sweater; Mr. V.P. gets off work early and disturbs the baby; finish-
    ing touches on the davenport.
83 The Johnson Family Hour: "Kids Will Be Kids"—P.J. learns to
    deal with his own homoeroticism; Nancy June is restless; the twins

break a window without setting off the alarm; Wolfie eats the
hard-copy notes for Virgil's thesis on Pindar.

Virgil proceeded on hands and knees down the carpeted upstairs hallway, having scoured every inch of his own room for the
scraps of shredded yellow foolscap that Wolfie had scattered
everywhere. Dad laughed at him from the top of the stairs.

"That'll teach you to use that old-fashioned pulp, Virg. You're
the only thing standing between America and the paperless future."

"Yeah, Dad," Virgil said, dropping to his belly at the entrance to
his parents' bedroom. From this rather rare perspective he could
see little flecks of the yellow stuff under the bed and piled in
corners. He groaned and started forward, his bony elbows aching.

"You coming down to watch the show?" Dad said.

"No, Dad."

"Why not? You edited this one, didn't you?"

"I want to rescue what I can of my notes before the vac-system
turns on at nine. And I didn't have time to edit the show; it's my
editing algorithm, that's all."

"Oh, one of those," Dad said, deprecatingly. "Colored filters
and slow motion shots of your mom opening insta-serves."

Virgil's hand closed on a triangular wad of three pages stuck
together; there were actually a few complete sentences visible.

"I think I outgrew trick photography some time ago, Dad."

"Well, no matter. Good luck with your thesis."

He heard Dad thudding downstairs like a bag full of rocks. As
far as he could tell, the rest of the notes in this room were a total
loss; the vacuum could have them. He backed out, got up on his
knees, and pushed on the door to P.J.'s room. There was a chance
Wolfie had gotten in—

"Hey!" P.J. shouted. The door flew back at Virgil, striking him with a dull sound in the temple and knocking his glasses awry. He sank back, rubbing his skull.

"Watch who you slam that on," he moaned. "Hey, what are you doing?"

P.J. backed up against the bed that took up most of his cubicle. He had just thrown a blanket over a pile of strange odds and ends, but among the items that poked out in places were tennis shoes, the cuff of a jacket sleeve, a jackknife. He tried to block it from Virgil's view.

"What are you doing, you mean?" P.J. said. "Don't you ever knock?"

"Sorry, I thought you'd be downstairs watching TV, so why bother? I'm looking for my notes."

P.J. looked scared, pale, worse than he had for the last few days. He nodded toward the corner behind the door. "Those them?"

In the corner was a swept-up pile of yellow scraps, the choicest fragments he had found yet. He grabbed them, rising, and stuffed them in his pocket. His head was starting to throb, and it looked like his glasses were bent out of shape: P.J.'s head was farther off than his feet.

"So, uh, P.J., what's going on?"

"Nothing," P.J. said belligerently. "Just get out of my room."

Virgil went toward the pile on the bed, and met full resistance from his brother. He avoided the first strike of P.J.'s arms, but a body block to his gut sent him sprawling back into the wall. This time he banged the back of his head.

"Jesus, P.J., what's your problem?"

As his vision cleared he saw his brother facing him, hands clenched, scowling, red-faced. "It's none of your business, Virgil."

"Ow." Virgil touched the tender spot on the back of his head, checked his fingers for blood. "What do you think I'm going to do? Go down and tell Dad you're cleaning your room? He'd probably throw a party."

"I'm not cleaning my room," P.J. snapped.

"Oh, then what? Come on, P.J., or maybe I will tell Dad."

"You better not." P.J. grabbed his arm and twisted it behind his back; Virgil knew P.J. could easily dislocate his shoulder.

"Let go," he said. "God damn, Peej. I'm your brother. If you can't trust me, who can you trust?"

"No one, apparently."

"I know what you're doing."

"Oh, you figured it out finally? Anyone else would have had it the minute they walked through that door."

P.J. let go of him and dropped down onto the bed; with a flourish, he pulled off the blanket, revealing a wad of clothes and spare possessions and a backpack he used for trips to the beach.

"You're running away?" Virgil said.

"You got it. You gonna go tell Dad?"

Virgil shrugged. "I guess not. I just can't believe you would want to."

"Believe it." He bunched up the blanket and stuffed a pair of socks into the pack. "I can't stay here anymore. I've had it with Dad and his typing tests. I can't believe touch-typing is going to make a difference when I put on the motor-stim verbalizers. But . . . it's more than that. I don't want that whole world anymore." He raised his arms. "This little world. Walls. It sucks."

"So how long can you stay on the beach? Are you even taking a sleeping bag?"

P.J. narrowed his eyes, his smile became ironic. "You really don't understand, do you? You're just like all the rest of them. I'm not going to the beach, Virgil. I'm going east. Outside. Over the wall. I'm breaking out of the neighborhood."

Virgil, leaning against the wall, let himself slide to the floor. "You're kidding, Peej." He was aghast. "You've really got to be kidding."

"You can't imagine anything outside your books, that's your problem." P.J. turned away, rolled up a pair of jeans, stuffed them in the sack. "Kurt Foster got assigned to perimeter security on his eighteenth birthday. I already talked it over with him. If I can get over the wall, he'll look the other way. He says the guards don't

34

pay much attention anyway. There's nothing to see outside, there's never been a threat. The people out there don't care about us."

"You're crazy!"

"Shh!"

"You're crazy," Virgil whispered. "The defense system is designed to track and kill anything that moves outside that wall; there's a no-man's land there, and you'd have to go through it."

"If Nancy June can sneak out of the house at night without Dad knowing she's meeting Arnold, I can get out of the neighborhood. Open sesame. The wall is there to keep people out. The walls that keep people in are all in here." He tapped his skull. "Mind games, that's what hooks the suckers like you, Virgil. Promises. If you work hard without complaining, you get to be like Dad. An asshole."

"You're too hard on him," Virgil said. "Besides, we both know this stuff about walls isn't the real problem at all. It's yourself you're afraid to face, so now you're running away. It's an overreaction, P.J., like your screaming jag the other day. It's hormones."

P.J.'s face turned white, lined in red. "And, my . . . my sex, is that all hormones too?"

"See, you're evading what really bothers you."

"I am not. I can't live here anymore, not with them." He pointed toward the family room downstairs.

"They're your parents."

P.J. shook his head. "I can never love them after what they did to me."

"They thought it was for the best."

"They did it without even asking."

Virgil laughed. "How could they have asked?"

"Laugh all you want, Virgil. You're just as much a product of their genetic specs as I am. And maybe there's some kind of time bomb in you, too, something you'll only find out about when you're good and unready for it. Because that's what it feels like, brother. I've got a time bomb inside me now, ticking away. All of a sudden I feel like I don't know anything, can't trust my own perceptions. I'm just waiting until . . . like, what if Kurt brushes against me or something and I find myself wanting to . . . to . . ."

"Peter." Virgil stood up and came toward him.

"How could they do this to me? To me?"

P.J. lowered his head, put his hands over his eyes, and began to sob. Virgil sank down next to him, put an arm around his shoulders.

"What does it matter?" he said softly. "What does it change, Peter John?"

"Everything," his younger brother whispered. "Nothing is the same now, not for me; that's why I have to leave. Outside there's a real world, with none of this programming, none of these walls, none of these sexual booby-traps. That's where I'm going. I want to get lost in it and know I can never come back, because if I did the guns would shoot me down on the way in."

"I'm sure they wouldn't shoot without asking who you were," Virgil said, "in case you wanted to come back."

P.J. raised his wet, mottled face. "Then you won't stop me? You won't tell Dad?"

"It's your life, P.J. Do what you want with it."

P.J. gave him an awkward smile, and leaned forward to hug him. But as their bodies touched, Virgil felt his brother stiffen and gasp, then spring away from him. His eyes were wide with inexpressable emotion.

"No," he said. "Look at what I'm doing. My own brother . . . I'm coming on to my own brother."

"Oh, don't be absurd," Virgil said, rising. "I've got to keep looking for my notes. You know, Peej, you'll probably feel better when you're a bit further out of adolescence. Maybe you should hang out for another couple of weeks."

P.J. shook his head, determined. "I'm leaving tomorrow night," he said. "And no one is talking me out of it."

"I wouldn't dream of it. Goodnight."

Out in the hall again, Virgil went back onto his knees. He started to think about what had just passed, but a low sucking sound startled him. It couldn't be nine yet. A few yellow curlicues tumbled between his hands, and the heap of large fragments he'd collected vanished under the wainscotting. A low-lying storm of foolscap and dog hair rustled through the rooms.

"Help," he shouted. Down the hall, he heard the twins laughing.

The widewall TV in the family room flickered like Christmas tree lights on the upturned faces of the Johnson family, minus Virgil and P.J. The twins giggled over their glasses of grape juice.

In the typically Virgilesque montage sequence, family faces whirled in a kaleidoscope of multicolored emotion, giving way to a silhouette of Dad at his PIJob; in the center of his head, Mom swayed against a starry blue background, a child's toy held in her hand like a microphone, singing the theme from the PIVacations commercial: "*Get away, on the wings of imagination. Get away, on a programmed Plug-In Vacation . . .*"

On the livingroom couch, Mom smiled over at Dad and squeezed his thigh.

"Hey, ow, you're pinching a nerve. I've got sciatica, remember?"

She leaned closer. "It would be nice to take a vacation, hon."

He shrugged, chewing a nail. "I've been thinking about picking up one of those new packs. Yosemite. I haven't seen it since I was a kid: it'd probably look nicer on PI, too. Not so much garbage, no mosquitoes."

"Sh!" said Nancy June.

Nancy herself appeared on the screen; there were variously angled shots of her progress down the upstairs corridor. She seemed to be walking on tiptoe past her parents' room. A digital clock in the corner of the screen showed the time as 6:54 A.M.

"Up kinda early," Dad said. The door to his room was ajar, and a shot from the hall showed him asleep on his back, elbow over his eyes, the hairs of his armpit stirring with each exhalation. The lens performed a slow, inspired zoom. This stuff had Virgil written all over it.

Risky spy music played background to Nancy's appearance in

the living room. Suddenly there was a sting of horns and Wolfie appeared, scampering up to her, wagging his tail, opening his mouth to bark. Nancy clamped her hands around his muzzle and dragged him with her into the kitchen.

"Oh, honey," Mom said, "you'll hurt Wolfie like that."

Nancy—the real-time Nancy in the family room—looked uncomfortable. "Virgil," she murmured.

The onscreen Nancy went straight to the wallphone and punched out a code that appeared at the bottom of the picture. The number looked familiar but Dad couldn't figure out where he'd seen it.

Arnold Smith appeared on the phone screen. *"Hi, Nan."*

"Shh! Arnold, you'll wake everybody up."

"Turn down your volume, dummy."

"Oh, God," Nancy said in the family room. "Oh, God, I can't do anything around here."

"I miss you, Arnold."

"I miss you, too, Nancy June. Are you ever going to get to come over without sneaking?"

"Well, I called—"

"This isn't real!" Nancy shouted, standing up in front of her parents. "The computer made this up out of its memory!"

"Sure, honey," Dad said, listening through her interruption.

"I called to say I could maybe meet you at the beach tonight."

"Great," Arnold said. *"What time?"*

"Ahem!" Nancy June shouted. "Everybody, Virgil made this up to get me in trouble!"

"Eleven?"

"Please sit down, Nancy," Mom said.

"Can you get out of your house that late without anyone knowing?" Arnold asked.

"Aiieee!" Nancy screamed. "Help-help-help! L.B.J. bit me in the leg, Mommy! It's bleeding, it's gushing blood! Look, Dad, please go get me a tourniquet!"

"Sure, with that little gadget you made the alarms don't go off at all."

Dad rose up from the couch. "That's enough out of you, young lady. There aren't going to be any midnight trysts with Arnold Smith."

"Daddy . . ." She looked desperate. "I haven't seen him in weeks."

He turned off the TV, and the twins started yelling. The juice stains on L.B.J's mouth did look a little like blood.

"Now look here, Nancy June," he said, "I'm not going to make you sneak around my house, or out of it. I'm not that kind of father."

Looking chastened, hands behind her back, she shook her head.

"What I propose is that you invite Arnold over here straight off. Ask him if he wants to come watch TV with us."

"Really?" she said.

"But there's one condition. I want to see this little device you're talking about."

"Oh, that," she said. "Sure, I'll get it."

She ran away upstairs, and Dad dropped down next to his wife, almost upsetting Junior from the end of the couch. "If that Arnold can get through my security system with another of his brain teasers, I'd hate to think what would happen if his invention fell into the wrong hands. His father's, say."

Nancy June returned with a remodeled kid's gun. Instead of making bright electric sparks when he pulled the trigger, it gave off a low hum. Dad was startled to hear the unmistakable sound of the tungsten-alloy lamellas opening at the front and back of the house.

"I'll be damned," he said. "Were the twins playing with this when they pried the windows open?"

Lyndon Baines and Lady Bird hid their faces.

"All right." He stood up. "Go call your friend and ask him to come over. I want that kid on my side."

"He likes you, Daddy."

"I'm relieved to hear it. Go on, you know the number."

Ten minutes later, Nancy went to answer the front door and returned with red-headed, acne-beleaguered Arnold Smith. Arnold's skinny arms were wrapped around a shiny polyboard box, out of which a coil of wires protruded.

"Uh . . . hi, Mr. Johnson, Mrs. Johnson," he said, out of breath, and dropped the box with a crash on the floor, startling Junior.

"I'll be right back," Mom said, hurrying away with the baby.

"I told my folks I was going over to Mike Brown's house to make science kits." Arnold looked up at Dad, such a serious teenager that Dad felt absolutely frivolous by comparison. "But Nancy June said you were watching TV, so I brought one of my things along."

"Something you made?" Dad said, hunkering down by the box.

"Yup. It's a ground-based satellite-pirate, with evasion, penetration, and retrieval capabilities."

"What does it do?"

Nancy stood next to them. "Arnold, don't talk about this stuff, let's watch TV."

"This makes TV even better," he said. "I'm sure you know this, Mr. Johnson, but Nancy might not. All our television channels in this neighborhood are restricted, Nan; we only get them through approved satellites—watchdogs. So in Laurel Woods and Cobblestone Hill together we get four national network channels; that's all we're allowed. Four out of hundreds that we could be watching. Plus there are local stations all over the place, aside from just the family channels we get to see. I mean, there are literally billions of channels worldwide, and when they're bouncing around overhead in the satellite nets, it's easy to receive them. But not with those watchdogs, boy."

"So what you've got here, I imagine, is a dog catcher."

"Sort of. It brings in the restricted stations. You wanna see?"

Mom came back with Junior and sat down again to watch the blank screen.

"I'm not so sure I want to see these things, Arnold, and especially not with my kids around."

"I've seen 'em," Arnold said. "It didn't hurt me."

"I have a reputation to protect," Dad reasoned. "Not to mention the ethical welfare of my family and the moral agreement

I've made with the community as a whole. Hell, boy, I was on the committee that voted for the restrictions in the first place. It doesn't seem quite right to watch the stuff just because we *can*. I could kill Connie right now, smother her with a sofa cushion, but I don't do it, and that's because I value my integrity. I decided years ago, for my family and myself, that I didn't need to subject myself to the disturbing images of the world beyond the neighborhood's walls—a world you've never seen, son—"

"But I *have* seen it," Arnold said. "That's all I watch. There're adventure shows, and business stuff I don't understand, most of it in other languages, and channels that are nothing but colors and shapes and music, and people preaching, and courtrooms, and channels that just play laughter or screaming, and war shows and naked sex channels and all this great stuff."

"It's a bit like going back on my word," Dad said. "I'll feel a little funny, that's all. Give me a minute to get used to the idea."

It was easily done, somewhat to his surprise. Blue light glowed out of the polyboard box, the TV image flipped, and Arnold sat down next to Nancy, twirling the dials on what looked like an old electric blanket control.

"A few channels I've programmed in," he said. "The rest is hunt and peck."

A surreal image of a woman's breast swelled out of the screen, a smile stretched across the nipple, but it went by too fast for Dad. He decided not to call it back until the kids had gone to bed.

"You're welcome to stay over if you can convince your parents you're somewhere else, Arnold."

"You can sleep with me," Nancy said. "Let's go right now—"

"Wait," Arnold said, dragging back as she pulled on his arm. "See that? They're all over the air, seems like half the national channels."

Dad looked up. On the screen was a vast animated cross, tilting toward him, soaring out of a supernal blue sky like his fondly remembered missile. Dad clenched the arm of the sofa and sat up straighter: there was something unholy about the sheer size of the thing, not to mention its sharpened tips. Stretched out upon

41

it was a withered, blackened thing with burning red eyes, barel[y]
recognizable as human. It enlarged steadily, the eyes burnin[g]
brighter, the mouth opening wider, showing sharpened stee[l]
bright teeth. The world rose into the frame, swelling, and Nort[h]
America rolled over the globe like a dog offering its belly to th[e]
plunging crucifix.

Dad's teeth ground tighter in his head, squeaking. He stare[d]
at the hot red eyes and jagged teeth, the figure's black mout[h]
gaping in starvation, as if it could eat everything there was an[d]
still continue to shrivel.

The stake was about to pierce the earth, but before it did th[e]
cross-rider's black mouth yawned to fill the screen with red
flecked blackness and a voice of thunder commanded, *"EA[T]
ME!"*

The twins, whimpering earlier, now screamed with all the[ir]
hearts.

Into the peaceful darkness of the screen, a bald head rose lik[e]
a sallow moon, and a pair of close-set watery blue eyes blinked ou[t]
at them.

"Brethren—" said the soft voice.

Arnold switched the channel.

"There's a lot of that," he said.

No one said anything for a moment. Stephanie had burrowe[d]
into the sofa. Dad got up, aware that he was shaking, and too[k]
the control box away from Arnold.

"That's exactly the kind of shit I was talking about," he said[.]
"That's exactly why I voted for restricted channels and brough[t]
my family up in a neighborhood like this."

"They call themselves the Christian Soldiers," Arnold said, i[n]
a much diminished voice. "I dunno. Their cartoons are pretty
good."

"Shit," Dad said. "Why don't you kids go fuck around?"

"Gee," said Arnold. "All right."

Nancy June and Arnold sat outside on the back porch, underneath a sky of mist and stars, their arms around each other.

42

"This is so romantic," Nancy said.

"I know," said Arnold. "Your dad's pretty neat."

"You think so? Everybody else thinks he is an asshole."

"Everybody who? Just 'cause my dad doesn't like him?"

"I think they're madder about the golf course than about what he did to your dad."

"I don't know," Arnold said. "I wish he hadn't crossed my pop. My dad is crazy. I mean really crazy, Nan. You'd have to put up with that if he was your father-in-law. He has a certificate. I saw it in his sock drawer once, and it says he's crazy. Some doctor signed it. Maybe it was a joke thing, like you'd put on the wall of your office with your diplomas and stuff . . . but it didn't look that way at all. I think he's really crazy."

But Nancy hardly heard most of what he said.

"Father-in-law," she whispered. "Do you really mean it, Arnold?"

"Well, someday. I'm only thirteen, and you're even younger, but next year, you know, I'll be seventeen. We have to think about the future."

"Arnold." She put her arms all the way around him, loving the smell of his acne cream. His hair was only a little greasy tonight, so she ran her hands through it. "I love you."

"Me, too," he said. "You know, I'm getting another speed treatment tomorrow. I'll be . . . accelerating again, getting a lot older fast. I hope you won't mind."

"Why should I? I'm getting mine soon, and besides, I'm more mature than you."

"I'll be different," he said. "But please, still love me, all right?"

"Of course I will. Oh, Arnold, we'll have a family and everything. I'll stay home and clean the house and you'll go on to your job, and the rest of the time we'll be together."

Lying back in his arms, she thought of the years ahead of her, and smiled. It felt like the way she thought her mother smiled. Someday she would be like her mother, so happy, so wise, with a husband and children and no cares in the world.

"Let's go to bed," Arnold said.

BETTER THAN BOTH WORLDS!
Ladies—Renovate Your Vagina!
Men—Imagine the Possibilities!
A GREAT GIFT IDEA!

Imagine the pleasure, the exotic sensation of a new orifice. New surgical internal-extension techniques now make possible a wide world of stimulating channels for bliss. This revolutionary process, developed and patented by Laurel Woods' own Dr. Ralph Edison, allows direct penetration of the perineum, exploring territory never before breached by microsculpting.

Combining the muscular control of the anal sphincter with the gentler pressures of the vaginal walls, Edison's trademarked RenoVag heralds a new era in sexual sensitivity, allowing the best of both worlds without danger of infection.

Husbands are raving:

"We always saved anal for special occasions. Now every weekend is great."—Frank Douglass, Cobblestone Hill.

"Thanks, Ralph. Your surgery is the greatest. I've never felt like this before."—Al C. Bloome, Laurel Woods.

Wives agree:

"Until I agreed to the renovation, my sex life was going nowhere. Now, thanks to you, Dr. Edison, my husband and I are closer than ever before."—Mrs. E. C., Cobblestone Hill.

"I had no idea of the potential of my own body until your special techniques opened me to perineal penetration. Now it's hard to remember what regular sex was like. I hardly ever have to use my old vagina any more."—Mrs. L. N., Laurel Woods.

Do you need to know more? Why wait? Call Dr. Ralph Edison today, and arrange an appointment for your own RenoVag™.

Special Introductory Offer: 15% discount if you schedule your appointment within the week.

"Thanks, Dr. Edison! I needed that!"—Mrs. T. B., Cobblestone Hill.

3

WALL
TO
WALL

CONNIE WAS ROLLED GENTLY from bed at 7:30 A.M. and deposited in a warm bath, where she finally awoke, thankful for automats that could rescue her from dreams. But as she lay in the foaming jets, bobbing gently, her pores were permeated by tingling stimulants, and images from her nightmares returned with terrible clarity. Her dreams were usually sluggish, confused things, like a jumble of television channels, and they fled at awakening to lose their way among other useless thoughts. But this morning the memories had a strange vitality, and she could not seem to awaken; the invigorants merely sent her into them with greater lucidity.

She had dreamed of watching television with Bill, but suddenly he was replaced by a full-grown Junior. The big baby had no interest in the sex station that his father had selected; fumbling at the remote control, he had switched channels until he found a repeat of that horrible cartoon: the plunging crucifix, the withered rootlike man, the poor world . . .

Without knowing why, she had snatched the remote awa
from Junior, but he leapt upon her, heavy and drooling, a giant
in diapers. He forced her to watch the screen, whereon appeared
the bald man with weak eyes and such a soft voice:

"Brethren and sisters," he said, addressing her in particular
pinned as she was by her enormous son and unable to look away
"Have you opened your eyes to the truth? Watch these previews."

Connie saw a farmstead, an orchard, dewy fields; heard a bras
gong ringing, as musical in its way as the sound of the creel
running through autumn-bright aspens. Trees, she thought. Why
it looks like my home.

But that was a silly thought. She heard the big baby giggle. I
couldn't be her home; it looked nothing at all like Cobblestone
Hill.

There was an old white farmhouse with porches running about
both stories, and ferns all around, and a brown cat slipping out
the side door followed by puffs of steam and the smell of baking
bread. She heard a woman singing, and it was a beautiful, familiar
song.

Why, that's my mother. I haven't thought of her in years.

She found herself floating out from under Junior, into the
screen, right over the side porch past the heaps of chopped fire
wood, into a hall where a pot-belly stove sat in the midst of a
fairy-ring of wet shoes and boots. As she warmed her hands
feeling her way into this dreaming body which seemed slight and
quick as a girl's, she heard the singing change inexplicably, a
though the singer were coughing up something bad; and there
was also some scuffling.

She drifted to the doorway and looked into the kitchen. A
kettle fumed, about to whistle. Sausage patties spat and hissed in
the cast-iron frying pan on the stove. Her mother bent over
behind the counter, but when she straightened, it wasn't her
mother at all.

It was the root-thing, gnarled and slithy.

She screamed and it turned with its cross dripping red and it
held out its arms to welcome her.

She flew in terror over the fields, to the little outbuilding with the brass gong hanging from its eaves. There should have been sounds of chanting, low and sonorous, and the smell of incense, but there were none of these things. Inside the temple, there should have been a dozen of her parents' friends wrapped in their heavy robes, eyes closed, heads bowed, chanting before the smoking altar with its big Buddha seated like all of them. Her father should have been there.

But this morning the grown-ups lay all over the place, and she did not see her father. She was glad that the candles had been snuffed; she could see too much as it was.

Then a little old balding man with very bright blue eyes stood up in the middle of the room, lit by his own spotlight. He came toward her with a crucifix in one hand and a hammer in the other, saying, "How sad, a child. What a shame, to have lost your youth —given but once—in an evil place like this. If you were very young, we might still welcome you into the fold. But . . . don't lose hope, child. There is always the promise of limbo."

And he came at her, forcing her out of the television screen, raising the cross above her as she lay on the couch in the den, trapped by her own huge son.

As the hammer fell, the whole dream cut away to bright block letters:

TUNE IN
SUNDAY MORNING
CHANNEL 666
BE THERE OR BE DAMNED

Those were only the previews.

When they were over, they started again, and after that again, each time more real, until upon awakening, here in the cooling tub, there was no way she could forget it. The memory was like a message written to herself.

She had lived it, hadn't she? Perhaps not the root-thing, but certainly the murders. Perhaps not the hammered crucifix, but something similar. All that had been before Cobblestone Hill, before meeting Bill at college and coming away with him, mortgaging her given name for a dream of safety. She had been Nirvana once, her parents Sam and Sara, gentle Buddhists.

The water sucked out of the tub, leaving her drying in a warm stream of air, wide awake but a bit dazed.

It was scary that she never thought of the past, that she accepted all this—her house, Cobblestone Hill—as if it were all that existed or ever had been.

Could she ever remember what had come before? Trying to think of the old days brought on a headache; fortunately, the medicine cabinet was near. She sat on the edge of the tub, twiddling a green caplet between her fingers, thinking.

First comes love, then comes marriage . . .

The neighborhood had been the plan of Dr. Ralph Edison, inspired by corporate philosophy. Work together, play together, live together—the company picnic taken to its limits and beyond. It had sounded so good in those years of fragmentation, when Connie and Bill had felt as if they were the last reasonable people in a mob of fanatics. It was a chance to take back the American dream—the dream that had become lost somehow among the splinters and the fringes, trampled by terrorists, syndicates, and social reform. The world at that time was not the sort of place where one wished to raise a family. But behind the walls of the neighborhood, there was peace and plenty, low-cost housing, the best in educational software, neighborhood health care: benefits, benefits, benefits. They had found a place among people like themselves, and had become so firmly settled there that eventually the rest of the world began to recede. There was little news of events beyond the wall, although Neighborhood Security constantly reassured them that they were safe from "danger." What danger?

There were so many things she didn't know.

"Bill?" she said, stepping to the bedroom door in her bathrobe. He was sitting up in bed, a slippery newssheet before his face.

"Bill, it's funny, but I can't remember, maybe you can. Did my

48

parents come to our wedding?" Or was that dream only a dream, she thought.

"You were in school on an orphan-grant, weren't you? You don't have parents."

"I was born before time-baking, Bill." But that answered her question. "What was my maiden name?"

"Johnson," he said.

"Are you sure?"

"Sure I'm sure. Johnson. We were made for each other."

Did I remake myself for you? she wondered. Did Nirvana do that?

She watched him, the news rising and falling slowly on his belly, his eyes still crusted with sleep, aging—she had to admit it —badly.

For you?

As she turned toward the hall, he said, "Hey, hon, are you sure you wouldn't like to try one of these renovated vaginas? Dr. Edison is having an introductory sale. No problem if you don't, of course."

She swallowed, numb.

"No," she said after a moment. "No, I really don't think so, Bill. No."

"Okay." She heard him sigh. "Up to you."

She moved on into the hall, hearing the children moving in their rooms. She opened the cupboard where Wm. D. Jr. slept and took a glance in. The baby opened his eyes at the touch of light, made a soft noise, tried to sit up. Despite herself, the memory of the dream came after her: she saw him full-grown and still in her care, still needing to be spoon-fed, still making those soft bubbling noises.

And Dr. Edison's explanation before his conception came back to her: "You'll need something to do in your twilight years, Connie, some strong link to the fruitful years of motherhood. I think you'll agree, when you reach that age, that a son who stays at home is a thing to be treasured. A good investment." She closed the cupboard and stood with her back against it, trembling.

Dad shook his head, as if reproaching his insta-serve pancakes, then looked up at Connie. "I'm sorry, hon, I have to work today."

"Saturday?" she said.

"I thought we were going golfing," Virgil said.

"Well, I'm sorry, this project just won't wait."

"Bill, that's a solid month of Saturdays you've had to work, and the Fuel Committee meeting will waste your day tomorrow."

"I guess I should see Elaine anyway," said Virgil.

"Mom, I'm staying at Mike Swanson's tonight, okay?"

"Just a minute, P.J. Bill, we had plans for this afternoon, don't you remember?"

"I said I'm sorry, hon, but I can't get around it. It's drudgery, but I'm under pressure to finish as soon as I can. Now five other guys are going to plug-in to sweat on this damn thing. What are they going to think if I decide to go golfing or swimming while they work overtime?"

"Mrs. Swanson said it was okay, Mom."

Dad pointed his fork at his oldest son. "Anyway, Virgil, you *should* be spending more time with that lady of yours. You've got to get used to her. The wedding is when . . . less than a month?"

Virgil looked uncomfortable, remote from his own body. "It's not like we have to spend all our time together."

"You don't spend *any* time together since you got engaged."

Virgil blushed. "It's different now."

"Bill, now look, what time are you going to be off? Leave Virgil alone a minute and answer me."

"I did answer you. I said I don't know. You think I'm going to hang around there any longer than I have to? Or any of us? It's Saturday for the other guys, too."

"Mrs. Johnson, could I have more pancakes?" Arnold asked.

"I'll get them," Nancy said. "You stay right where you are."

Dad watched his wife glowering at her placemat. He knew it was useless to argue. He looked at the clock.

"I'm sorry," he said, and got up, leaving the table to sort itself out. "I'll get back when I can."

Dad reminded himself that his lies were well justified: Doctor's orders. The era had long since passed when plugging-in was an economic necessity; there were only "pleasure" programs now. Doc Edison insisted, however, that Dad and the other men of the neighborhood plug-in regularly: the daily work pattern must not be altered if the nuclear family were to remain stable. "Take away a man's role as breadwinner and you take his authority," Doc had said once, and on that point Dad had to agree.

Upstairs, in his study, it was peaceful, the sun warm on his desk. He flipped the switch on his console, called up the job entry, and pulled on his working suit. With his eyes covered, his hands in the pads, he walked down a long featureless corridor lined with doors. The first one he came to had his name on it, but it was only a decoy door, programmed to detain anyone who came looking for him without authorization. He went past it to another labeled CENTRAL FILES.

Inside, there were several rows of metal shelves, and past them a door labeled *Men.* He went through that, took a step, fell.

Howling his laughter, he plunged down the slick red slide into a frenetic jungle of color, light, and sound. His body changed as he accelerated. Balls of lightning showed a much younger William D. Johnson, his stomach firm and lightly haired, his naked legs slim and fluent with muscle. Suddenly the slide ended in the midst of an electric blue vapor, and he flew into space, flapping powerful wings.

"Hey, Bill."

He looked across the color-cracked abyss and saw his four co-workers gliding toward him, all of them naked youths with angel wings.

"You're late," yelled Marv Coolidge, a smooth-faced kid with curly blond hair.

"Give me a break," Bill said. "You gonna dock me five minutes' overtime? This is volunteer work."

Marv circled around him playfully, but there was an uneasy look in his young features. "I hear the Lodge Council is planning an inquisition, Bill. To settle accounts between you and Jock."

"Do you believe everything you hear, Marv?" Dad slapped him above one wing. "What're you trying to do, spoil my afternoon?"

"Well, you know I'll always vouch for you."

"Marvin, sometimes you surprise me. You're taking it too seriously."

Coolidge shrugged and broke into a high-pitched laugh. "If you say so."

"Hurry up," shouted Dave Hiram. "Wait'll you see this new routine. It's straight down, Bill."

They folded their wings and dropped like arrows, five angels centering on a target of high crystalline spires whose tips flashed up from the emptiness below. Their meteoric flight ended on a narrow balcony, outside an arched doorway. Inside were the sounds of laughter, music, the smell of intoxicating smoke.

Marv tapped Bill on the back, between his wings. "After you, pal."

Bill went in and was stunned at first by the seemingly impossible display of raw sensations that met him: kinesthesia—his body relaxed into it, dissolving, fusing with the light and the taste of liquor and the smooth touch of sweat-slickened skin. There he was, a mote, an angel—alone, but only for an instant.

Then the women appeared: five, nine, a dozen, twenty, more and more, flitting through the high-domed chamber, lascivious sprites, all wanting him. With a laugh he sprang into their midst, and the nuptial flights continued through the long Saturday afternoon.

It was a stunning day, the first that actually felt like summer, and Virgil could see that the green of the grass on the hills beyond the wall was well on its way to being replaced by the straw color more typical of the season. Only in the neighborhood would all the grass stay green, for only there was all the grass confined in regularly watered lawns. The wind off the sea kept the sun's heat from reaching them, but its light was unobstructed.

"What is it, Virgil?" said Elaine Wesson. "You seem distracted."

"Hm?"

He looked away from the wall that edged the eastern limit of the golf course and reminded himself that he was supposed to entertain his fiancee. But his smile, when he allowed it to be seen, felt artificial. The worst thing was that it had nothing to do with her. He couldn't stop thinking about P.J.

"I'm sorry," he said. "I didn't sleep well last night; I keep drowsing."

"You need stronger prescriptions," she said. "As you get older, I mean."

"I guess you're right."

Elaine looked especially suggestive this afternoon. Her wide-brimmed bonnet was wrapped to her head with a pale scarf, and with the accompanying traditional veil she resembled a bee-keeper; the wind had flushed the cream from her cheeks, he thought, but it was hard to see her clearly. He rather regretted the engagement attire, meant to increase his suspense until the connubial unveiling. His memories of Elaine in her swimsuit, before his proposal, were almost painful. The many layers of her dress beat like flags, slowing their progress across the slopes from hole to hole, and the ballooning of her sleeves had made it impossible for her to wield a club; so instead of playing golf, they strolled arm in arm over the course.

The wind was strong enough to dissuade others from playing. There had used to be a windbreak afforded by tall pines and eucalyptus along the seacliff, but that was gone now, just as the lip of the cliff was gone. They stood rather close to the upright tail of the missile, half-buried in an oversized gopher hill of piled-up earth: the mound and its accompanying trench made up the new sixteenth-hole trap. The missile awaited removal by his father, in which case, Virgil thought, it would wait a long time, until it became a sort of monument to his perverse ingenuity. After their initial uproar, most of the men in the country club had admitted that the new trap added something to the course.

At last they stopped at the gouged-away earth slide above the sea. Virgil gazed in fascination at the strata of jumbled yellow stones, like rows of crooked stained teeth jutting out from under the rough hem of the golf course. He felt a sudden vertigo and stepped backward, pulling Elaine with him. She shrieked, but it turned to a laugh as they ran downhill, out of the wind, toward the remaining trees.

They came to a stop, breathless, and Elaine swung toward him. He was sure she would have kissed him, if not for the veil.

"Virgil," she said, "please, dear heart, what is it? You look so worried."

"It's . . . it's nothing," he said. "Nothing to do with you, Elaine."

"But can't you confide in me? You should learn to trust me, Virgil. I am the partner of your heart. Shouldn't you share your heart's concerns?"

His jaw tightened and he felt vulnerable, unfairly matched, for her face was completely hidden and his was bare. Perhaps it was the marriage that disturbed him, more than P.J.'s secret. She seemed like a stranger now, no more the laughing girl on the beach.

"Virgil," she said, "what is it?"

"I . . . I . . ." He shook his head in agony, stumbling away from her. He heard her gasp, felt her hand tighten on his elbow, then she pulled him straight up, forced him to face her, and her words came out of the shadow of the veil, urgent and terse, but whispered:

"Virgil," she said, "tell me . . . or I'll tear your face off."

P.J. huddled in the shadow of the wall, the night wind cold in his hair, his face wet with saltwater that blurred with the tears in his eyes. Footsteps passed overhead, but he was among shrubs, invisible. When the shape of the watchman had gone on, he stood and continued through the bushes until he came to a tower built into the wall, with windows in its heights and a door in its base. Kurt would be alone in there now. He pressed a button near the door, and after a pause it buzzed and swung open.

Above him, at the top of a spiral stair, his best friend looked down. He looked pale, as frightened as P.J.

P.J. said, with as much bravado as he could manage, "I'm ready if you are."

"You're really doing it, huh? I thought you'd back out."

P.J. shook his head. Kurt said, "Well, good luck," waved briefly, and tried to smile. He did not come down the stairs to say goodbye, not even to shake hands; he had seen the Johnson Family Hour last week and knew the reason behind P.J.'s flight.

"I won't be seeing you again, Kurt. Doesn't that mean anything to you?"

Kurt twisted his lower lip, sucking it. "No more flag football?"

"Goodbye, Kurt."

P.J. turned around and went back out, and pressed the door shut behind him.

On the other side of the tower, a tarmac road began at a solid metal gate and went straight into the middle of Laurel Woods. Robot-driven delivery trucks sometimes came into the neighborhood this way, as well as Cartel people. The lights of the houses dimmed in clouds of mist, the juniper bushes bowed their farewells, bending low and whipping up again. Cobblestone Hill was visible above it, to the north, the humped back of a sleeping dragon. P.J. turned away from the secure homes and hurried through shadows until he came to the side of the gate.

From his pocket he took the toy gun that Arnold had rewired for the purpose of his midnight trysts with Nancy June. As he approached the gate, he pulled the trigger. The hum of the gun was joined by the groan of the gate, as with a jolt it began to open.

There was no need to wait: the gap was already wide enough for him to pass through. For a moment he was caught under bright lights, then the wind pushed him through the slit and the rumbling metal plate eclipsed the glare. The wind stopped, the air was still and dark, and he had nothing forcing him but himself.

Ahead there were three lamps to pass before he reached the darkness of the east, beyond the security perimeters. He hurried for the first, staying on the far side of the road, and had not gone far before the wind scooped down to the road again and got under his feet to help him along.

The first lamp flew past opposite him. He felt like a moth, a specimen held out in the darkness to any eyes that might have strayed toward the road. Kurt saw him, he was sure; but as for any other, he would soon know. He waited for shouts or, far worse than that, the silent lancing of a laser into his heart; but that was stupid, they would not fire on someone leaving the compound—only follow. Better death than that. If they chased him, he would run into no-man's land, into the total dark, off the road where the automatic sentries would shoot him without inquisition.

The second lamp was behind him.

His lungs ached, the knapsack banged his ribs. He stumbled, almost fell into the splash of light beneath the third lamp, but then caught himself and came up laughing, nothing but night ahead of him now. Only Virgil and Kurt knew that he was gone. No one knew where he was going. With a kind of delight, he realized that no one included himself.

FROM VIRGIL LAMARK JOHNSON'S *PINDAR*

". . . ravages of prehistory, the savage bite of a caveman's quill pen, from whose tatters arise the tradewind institutions of early classical man, among whom . . . nearly incomprehensible to the modern sensibility, given his reliance on an antiquated metric scale, the . . . *Odes* themselves take on a fabulous light that is half their own inner luminescence, half the . . . sail on a fragmented sea of Homericana . . . comic-opera melodrama, rare forms of driftwood, kraters of olive oil once carefully preserved, now clogging the depths of the already slimy . . . filter of Roman insensibility to the archaic themes of . . . fiscal responsibility for the heroic lads who braved . . . priapic dances . . . drunken heaving of the wine-dark . . . voice of . . . Pindar would perhaps remember with distress the . . . trophies of a noble, more intelligent, masculine yet sensitive . . . horse race, in a style rendered lucid by comparison to . . . more evocative computer translation still fascinated . . . too many . . . city-states . . . *agon* beyond shame or guilt cultures . . . the randy poet . . . kept from the windows of the courtesans, singing his . . . even so . . . ng . . ."

HYPOCRITICAL MASS

NANCY STILL HAD A lingering urge to sneak to the back door when Arnold whistled from the side of the house, but there was no need for secrecy around here now. It was only from Arnold's father that they needed to hide their affair, and as long as Arnold came around the back they were safe.

She walked straight through the kitchen where her mother was swabbing the breakfast table, through the family room where Stephanie was trying to get off her leash, and opened the back door.

At first she didn't recognize him.

"What's the matter with you?" he said, in a voice that had an unaccustomed gruffness. He shouldered past her into the family room and pointed at his satellite-pirate on the floor below the TV screen. "I want that back."

"Arnold?"

He looked a size too big for his clothes, which he probably was. His hair was oilier and lay flat against his scalp, and his acne was inflamed. She also saw, with something of a start, that his jaws were covered with pale wisps of coarse-looking fur. His teeth looked crooked.

"Don't stare," he said. "I know what I look like."

"But . . . I'm sorry, I won't stare. You can laugh at me when I get my injection, all right?"

"There's nothing to laugh about," he said, with a sullen glare at Stephanie. "Leashed," he said angrily. "It's just another of the restraints slapped on all of us. And I've about had it with—" He broke off suddenly, hearing Mrs. Johnson approaching. "Quick, outside." He grabbed her elbow and pulled her with him through the back door, and around the corner of the house.

"Arnold, what's happening?"

He gazed up at the sky, raising his chin to the wind. "I'm not sure I can explain all of it."

"You're different now," she said. "That's all."

"No!" There were depths of anger in everything he said. "I'm not different—I'm more myself than ever before. I can see things more clearly now; I can see the pressures I've struggled with all these years, unconsciously. It's so obvious, so pitifully obvious, so hopeless . . . so futile."

She put a hand on his shoulder. "Arnold, don't talk like that."

He shook his head. "No, I've found hope, Nancy. There *is* a way. All my life I've been repressed, you see. All of us have, here in this damned armed camp of a community, this—this monument to fossil values. From before I was conceived the ideals of my parents have been foisted upon me, cramping me. I rebelled the only way I knew how, for I was young and weak, and thought I was helpless. I rebelled through my intellect, creating the perfect wall to demonstrate the frailty of *their* walls, inventing tools to slip through their security nets and all their other restrictions. I dreamed without knowing it, Nancy, with never a memory of what it was I dreamed when I awoke."

Nancy listened in awe, awaiting every new word of this intense manifesto of puberty.

"But now I am awake, and I remember my dream all too

clearly. It is a dream of freedom, and no longer will I merely dream it. I will live my dream. My mind has taken me this far . . now my hands will finish the work."

She felt dizzy, as if he had led her to the brink of a new land named "Freedom," and said, "It's all ours."

"Arnold," she whispered. "What are you going to do?"

"I am going to build a bomb."

"No one in this community would have any use for a nuclear device," said William D. "Dad" Johnson to the assembly at the other side of the neighborhood. "Except, possibly, to heave at some threat outside our walls. I maintain, in any case, that the so-called dangerous plutonium pellets would be kept in a high-security compound. There is no more secure place in all of Cobblestone Hill and Laurel Woods than my garage."

"For all I care, you can keep it under your bed," Jock Smith said, standing up long enough to meet Dad's eyes. Smith smirked and welcomed the little wave of laughter that came from the sycophants in his Natural Gas Brigade, all of them wearing their little Blue Flame badges that said, "Ask Me About Gas!"

Dad jabbed a thumb downward. "History will laugh you off the page, Smith."

The men from Dad's side of the street chuckled their agreement.

"Gentlemen, gentlemen, please," said the Cartel man on the podium at the front of the Whelk open-meeting hall. Mr. Ashenwriste was a tall, trim man, with distinguished silver panels in his black muttonchops, and deepset dark eyes. "Please keep in mind that there is no financial reality for your rivalry. The Cartel will serve any and all of your fuel needs, no matter what type you require. If only one of you desires the garage-based nuclear unit at this time, then only one will be installed."

"That's right," yelled a Blue Flame. "There's only one crackpot."

Dad stood up to see who had spoken. "I'm not the only one considering the installation," he said, "even if I am the pioneer.

61

Look at all these other fine men who share my ideas, all thes
courageous souls who'll join their names with mine on the firs
order for installation."

He turned and surveyed the faces of his comrades, and wa
annoyed by the eyes that wandered away from his, the mouth
that refused to return his smile. Marv Coolidge, Dave Hiran
Gary Blankenship, his nearest neighbors. They couldn't all hav
been giving him lip service, he thought. Could they?

It didn't matter to him. He would go it alone if he must. Bu
he wished someone could explain to him how, in trying to be
regular joe, he had ended up a maverick.

Charlie McCormick stood up in a rear corner of the room. H
was the oldest man in the neighborhood now, after the Rober
sons had been farmed back to Sunset Ranch at retirement, an
his words were taken in silence by the other men:

"The simple fact is, divisiveness will push up prices for all o
us, Bill. Whether we're going nuke or natural, the more of us i
on the deal, the bigger the discounts. A dozen separate installa
tions spread over time will cost about five fortunes more than ,
dozen installations done at once from a central distributor. No
stick that in your pipe and smoke it."

"I'm sorry to disagree with you just this once," Dad said, an
he was. "But money is a yardstick for courage. Every great innova
tor has had to make an investment. What would have happene
to Columbus if he decided to keep the money for his trip in ,
retirement account, where it would be safe until he was ready t
use it?"

"It wasn't Columbus's money," Charlie snapped with the au
thority of history itself.

"Gentlemen," said Mr. Ashenwriste, and as always the me
gave his words their full attention; he was the one who would b
taking their money whatever they decided. "Let me remind yo
not to dwell on your hostilities, whatever their cause. You know
me well by now. I have been your liaison for how many years? An
have we not always reached mutually satisfying arrangements? Le
me say that I have your interests at heart: I have feasted with you

families, played softball in your Sunday picnics, golfed on your course, and walked your dogs." He put a finger to his lips, though no one had made a sound. "Do you not think I know you by now?"

The men looked at the floor and scuffled their feet as if ashamed for having forgotten their old friend the Cartel in the heat of their personal grudges. Finally someone asked, "Well, Mr. Ashenwriste, what would you suggest?"

"I say let Mr. Johnson install his nuclear unit. Let it be a trial run. He has a daughter on the way, genetically fitted for the explicit purpose of meeting the family-oriented nuclear future head-on: he has already prepared himself for the nuke's arrival, welcomed it into his home."

Dad inclined his head. "Well, I'm not looking to hog the limelight. These other gentlemen—" He blushed, aware that Ashenwriste's diction was phonifying his own. "—also want to sign up."

He looked at the "gentlemen" in question, and again they seemed rather interested in the door, the clock, the high dark corners of the building.

"Well, don't you?"

Marv smiled as if he were about to do him a big favor. "Well, it could run into some money, Bill. And while that's all very well, I may not be able to lay down much until there's a bigger customer base and some kind of discount. It makes sense to do it as a neighborhood thing."

"A neighborhood thing?" Bill said. "What are you, cattle? Where's your goddamned independence, Marv?"

Marv didn't answer. Dad decided not to play angel games with him for a while.

Dad looked up and saw Smith gloating.

"You're going to regret it, Jock, when you're squashed in the skid marks of history." He paused and had to think about what he'd said: he'd meant history would be taking off fast, but maybe it sounded like he'd meant it would be coming to an emergency halt.

"History, shmistory," Jock said, betraying some kind of Jewish heritage. Dad would have to take that up with the Ethics Committee. "I just know that plutonium is dangerous and I won't have it in my house. I don't even want it on my block."

"We discussed that, Smith. Right, Mr. Ashenwriste? You have the proof. Nuclear waste nowadays is about as dangerous as wet coffee grounds, especially with that new aerosol decontaminant they'll be coming out with pretty soon. All I have to do is store the waste somewhere safe until that stuff's perfected, and the rest of the time I'll be laughing up my sleeve." Unfortunately, he was in short sleeves because of the heat; once more, his imagery had backfired on him: laughing at his armpit indeed.

"It is the safest waste ever," Ashenwriste agreed.

"That's right," Dad said, "listen to him. And look at me. I'll give you the kind of proof that gets through your thick, numb skulls."

Dad walked up past the podium, to the high table where Mr. Ashenwriste's briefcase was laid out among the tables and charts for overhead projection. From the open case he took a small metal bottle marked with a sign that indicated the contents were potentially radioactive.

Dad picked up the bottle, unscrewed the cap, and tapped one of the little blue-sheathed pellets into the palm of his hand.

He held it up for all to see, holding them hypnotized. He moved the pellet from side to side and their eyes followed it.

"It's tiny," he said. "It's got a protective coating that only comes off in the reactor. It's as goddamned safe as a goddamned jellybean."

He popped it in his mouth.

It went down like a vitamin, without water. He almost choked, but kept smiling.

Mr. Ashenwriste nodded to him, then to the assembly. He stepped off the podium, gathered his papers and samples—capping the metal bottle with silver-gloved hands, Dad noticed—and slid them all into his briefcase. Then he walked quickly from the room.

"It was a sample," said one of the Blue Flames. "A dud. No

plutonium in it. You're the royal bullshit artist of them all, Bill Johnson."

But they had all seen Mr. Ashenwriste's hasty departure, and judging from the look they gave Dad, he knew his demonstration had convinced them of something.

Dad swallowed again, fixing his eyes on Jock Smith. "Don't you believe me, Jock?"

Jock grew pale as Dad started toward him. Something in his eyes seemed to crack. In a moment he had backed through the crowd and vanished out a side door, leaving his Blue Flames to stare after him.

Good, Dad thought. Let 'em see what stuff he's made of. Let the Lodge Council call us up on trial. Then we'll really see something.

"So, Marv," he said, noticing the man's eyes resting uneasily on Dad's stomach. "You're not ready to go nuke, eh?"

"Sorry, Bill, I just remembered a, uh, picnic I had to help with." Marv slipped away.

It was the same with his other friends: "Sorry, Bill." "Later, Bill."

He watched them leaving him alone, wondered what had gotten into them. Meanwhile, in the depths of his belly, he could feel the mother of all belches coming on.

"Where's P.J.?" Dad asked, and then let loose a terrific burp that masked the sounds of Virgil's sudden choking. Peter John's place was conspicuously empty at the dinner table; Wolfie kept jumping into the chair.

"I got a call from Kurt Foster," Connie said. "You remember, that handsome blond boy. P.J.'s staying at his place tonight."

"What's the matter, he can't call himself?"

"It doesn't matter, Bill," she said. "The important thing is that he's seeing more of his friends again . . . his boyfriends, that is."

"Oh." Dad dipped a forkful of pork chop into the applesauce. "I see what you mean. That Kurt is a pretty, uh, good-looking kid. Rugged features. I like that in a boy."

"I guess P.J. does too," Connie said.

Dad belched again. His breath smelled curiously antiseptic. He pushed away his insta-serve, chewing the inside of his mouth, then shook his head and pulled the insta-serve back. Those damned Blue Flames were trying to make him neurotic. Jock Smith especially: that business about plutonium being too dangerous to keep around the house. What did people think Jock would be stuffing into his warheads—confetti and party favors?

He forced himself to finish the meal. A hearty appetite was a good sign, or so he thought. Encouraged, he polished off a pint of ice milk.

Dad wondered why he was so nervous. Who's making me nervous? There's no need . . . stuff's safe . . . safe as cotton candy.

He went to sleep early, thinking it would be the best thing for his indigestion, and with the aid of a double dose of Num-Tums was soon dreaming. They were not pleasant dreams, and he awakened sometime after midnight, clutching his stomach. He forced himself to relax, patted his belly to soothe it.

His intestines shook thunderously, then began to speak in a modulated voice, high-pitched like the squirting of bubbles.

"Bbbilll . . ."

"Oh, Christ," he said. He looked at Connie to see if she had heard, but she slept on.

"Lisssten to meeee, Billll."

He rolled over, hoping that Connie would waken, and clamped the pillow over his head. But the sound was in his body; it resonated on his diaphragm, echoed on up through his bones.

"Forrrget abbbbout gassss. Weee cannn have ssssuch ffffun togetherrrr."

"Who are you?" he yelled, sitting up.

Connie rose onto her elbows. "Bill? Are you having a dream?"

"Yeah," he said. "I'm awake now. It's all right, hon, go back to sleep."

He was covered with sweat. As she sank back into the bed, he slipped out and padded into the bathroom.

He slammed the door shut but did not turn on the light.

Dad sank onto the toilet and, with a shudder, voided himself. His bowels whistled with relief.

"I." Squirt. "Am." Squilch. "The." Pft. "Fffuture."

As Dad sat listening to the dying complaints, Connie turned on the light in the bedroom. He remembered, then, that he had shut the door. Slowly, he opened his eyes.

The light, sickly and bluish, was coming up through his legs. His shout woke him once more, this time for real.

At that time P.J. was also living a nightmare. His journey had gained a heightened, hallucinatory quality due to his lack of sleep, yet his suffering was the most real he had ever experienced. There were no drugs to comfort him, no bed to crawl into, no footsteps to retrace, no light to guide him either forward or back or in any direction. He was lost, starving, freezing, and now drowning.

The previous night had been nothing like this. There had been a chill in the air but no rain, and he had kept warm by marching northward, following the coast, traveling near the road but not on it. There was no traffic on the highway, but once he saw stationary lights ahead of him—houses—and he went far out of the way to avoid them. He went into the hills.

At dawn he had still been in the hills. He wondered if he should sleep in one of the dry ravines, but his excitement at freedom was too great. Seeing ramshackle houses on the hilltops, he stayed in the ravines wherever possible, hidden. The day passed slowly. Sitting on a sun-warmed rock, he tore the lid from an insta-serve and found the contents cold and desiccated, inedible.

By dusk he was ravenous. He kept walking to keep his mind off his stomach. Reaching the top of a hill, he found that mist had obscured the coast and was climbing swiftly up the slope to meet him. There were houses down by the road, but he was not ready to give himself up to them. He turned and ran along the inland side of the hillcrest, toward a forest. It was there, when night fell, that he became lost. Trees and bushes tore at his skin, the rain turned everything underfoot to mud, and he found himself sliding into a ravine. In the dark he could not scramble free, and so he followed its course. The downpour filled the ravine with water drained from the hills; he was knocked down more times than he could count by things washing into him from behind, and sometimes he clung to them to keep from drowning in the deepening torrent. He had lost his pack—he had no idea when. He thought that he was bleeding, torn in a thousand places, he thought that he would certainly die.

And then he saw the bridge.

It stood out against a tangle of wind-thrashed trees and patches of sky, thanks to a lamp burning above it. In that light he saw that the stream was partially dammed by branches and bushes that had become tangled in the shadow of the bridge; he thought that if he could climb through them, he might be able to pull himself up and out of the stream.

The current finally carried him into the dam. Lamplight shone on the churning water several feet away, but he felt too weak to move that far against the flood. Still, he tried, and succeeded in falling backward into the mass of loose wood that clogged the channel; his thrashing tore it loose, and he was swept away again.

At the far side of the bridge he saw the lamp again and cried out, reaching toward it. His hand caught a thick, hard fiber, like a smooth rope; he saw it was a root that dangled from the side of the ravine.

For awhile it was enough to hang there, gathering strength, but when he had to move again he believed that resting might have been a mistake. His greatest desire was to sleep. But he dragged himself hand over hand up the root, caught the other twisting anchors of the same tree higher up the bank, and finally dragged himself over the mud onto high ground.

There was no respite. He could hear the earth behind him sloshing into the river, dragged down by the constant erosion and perhaps helped along by his transit; so he had to move before he was sucked away again. He crawled back toward the light, haunted by its twin image reflected in the metal surface of the bridge: a drowned lamp. When his hand touched the lantern post, he slowly stood upright and looked over the bridge to see where it led.

The rain let up, then stopped completely, leaving a hush.

Against the clouds he could see a hillside, trees growing along its rounded silhouette as evenly as the pickets of a fence. Where the trees ended, higher on the slope, he saw with startling clarity row upon row of crosses.

Crosses. There must be a church somewhere near. He was almost physically overcome by a memory of warmth, of Christmas services in the neighborhood, of voices singing hymns and heads bowed in prayer.

Water drizzled from the trees, spattered on the road. P.J. turned around, still clinging to the lamppost, and looked in the other direction. Through the trees he saw a squarish gleam, like a sheet of water or glass. A dark window.

His tennis shoes squeaked as he hobbled down the road. The trees drew back, until he could see a row of houses between them. The road wound down past the houses and out of the trees, onto open land. Because the houses were dark, he kept going until he was out beneath the sky. The clouds had begun to thin, and clear air and stars were appearing in patches, when ahead of him he saw the church with all its windows lit.

Voices murmured through the walls of the building. It sounded like singing. He hurried, but when he reached the church he discovered that he was at its rear.

It would be safe. Churches were refuges. He must be far enough away from the neighborhood by now that it would be all right to accept a little hospitality, make some human contact.

The windows were of dark glass, scarlet and violet, even black, like captured lightning. As he walked alongside the church he could make out the shapes—distorted through the windows—of the singers standing in rows within. The music was familiar, though the words were unclear.

" 'Onward, Christian Soldiers,' " that was it. He started to hum the tune, but he couldn't remember the words without a hymn-book in hand.

He had a bad moment when he realized that he had walked out into the middle of the coast highway without seeing it coming. The dotted line ran as far as he could see in either direction. In the moonlight that peeked through the clouds he saw that the road was deserted. He was still safe.

If he had been afraid of approaching the church, his sight of the front door took away any doubt. It was brightly lit, the doors were open wide on the vestibule, and above the entryway were blue neon letters: THE CHURCH OF THE OPEN ROAD.

Below that, smaller painted letters on a pair of opposing signs informed him that "Good Sam Presides Herein" and "Travelers Are Welcome!" There was another sign that he thought he was misreading somehow; it implied that services ran twenty-four hours a day.

The singers finished their rousing chorus and the church grew as silent as a television with the picture on but the sound turned down. P.J. was a little nervous about walking into such a silence, so he went only as far as the vestibule, thinking that he would wait for them to start the next song. But no sooner had he stepped out of the wind and set a foot on the deep red carpet, than the doors at the far end of the chamber swung open on the interior of the church, revealing all the singers with their backs turned to him. He stepped forward—expecting that whoever had opened the door would be coming out—and the doors shut.

Only then did he notice the electric eye at the entrance. It was an automatic door.

For some reason he felt more nervous than before. He looked back at the road and remembered the chill of the wind, and the possibility of more rain. His clothes felt frozen to him like a second skin.

He continued on past the threshold, the inner doors swung open, and he went on through. The next hymn was just starting.

He stood against the rear wall. Warmth filled him, the air resonated with the sound of voices lifted in prayerful song. He closed his eyes and gave thanks that he had survived the storm. His stomach was boiling with hunger . . . but he was alive.

Thinking of what a mess he must look, he opened his eyes. Fortunately no one had turned around to stare at him. All of them —all the dads and moms, grandparents and kids ranked among the pews—were staring toward the front of the church, where a cross hung high up in the shadows, glimmering with red jewels.

He shuddered, suddenly weak. The events of the last two days had drained him, but until now he had not found a moment to pause and rest. Before his legs gave out, he decided to get to a seat.

There was a space at the end of the hindmost pew. He limped to it, readying himself with a smile to greet the old man who stood there.

One hand on the back of the bench, he turned to look down the row. He stopped, stared, and did not move for a full minute; but he was not nearly as motionless as the rest of the congregation.

They were lifelike statues, manikins, cast into poses of worship and fastened to the floor. Blank eyes staring, filled-in mouths gaping, blank hymnals in their pawlike plastic hands. Now he saw the speakers along the edges of the pews, spewing forth the songs.

In mid-verse, the song ended.

P.J. backed out of the pew. The speakers crackled, and an organ note began to vibrate the floorboards. Above the note, a calm voice said, "Welcome, traveler. The Church of the Open Road welcomes you to take your fill of spiritual and physical nourishment. Join us in our songs, join us in our prayers. You will find holy refreshment at the front of our church—an offering to you, brother or sister. Welcome."

P.J.'s eyes fixed on a brass collar hung around the throat of the gray-haired manikin nearest him. Engraved on the collar was the name WALTER S. TELLER. The matron beside the first manikin was ESTELLE V. TELLER. All the dummies had names.

The church filled with song once more. P.J. stood in the middle of an aisle, looking back at the door through which he had come.

Refreshment, he thought. Food.

Was it worth it to stay in a church full of statues if he could get something to eat?

His stomach howled at him. Yes!

He turned away from the door and walked down the aisle, convinced that the dummies were watching him with painted eyes.

The pulpit was empty, but before it was a huge white chest with a silver handle. By the time he reached it, he was almost used to the idea of the manikins: at least there would be no one to see him, no one to tell the neighborhood that he had passed through, no witnesses. He grasped the handle, which was icy, and pulled up the lid.

A cloud of frosty air rushed over him. Through it he could see platters of food, bowls of fruit, a huge bottle of red wine, cold cuts. He reached for a cube of some pressed, pale orange meat and was already reaching for another by the time it touched his tongue. It was firm, slightly fishy-flavored, like a mild salmon. He crammed an apple in his mouth, but it was mushy and he dropped it after one bite. More of the orange meat. He pulled the cork out of the wine bottle and took a huge swallow, washing down several more of the resilient salmony cubes.

His gut clenched as the wine reached his stomach. He gasped, dropping the bottle; he had eaten too fast. Or . . .

His knees hit the floor, the edge of the chest banged his forehead. He grabbed the cold rim of the chest, looking up at the pulpit through swimming eyes. A small beam of light illumined the cross in the peak of the roof; red eyes glinted down at him, and the black chasm of a voracious mouth yawned like a little pit that had begun to swallow up all the light in the room.

The last thing he saw was a bald manikin head rising over the pulpit, its shiny blue eyes lit from within.

"Welcome, brother or sister," said a gentle, wavering voice. "You have tasted the kingdom to come, the savor of our savior. Now you shall hear the songs on the flip-side of life. You will fight among doves. You will live in death forever, for having eaten you may never leave."

The ice-chest slammed shut on his fingers, and P.J. fell backward in the middle of a scream that would still be waiting for him when he woke.

WHY ACCELERATED GROWTH?
A Pamphlet
by Dr. Ralph Edison

You might as well ask, "Why an accelerated world?"

Every day, each of us is faced with a seemingly endless series of complex issues—moral and logistical—many of them new to the earth. If asked for answers to modern problems, metaphysicians can only grope for answers, rarely admitting that they don't even understand the question. Often the mystics hedge by telling us that we *cannot* know. Science, on the other hand, acknowledges that while we do not know all the answers, or even all the questions, there is always hope.

The world changes quickly, but we can keep abreast of the tide by changing at a slightly faster pace. New men have new minds, they won't accept old answers, they don't see things strictly in terms of the old-fashioned points of view.

Consider the microbe. Consider the pest. Reproducing in vast numbers, living brief but busy spans of time, bacteria and insects have outlasted the dinosaurs, seen the earth through a procession of geologic and climactic upheavals, and remain today to share a mute lesson of survival with those who can interpret their dumbshow.

There is a chain of being and nonexistence: birth, life at its harshest and mildest extremes, reproduction, and then death. Somewhere in this ever-repeating chain, something called adaptation occurs. The tiny, swift creatures are masters of the art.

They live in colonies. They live in hives. They reproduce by fission, or breed under circumstances of extreme compression. There is no privacy: everything must be shared. And yet the strongest in the system continually weed out the weak, doing a better job at ensuring survival of the fittest than the random threats of nature; for the citizen wasp knows the weak points in his hive much better than, say, a stray tidal wave or rogue plague.

The system is intensely self-aware, though perhaps not in a sense we normally associate with awareness; it picks at its flaws as a boy picks a scab, making way for new growth.

The system is dynamic. It maintains its integrity over the epochs, becoming an ever more perfect specimen of itself, even while the individual cells—the single locust, the herpe solipsist—are born, live briefly, slough away, and are no more remembered except for their fleeting contributions to the social continuum.

This is our goal: to learn from the microbe.

To play the game of our chromosomes—lethal to losers—at their own level.

To survive.

5

SOMETHING FROM THE OVEN

DAD GOT TO WORK late Monday morning, but it was no big deal. A datastorm had kicked up in the rush of the first hour, and by the time he arrived his co-workers were soaring around with nets as light as cobwebs, catching the few stray bits and shaking them into wide-mouthed chutes. He was just in time for the first break, although there would be plenty of processing to do later. He sat on a lavendar cloud next to the shapely simusecretary, smiling at the feel of her hand on his thigh, while around him warm currents smelling of scotch and expensive cologne bore faint erotic images like old blue-movie reels unrolling in the air. His sour stomach was literally in another world, in an aging overweight body. Of course, it would be waiting for him when he got off work.

The simusec'y had just begun to follow his lead toward a more fantastic use of their fifteen simulated "minutes" when the tousled head of a husky adolescent peeked over the edge of his cloud and said, "Bill? We've got some trouble."

"Hal Frost? Haven't seen you here in dogs' years. Whatever it is, it can wait. I'm on my break."

Frost jumped up onto the edge of the cloud and Dad protested as he felt the girl evaporate.

"What's the big idea?"

"This is off-line trouble, Bill. It's about your son Peter John, and mine too."

Uh-oh, Dad thought, imagining the scenario: Hal barges into Kurt's room and finds the boys tussling with a bit too much skin showing. He began to wonder if he should have listened to Doc Edison so much when they were planning the family; maybe a second opinion would have been a good idea, all those years ago. But there was no one in the neighborhood to give a second opinion.

"I'll meet you at your place," Frost said.

Dad felt the cloud solidifying beneath him, turning into a desk and chair. He found the door and went into the hall, leaving Frost to find his own way out. In the dark curtained area at the end of the hall, he closed his eyes and felt for the pads on his head and hands. Disengagement was accomplished with an electronic squeak and accompanied by a sudden attack of heartburn. His stomach was worse than ever.

There was a memo from Connie waiting on his desk: "Come to den."

A sharp black piano wire of pain seemed to thrum between his heart and his gut for a moment. He held himself upright against the desk, reached for his pack of Num-Tums, and swallowed half a dozen of the pills in a single gulp. By the time he reached the den he was yawning from the medication, and Connie's inexplicable tears only made him smile and look slowly around the room for something that might calm her—say, a soft animal toy. The first rush of comfort, however, was fleeting.

Aside from Connie, there were in the den a half dozen people he had not expected, including Hal Frost, who after all must have sent a sim to fetch him from his office. He was momentarily irked at not having been summoned in person.

Hal got up from the couch, leaving his wife and son sitting, and grasped Dad's shoulders as if to steady him. It looked like a lynching: every one was so grim. Dad stifled a burp, which broke the mood—his mood, anyway. The taste of Num-Tums chased away his doubts.

"Bill, we have something to tell you."

Dad looked past Hal Frost at Connie, who seemed unable to move with Wm. D. Jr. and Stephanie weighing down either leg. She stared at him, her mouth trembling, her hands scrabbling like nervous claws over the kids' scalps.

"You want a Tums?" he asked her.

"Bill, I know this is hard for you," Hal said, getting in his way. "Maybe you should be with Connie right now."

"Don't beat around the bush with the poor bastard," said a man he had never expected to see in his living room, a man with a wound-up face and an entertaining collection of nervous gestures. Douglas Taylor was chief of Neighborhood Security.

"So I'm a bastard, am I?" Dad said mildly. "You all storm into my house to call me names? Who let you in anyway?"

"Your son P.J. got out of the compound," said Taylor. "Night before last. Kurt was covering for him, but the records don't lie. The gate was opened and something bigger than a dog went through." Taylor glared over at Kurt Frost, who could not possibly have sunk any deeper into the sofa than he had. "The monitor tapes were blank for several minutes."

Dad stood smiling, feeling his stomach relaxing at last. His thoughts drifted on a pleasant, placid tide, in and out: through his heart, then to his fingertips, through his lungs, feeding his brain. In and out. P.J. was a good kid.

"He's outside, Johnson, didn't you hear me?"

Taylor came closer, with one of his deputies. Hal Frost turned around and grabbed Kurt by the shoulder of his jacket and yanked him to his feet. Dad was a little disturbed to have the youth thrust at his face and shaken by his father.

"I-I-I'm sorry, Mr. J-Johnson, b-but it was P-P.J.'s id-d-dea!"

77

"It's sewage treatment for you, kid," said Douglas Taylor. "Forget about going into hydroponics."

"Shut up, Taylor," said Hal, shoving Kurt back at the sofa. "I don't know what to say, Bill. There isn't any way I can see of making this up to you. He's gone out."

"Out there," Connie whispered. "Out . . . there!"

"That P.J.," he said loudly, beaming, and they all stared at him as he gave a great laugh. "He's really something, that kid. I always told him he'd go far, you know it?"

"He's gone to his death, you clown," said Taylor.

The insult almost upset Dad—almost. By now he was getting used to the Num-Tums. He could take over and keep himself afloat, didn't need no paddles, no life-preserver, no. He could face the big reality. Yep. He could handle it. He was big. He was tough. He was Wm. D. Johnson. He was Dad.

He caught Connie's eyes and something shot out of them, ricocheted through his head, punctured skull and soft tissue in so many places that he felt himself deflating slowly, slowly, as with his hands he tried to cover all the holes in his face and stop the high-pitched whining, like a baby's screams, that was coming out of him. Bad luck. No more Tums. He was coming down hard without a parachute.

"Outside?" he heard himself whisper. "Where the hell is that?"

Later, the Johnsons sat in their den with the widewall TV turned almost all the way down. Neighbors and authorities had left them to their grief. Stephanie wept because her mother wept. Nancy June stared out the window at the fence around the back yard, sniffing. Virgil sat with his head in his hands. The twins were watching TV.

"Peter John," Connie whispered. "What did we do to you?"

Her husband squeezed her and gave a grunt of resignation. "It was his decision, Connie."

"P.J.," she said, shaking her head. "He had no idea what it was like out there, Bill. No one ever told him . . ."

"That's because no one knows. How long has it been since any of us have been out?"

"Maybe," Virgil said loudly, "maybe he'll run right into another neighborhood like ours, and they'll take him in."

Dad shook his head. "There just aren't that many, Virg."

Virgil let his head sink forward, looking miserable.

"Let me show you," Dad said. He got up and went to the TV, carrying a finger-sized cylinder that Douglas Taylor had lent him with a laugh when Dad had suggested starting a search. He slipped it into the tape-cradle and closed the cover, ignoring the complaints of the twins.

The wall lit up with an abstract illustration: luminous dots of several colors, green and white stripes, black patches, huge stains of blue overlain by silvery whorls. Dad kept on the controls and the image shrank, becoming a globe for a moment: it was planet Earth, but retouched by a crazed cartoonist with a penchant for india ink.

"Wrong way," Dad muttered, and the image began to grow. He centered on the western coast of North America, and it became immediately obvious that aside from the superimposed silvery vectors of wind, and the deeper dark blue ones indicative of ocean currents, there was little to see. Virtually all of the continent, with the exception of a few white mountain caps, was smudged or overlain with glossy blackness, as if tarps of all sizes had been thrown over the countryside. In places they did not quite meet, and here a few glittering dots appeared. America was the new dark continent.

"What's wrong with the map?" Virgil said.

"It's been censored," Dad said. "The question is, did Taylor's department do it, or has everybody on the planet thrown up screens to keep the photosatellites guessing? That I can't answer. Let's see what hasn't been hidden."

He touched one of the glowing dots near the coast, a diamond eye winking out between the unmatched corners of four black sheets. The voice of the map said, "Ruined sheepfold, circa

1987." Another: "Municipal dump: no current activity." Another: "Overturned pickup truck, probably a Studebaker."

"The sats have good eyes," Dad said, "but it doesn't sound like there's much to look at. Guess it's calmed down since we left it. Anarchy or tyranny . . . it was hard to tell what was going on when we moved in here. I've never looked back."

As he brought the picture closer to home, one little light grew brighter than the rest, and finally it resolved into a satellite image. The charm of familiarity captured his attention, momentarily lifting the weight of oppression and fear that the censored landscapes had drawn down on him, and Dad stood back from the screen to watch his neighborhood running itself like a living toy. Mercurial waves flashed in the crescent bay, the beach itself gleamed as though coated in glass. The streets, and the roofs running alongside them, resembled a rather unimaginative schematic for silicon circuitry. There was also the movement, almost too tiny to discern, of humanity. He saw his lodge, a brick-red cross with alternating rings of gold and white at its center. He sighed, looking for his roof, but then his spell of fascination was broken by a memory of P.J. getting a globe of the world for Christmas, and his eyes flicked to the thin black line that surrounded the neighborhood on all sides save the seaside.

Beyond the wall were roads, fields, hills, forests, all identified by illuminated letters; otherwise, he would not have been able to tell one from the other at this angle. He panned away from the wall, following the road to the north until it ended in a field of black.

"Taylor was right," he said. "How can we search for him in that?"

"Can't you do anything?" Connie said. "Bill? Do you mean to just leave him out there?"

He turned to her, and met her eyes, but there was no force in his words. "I can't follow him," he said. "There's no one in this community willing to go out there. The roads go who knows where? To robot plants somewhere? P.J. must have been crazy to leave, but it would be crazier to follow him. Don't you understand that, Connie?"

"I understand," Virgil said. "It's okay, Dad. No one expects you to do it."

"Well," Dad said, and shrugged, as if that would relieve him not only of responsibility but of pain. Biting his lip, tears in his eyes, he looked back at the map that was mostly black, and realized that he was the one who had most expected himself to go out through the gate on his own, to find his son. He glimpsed an endless option that flickered and forked like lightning in his mind, the possibility of following P.J. into a hidden world where anything might happen.

That was a harrowing moment. He stood paralyzed before the television until, with all his will, he had dismissed the idea as impossible.

With a quick jab of his thumb, he extinguished the map, and went to sit down next to Connie. He took Junior from her lap and held the baby's bottle while he drank. Anything, he would do anything to feel useful. Anything but—

"Oh my God," said Connie, starting forward so quickly that Stephanie almost spilled to the floor. Seeing her expression, Dad sniffed for the smell of burning food, thinking that she must have left something in the oven. But he smelled nothing, and there was no reason she would have had anything but insta-serves planned for dinner.

"My God, Bill, I just remembered." She planted Stephanie in his lap, next to Junior, and stood up, smoothing the pleats in the hips of her pants suit. "What a time . . ."

She looked frantic, but her eyes were brighter than they had been all afternoon.

"Bill," she said, "we have to get Erica today. Labor starts in twenty minutes."

His grip tightened inadvertently on the plastic bottle, forcing too much orange juice into Wm. D. Jr.'s mouth. The baby choked, juice spattered his shirt. He shoved the boy at Nancy June and hurried into the kitchen after Connie.

"It can't wait?" he said, catching her by the cabinets.

"We can't put her on hold this late. We have to be there— all of us—when she comes out." He was startled to see her whitened mouth work itself into a slow, rigid smile. "And we have to be happy to see her."

"Happy?" he bellowed. "Happy is the farthest damn thing from our minds. Just look at them." He pointed into the den where their children formed a family portrait of misery, framed by the sides of the door. The twins were the exception, but they were beginning to realize what had happened.

"They've got to cheer up," Connie said. "Get the car ready, would you please, Bill? I'll get something to raise their spirits—"

He caught her by the wrist. "No medicine."

Half turning to him, she said, "Why not?"

"I—" He was thinking of the Num-Tums, of how hard he had come down, and the distorted happiness he had felt upon learning of P.J.'s disappearance. But he couldn't explain all that now. "Let's do this without drugs."

"I'll just get my purse," she said. "Oh, hurry, Bill."

She ran on upstairs, and Dad went into the garage through the door next to the fridge. The mammoth Venturon recreational vehicle took up half of the hangar-sized space, its spiraling aerials and bristling antennae almost scraping the ceiling. Dad avoided the treacherous-looking path between toppled bicycles and went straight to the family car, a sleek, segmented red roadster with chrome tailfins and a detachable compartment for the kids. He touched the garage door opener and reached into the car to start it up; a fan whirred, the panel lit and bleeped until he prompted it to idle. Misty sunlight crept through the opening door and over the floor like a wave with corners and straight edges. He found himself staring into the glassy eyes of Jock Smith's binoculars in an upstairs window across the street.

"I'll get around to you, you vulture," he muttered. Jock seemed to lean closer. Dad suddenly thought of the delight the Smiths would take that evening, when they watched the Johnson Family Hour and saw William D. Johnson break down.

"Read my lips," Dad said, and held up his middle finger—or tried to. His fingers were crabbed and wouldn't cooperate. With a curse he went back into the kitchen.

Connie had rallied the children around the table to give them a pep talk, which she now finished with an admonition: "And if you can't manage to be happy, your father will take you aside and give you something to cry about. Dry your eyes, Nancy June; Virgil, tuck in your sweater."

The family trooped together to the waiting car, which greeted each of them by name as they found their seats. Dad glanced over his shoulder into the attachment and winced at the empty spot where P.J. should have been sitting. Jock, he noticed, had deserted his post.

As the car drove into the street, Dad saw an arrow of glare floating in the misty air beyond Connie's window. Unusual. The windows darkened automatically in the diffuse sunlight, and suddenly he could see the beam with ease: a tightrope stretching from the eaves of Smith's house to somewhere behind the car. Dad nearly pinched a nerve trying to look around, but all he saw was the garage door falling like a portcullis. Now there was no stray laser fire to be seen. He checked Smith's windows, but they were still empty. Eyestrain, he told himself, though he half expected to see Smith lying sniperlike among the junipers.

"Our crusing speed will be twenty-five miles per hour," said the car. "We will reach the input destination at 4:57."

"Erica's due at five ten," Connie said, giving Dad a brief smile that had something of real pleasure in it. "But I should be there for the labor at five."

He shrugged. "I don't see why they can't just send her over when she's ready."

Connie sighed. "Men."

Nurses in powder-blue frocks scattered before them like pigeons, nearly spilling their cups of coffee when the Johnsons rushed into the predelivery room. Connie looked for Dr. Edison, expecting to find him sitting down dunking a donut into a steaming paper cup, as was his wont when she came to pick up a child. She was surprised when she finally looked through the glass partition making up one wall and saw him out on the floor among the machines, near the row of time-bake units, an electrical plug in one hand, a pair of shiny tongs in the other.

"You can go in, Mrs. Johnson," she was told by a nurse. "He's expecting you."

"I'm gonna feel sick," Dad said. "I'll meet you in the waiting room, honey."

"I'll go with you, Dad," said Virgil. "I want to read the magazines."

By the time she looked back, they had deserted her. She understood that Bill was disoriented by the delivery room, with its aisles of machinery—strange looking waldos with claw-hands that lifted instruments and set them down and directed narrow beams of colored light into dilating apertures—by the heat of the incubakers and autoclaves, and the heterogenous muddle of mucky sounds and tangy birth smells. She understood: this was a woman's place, or would have been if not for Dr. Edison.

She told the other kids to follow their father—Stephanie had already been left in a nursery—but Nancy June protested.

"No, Mom, I want to see the birth. Can I, please?"

Connie sighed, but she was touched. "If I say yes, will you take Junior and the twins back to the waiting room first?"

"Sure!"

"Okay, then."

Nancy took Wm. D. Jr. from her arms, hefted him over her shoulder, and whirled through the swinging doors, herding Lyndon Baines and Lady Bird ahead of her. A moment later she was back to take Connie's hand.

"If only P.J. were here," she said with a brave, sad smile.

"Please, Nan, not now."

They went into the delivery room together.

Dr. Edison's voice rose above every other sound in the long, cluttered room. It was loud but not deep, and authoritative without sounding certain. Connie had a sense of recklessness as she steered her way through the robot carts, but she was unsure if it was the doctor's or her own; everything in his offices seemed a little bit out of control, as if to make up for the restraint that usually pervaded the rest of the neighborhood.

"Where's the mother?" she heard him say. "Damn it, nurse, get out of my way!"

As Connie came closer to the focus of the room's flurry, Nancy June's hand tightened in hers, and she glanced down to see her daughter looking terrified.

A woman's scream cut through the clamor, silencing no one. It came from a speaker on the wall above the oven door, where Dr. Edison now stood looking at his watch.

"All right," he said. "Induction."

He flourished the electrical cord in his hand and plugged it into an outlet near the door.

The screams were coming regularly now, vibrating the light bulbs in the hooded lamps that cast angular shadows all about this end of the room. Now the lights began to dim and a blue radiance softened the edges of the tables and waldos. Dr. Edison turned, a ghost in a luminous white sheet, and spotted Connie coming toward him.

"You're late, young lady," he barked. "Get over here and do your thing."

The next thing she knew, a nurse had separated her from Nancy June and slipped a microphone into her hand.

"Go on," the doctor said, "yell your head off."

She had forgotten about this, the pre-birth screaming that Doc Edison said strengthened the bond between mother and child. How, precisely, it strengthened that bond, Connie could never quite figure out. The speaker above the oven fell silent, waiting for the real thing. She paused to take a deep breath, and Dr. Edison took a step toward her, brandishing his tongs.

"Yell, I said!"

Connie screamed with all her breath, stripping the interior of her throat.

"Louder, Connie! Again, again!"

She screamed, screamed, screamed. P.J.'s face came to mind, coupled with the thought—recently inseparable—of the sharpened crucifix coming down hard beneath the blow of a heavy hammer. She screamed at that. She was thinking of the wall now; the wall that surrounded their houses, their golf course, their beaches; the wall that kept all of them in and everything else out; the wall that poor Peter John had breached; and all she could do was scream. Eight children, nine children, ten, how many more? Screaming, bellowing. Families on every side, they have eight kids, we'll have nine: a senseless howl. Now she was shrieking, she was pain and little else. Insta-serves: help! And sleeping pills: no, please, the agony! Something for the pain? At last she could scream, only here, only now, only for this single, small, all-too-rare occasion.

"Goal!" cried Dr. Edison.

He tore the microphone out of her hands, prying it from her fingers with a special tool made for the purpose. In the next instant he had forced her down on her knees before the oven, spread her arms wide to receive the gift. Everything was silent, though she heard Nancy moaning.

Ding! went the timer.

With a raucous laugh, Dr. Edison yanked on the oven door. A light went on in the chamber.

"Looks done," said a nurse.

"Of course it's done," said the doctor. "She's done, I mean. To perfection, no thanks to you. If she were a soufflé, she would have fallen."

Dr. Edison grinned down at her, looking as though he'd had to chip away parts of his dry, wrinkled face to accomodate the smile. "You know, I usually don't give a birth this much attention, but this is a special day for the neighborhood. Get ready, my dear."

Connie put out her hands. Doctor Edison reached into the chamber and took out a silver bundle that looked like a huge potato wrapped in aluminum foil. With his tongs he tore into one end of the package. A puff of steam fogged his eyeglasses.

86

"Ah, a beauty," he said. "Come on, you take her from here."

Connie received the crinkly silver bundle without hesitation; it was only when she saw her daughter's face that she trembled.

She had seen seven children come into the world, the last four of them from the oven. They had all looked much the same: mottled, frail, glistening with blood or incubation fluid, red in the face, hollering with powerful lungs.

Not Erica. She has none of these things. As the last of the steam wisped out around her face leaving only a few beads of moisture to dry in an instant, Connie saw that her daughter, so silent, was a solid shade of blue-gray.

It's the light, she thought, but the bulbs were reverting to white and the change made Erica's color even more obvious.

"She's gray, Mommy," Nancy said. "What makes her gray?"

"New blood," said Dr. Edison. "The latest. Believe me, she'll need it."

Erica's pupils were dull silver rings, like lead washers.

Connie swallowed, unsure if she wanted to peel away the rest of the foil. The decision was made for her by Erica, who began to beat at the covering from within, denting the wrapper with punches of her little hidden fists: first one hand burst into view, then the other, and she shredded the foil from her chest.

"Perfect," said the doctor.

"Why doesn't she cry?" Connie whispered as the nurses bent over her.

The flat gray eyes sank into Connie's consciousness.

"Smile, now, mother. Let her know that you love her."

That was harder than Connie would have thought. When she believed she had summoned a semblance of motherly love, she said, "Come on, little love-child, come on, please cry, do something."

Erica narrowed her huge eyes, as if she understood, and slowly drew her lips back into the rictus of a molested dog. The surgical lamps shone on a full set of sharp teeth the color of graphite.

"She has nothing to cry about," said Dr. Edison. "Shall we take her to the party?"

In the midst of bright party lights of all colors, where the air was full of wild music and a constant drizzle of confetti, Dad felt like a dead man. In spite of this, he forced himself into jollying the children and greeting Erica Valentine Johnson with laughter as loud as he could manage. He took the little silver bundle in his hands, tossed it in the air, and was startled to hear a snarl from his newborn daughter at the peak of her trajectory.

He almost dropped her.

When she was safe in Connie's arms again, he looked at his family with a questioning eye. The twins looked startled in identical ways.

"She's gray, daddy," said Lyndon Baines.

"She's blue," said his sister.

"She's like that because she's not like us," said Nancy June protectively. "She's better."

"Now, Nancy," Connie said, "It's not that she's better—"

"Better?" said Lyndon, looking disgusted. He started to grab at Erica, as if he might run and throw her out the window if he could get her away from Connie, but Connie pulled her out of his reach.

Dr. Edison stepped between Lyndon and Connie, his eyes turning angrily to Dad. "Johnson, keep a rein on your kids. This is no time to squabble. Line up and I'll give you all pep-shots."

Dad mumbled, "I don't want another shot."

"What's that? Speak up, Bill."

Dad felt himself blushing like a teenager.

"I said I don't feel like a shot," he said, a bit louder, all too conscious of this rebellious tone. His embarrassment made him bluster.

Edison smiled as though he were biting his lips. It was a smile that said, "I know what makes you tick, Wm. D. Johnson the Elder. I know all about you and your family. I know, psychology-wise, why you have the number of kids you do, and I've seen your scraggly chromosomes—which look like unraveling sweater sleeves, by the way—and I've lit up much more of your lovely wife than you have. I know all about what went on between you and

Doris Smith, and why you really have it in for her husband. Why, Bill," that smile seemed to say, without even unsealing to speak, "I even know your middle name."

No wonder Dad felt nervous in Dr. Edison's presence. He had the dirt on everyone.

"Bill," the doctor said gently, "I wonder if I could speak to you in my office."

With a nod to the nurse, who approached the Johnsons with a ready hypodermic revolver, Dr. Edison turned and headed toward the exit. Dad found himself following, unwillingly.

The doctor's office was crowded with devices, some only half-unpacked from their shipping containers: complicated configurations of lenses, plastic waldos, tweezers mounted on hover-jet dollies. An open cupboard, above a well-stocked wet bar, was crowded with vials and syringes in brilliantly labeled packages: FREE SAMPLES! . . . TRY THESE AND YOU'LL NEVER GO BACK TO . . . TRIAL DRUGS . . . NOT FOR RESALE . . . TOY SURPRISE INSIDE!

Dad looked for a place to sit. The visitor's chair was occupied by a microscope the size of a small boy.

Dr. Edison tugged a Dixie cup from a dispenser, peered into it, and blew out a bug or something. He reached for a flask of amber alcohol and looked inquisitively at Dad.

"Drink?" he said.

"No thanks, Doc."

The doctor's expression narrowed. "You feeling well these days, Bill?" He poured himself a drink.

"I'm fine," Dad said.

"You've put on weight, I see. More than I expected. You don't get much exercise. I'm tempted to try you out on a new exermatic contraption I picked up last month: hook it into your PI and it gives you a workout while you work."

Dad shrugged, still nervous.

"Look, Bill, have a drink." He held out the paper cup.

"I really don't want any," Dad said, suddenly angry. His eyes locked with Dr. Edison's, and they stared at each other for a full minute. Dad couldn't read anything of the doctor's thoughts, but he felt as if Edison were learning everything that was going on inside of him. Finally, the doctor nodded and raised a finger to Dad's left cheek; he let it rest just under the lashes of the lower lid.

"Iridology," he said. "That's the diagnostic tool of the future. It barely keeps up with my intuition, of course, but it's better than a lot of those damn machines the salesmen keep pawning off on me." He pulled the finger away and pointed at the microscope. "I mean, look at that. What can I do with a microscope these days? Watch matchheads and pretend they're the surface of the moon? I'm thinking about donating it to the museum. I mean hell, Bill, I've got a little box the size of your finger that will take holographic infrascans of your cells and float the images right in front of your eyes thirty seconds later, along with a damn clever little legend that points out any dysfunction. Teensy-weensy mitochondria blown up big as dimes. Sure you don't want a drink?"

Dad shook his head. "No, no, I don't want to confuse things any more than they are, Doc. You know what I mean?"

If Doctor Edison had worn eyeglasses, he would have been peering over them now. "I know what you're going through, and that's a different matter. Your eyes tell me that you're in the early stages of massive withdrawal: from what, I can't quite make out. The drug ring, which in you is normally a dark olive in color, seems to be . . . what color is magenta? I can never remember."

"I haven't had a Num-Tum in a few hours, I guess that's unusual. The last one didn't settle well."

"Digestive trouble," the doctor said, still examining his eye. "Eaten anything that might have disagreed with you?"

Dad pursed his lips.

"How about your sex life? Getting enough lately?"

Dad shrugged.

"You did ask Connie—"

"I asked her and she wasn't interested, Doc. That's her business, all right?"

Edison shrugged and turned away to replenish his drink. "I keep telling you, health is the whole family's business. You don't want to raise a crew of schizophrenics and catatonics."

"I feel like . . . I feel like the family is breaking up."

Dad's throat burned, but there—he had said it. It had come out easily, but until it was admitted, he hadn't realized that it had been nagging him since P.J.'s tantrum. Now his son was gone. So much for homosexuality rounding off the edges and bending the lines to bring them all together, to make the Johnsons converge into a neat little cohesive unit. With one of them gone, the whole thing seemed unstable, unworkable.

Suddenly his face was in his hands and he sank down onto the chair, forgetting the microscope. With a groan, the doctor lifted the device, making room for him, and then Dad felt a conciliatory pat on his shoulder. He sat there, hunched over with embarrassment, his palms filling with tears, trying to make as little noise as possible.

Breaking up, he thought, letting himself feel the possibility for the first time, savoring the pain of it as if that were the only way he could really experience his sorrow at P.J.'s absence. This is it. My family. Everything I worked for . . . breaking up.

"Bill, I hate to see a man drive himself crazy with worry. I'm going to give you a prescription and I want you to take it. I understand what you're going through; I've been watching your show for a few weeks now, and I think I saw this coming. Here, take this."

Dad felt a slip of paper pushed into his hands and he opened his eyes, thinking it would be a Kleenex. It was a prescription.

"Just remember that everything changes, Bill. Peter John has flown, but Virgil is about to marry. That will be like welcoming a new daughter into your home. And Nancy is due for her treatment. You're going to be dealing with a very different person there, I can assure you. She's been a little girl up to now. Your hands will be full, Bill. In the next couple of weeks alone, you'll find yourself forgetting about Peter John. You will forget him. You will forget . . ."

91

Dad nodded and with a final sigh, boosted himself to his feet with both hands pushing on his knees.

"In the meantime," the doctor said thoughtfully, "I'll have a talk with the Whelk Elders. There were plans to call you and Jock up for inquisition, but I'll see if that can be postponed."

"Thanks, Doc." Dad felt mysteriously relieved—perhaps reprieved. Had he been afraid of that inquisition, in spite of everything?

"You go on out there and welcome your daughter," said Dr. Edison. "Have a good time, Bill. Loosen up. Now, I have things to attend to here. You know the way back."

He clasped Dad's hand and winked. "You're about due for a treatment yourself, you know."

Dad stiffened. It had been years since the last one. He felt a physical pang—adrenalin, fear—that reminded his cells of the abrupt transitions from youth to maturity, from maturity to middle age and the beginnings of senescence. Another treatment . . . he should have known. He couldn't coast through his middle age forever. There was another reason he dreaded Dr. Edison: he held the needle that brought about rapid, painful transformation.

He found himself walking down the hall toward the sound of his family's laughter, but he was in a daze and was hardly aware that he had greeted them until he looked down and saw that Erica was sleeping in his arms. She looked unreal, gray-blue.

Here she is, he thought. My daughter. My idea, too. But I don't know that I'll want her in the house.

The Johnsons returned to their car through the slowly dying light of the long summer day. One more interruption awaited them, in the person of a tall man, elegantly dressed in subdued twilight colors, his hair dark yet silvered. He was standing near their car, looking toward the sea.

"Mr. Ashenwriste!" said Lyndon, running on to meet him. "Hey, Mr. Ashenwriste!"

The Cartel man laughed gently and tousled the boy's hair. He had played soccer with Lyndon and other neighborhood children in previous years; they were used to seeing him at picnics, drifting from table to table like every family's favorite eccentric uncle.

Now, though he smiled for the children, he avoided their attention and addressed the adults directly.

"Mr. Johnson, Mrs. Johnson, I have come to extend my sympathy over your son's departure. I'm sure this is a trying time for you, no less so with the birth of this child."

"Thank you, Mr. Ashenwriste," said Connie.

"The Cartel feels a debt of gratitude to both of you, for being such champions of home nuclear power."

Dad shrugged, flattered, at ease despite his worries. "Oh, the guys will come around eventually."

Mr. Ashenwriste gave a little bow. "Even so, we would like to help you as you have helped us. Your son, Peter John, is somewhere out there." He inclined his head toward the hills in the east. "Naturally, you cannot follow him."

"Well, my work load is pretty heavy."

"Please let us lift some of that load. Cartel personnel move freely, and there are many of us. We would make this offer whether or not you had decided to install the garage unit, sir, as a humanitarian gesture; but it will mean even more to us because P.J. is a Johnson. Erica should grow up to know her brother."

Dad looked at Connie and saw that she was crying. She tucked her hands under his arm and pulled herself close to him.

"Thank you," Dad said gravely, softly. "Thank you very much, Mr. Ashenwriste. I—we're very touched."

Ashenwriste bent and extended his hand until Connie withdrew one of hers and held it out, whereupon he kissed it.

"It is the least I can do," he said. "The Cartel is behind me in this."

"Well," said Dad honestly. "That, if nothing else, gives me hope."

6

BLACK SHEPHERD

"Rise and shine and give God the glory, glory!"

P.J. awoke to the clamor of reveille, and saw through half-shut eyes that it was still dark. His breath had condensed on the icy window next to his face, and candlelight caught in the beads of moisture. The heavy black bulks of trees crowded beyond the glass, as impenetrable, forbidding, and shapeless as his dreams. All around him, the boot-camp acolytes were stirring slowly, like pallid taffy things pulled from a writhing morass of flesh—it could have been the landscape of hell or another PSA flashback. Parascopalamine (or "the Periscope," as Good Sam called it) had been the mainstay of his consciousness for the past . . . how long had it been now? A week? A month since he'd strayed into the fold along the dotted line? The Good Samaritan's injections had blurred the borders of light and dark during the first part of his stay; day and night had less meaning than black and white. In his interrogation sessions, whirling lights befuddled him; he was made to chant hymns until hyperventilation propelled him be-

95

yond the time-bound membranes of his rational cells; he mumbled prayers on his hands and knees; and already he had learned to dissemble, clean, and reconstruct a DOV missile hand-cannon with his eyes closed.

Finally, in the course of picking P.J.'s memories, Good Sam had found that P.J. was a proficient ideomotor responsive typist, and since then it had been more of the same old grind he had left home to escape. The day started earlier, that was the biggest difference. There was an endless procession of memos and military reports, all encoded into alphanumerical nonsense beyond his understanding. One little typo could earn him a drug-enhanced punishment that went on for eternity. Looking through the Periscope, he had seen hell more often than he liked. Heaven, on the other hand, remained a transcendental carrot to be hung before the noses of the good rabbit soldiers. Crosses on a hillside: that was the be-all to end all around here.

Memos, memos, memos. Yet P.J. had the suspicion that Sam was priming him for something greater. Why else would he take such interest in a vagabond, no matter how great his typing speed?

"Brother Peter John," said Michael, the sepulchral adolescent whose cot was nearest P.J.'s, "get up."

P.J. mumbled. "I don't want to get up."

Michael pulled his khaki robe over his head and ran a hand through his stringy black hair. Despite the colorful cardboard placards all over the wall of their dorm and classrooms, reminding them to "Wash your body and your hair—God has noses everywhere," most of the grunts in Camp Samaritan had terrible acne and body odor problems. At first P.J. had been aware of a constant fishy reek about all of them; now it was his smell, too, and only rarely did he notice it. He thought it was related to the orange pressed food that composed the bulk of their diet: the Host, they called it.

Tardily, but not so late that he would incur the wrath of the Monitor, he rolled out of bed and dragged his robe and slippers toward him. For the moment that he sat there naked and shivering, too weak to finish what he had begun, he noticed that Michael was watching him sheepishly with sleep-crusted eyes. Seeing P.J.'s curiosity, the younger boy blanched, turned away with a jerk, and began rolling up his blankets.

"You shouldn't be so tired," Michael said, sounding out of breath. "You get to stay in the office all day while we're out training in the hills. You're lucky."

"I guess," said P.J. He yawned and stood up, and sudden dizziness disrupted the morning routine: he saw the long barracks room stretch to eternity, with a multitude of mussy, half-dressed boys flicking dirty stockings at each other to kingdom come.

The buzzer for morning prayers brought him back to his more mundane, but no less surreal, confines.

Hurrying out into the cold morning, in file, P.J. was surprised to find a tremor of pleasure in his steps. But the sky was like a sliver-thin sheet of beautiful blue marble, where the moon hid all but a sickle of its face among clouds. Ahead of him, in the crease of the valley, the low metal buildings were smudged by ground mist into ghostly gray forms.

The girls trudged out of their barracks and fell in alongside the file of boys; there were no smiles exchanged, though a contagion of yawns spread quickly. All slippers flapped and shuffled in unison on the paved road. P.J. stared at the back of their dorm monitor's close-cropped skull, firing imaginary white defensive open-vector missiles into the nape: there went a swift salvo of DOV's, wings unfolding, bright sharp-nosed blurs right on target. The monitor's head exploded like those of the practice manikins. He could always dream.

Before the chill of the damp air had time to get into his bones, P.J. was inside the chapel. The stuffy, overheated air instantly dried his sinuses and made his eyelids rasp. He found his place among the pews, Michael to one side, a skinny weasel-faced individual named Jeremy to the other. Jeremy's problem was not some innate, weaselish character fault that had manifested in his features; it was malnutrition. He was allergic to the Host, the staple of their diet, and never got much to eat.

As the organ played, they bowed their heads as if to let the melody roll over them without meeting resistance. P.J. closed his eyes and found himself dreaming again.

There was the neighborhood. It was the first time he had thought of it since the last PSA interrogation; all the details of his past had been confiscated by Good Sam. Only in dreams did he see them now.

He drifted like a seagull over the familiar roofs. He could see Dad starting the lawn mower, and Mr. Smith in his backyard fiddling with his missiles. And his mother. He dived close to her as she scooped up Wolfie's turds from the backyard.

Mom, he tried to cry, I'm sorry I ran away. I should have stayed and tried to learn something more about myself. Maybe you could have answered the questions I was too scared to ask.

But she didn't see him, intent on her task.

Nancy? he called, and swooped up to her bedroom window. Shapes moved under the sheets. Arnold Smith's head appeared briefly, smiling, then ducked back. Floating in the open sky, he imagined muffled laughter underneath.

Virgil?

The breeze lifted him up until he could see the shore. Down in the bay, Virgil hauled his sailboat *Argos* into the waves. P.J. breasted the wind and descended as though down a flight of invisible stairs, a succession of soft bumps. But before he could come close enough to talk with his brother, a pointed elbow jabbed him in the side, and he straightened with a gasp, remembering where he was.

Good Sam's blue eyes stared down at him from the pulpit, but it was an impersonal stare, meant for all of them.

"Good morning, little lambs," he greeted his flock. "This day, let us give thanks for the savor of our savior, the eucharistic flavor, which we all shall eat on toast, his holy sacrifice, and pack in our lunches, plain or deviled, if you'll pardon the expression."

No one laughed. It was too early.

"A moment of silence," said Good Sam, undisturbed by the lack of response in the chapel.

A moment of coughing ensued.

"And now our prayer."

All rose, put their hands together, and intoned to the red-eyed figurine crucified at the head of the church:

> "We pledge artillery to the flag,
> Of the United States of Armorica,
> And to the revision for which it stands,
> One reason under fire, inaccessible,
> For everybody everywhere to love. Amen."

The figurine, swaddled in the rags of Old Glory, returned their cold stares, but did not answer.

"And now our little hymn. Just to stoke your appetites."

> "Onward Christian Soldiers,
> Marching into war.
> With the guns of Je-e-su-us,
> Spreading hope, and more . . ."

"Creamed chipped Host on toast again?" someone complained, very quietly, as they entered the boys' cafeteria.

"Holy shit on a shingle."

Jeremy, in line next to P.J., made a gagging sound that he thought was in jest at first; but when he looked around, he saw Jeremy run out the door with his hand clamped over his mouth.

"Guess his allergy is getting worse," said Michael.

"So is the smell," P.J. said.

"Smells good to me," Michael said, "I'm used to it, I guess."

He moved toward the steam-trays full of the orange chunks floating in thick white sauce, which was ladled over brittle squares of toast. The workers who dispensed the food and stood in the steam wore rubber gloves and filter masks. P.J. received his meal without enthusiasm, and waited for Michael to pour himself a glass of orange juice.

There was a crash at the door to the cafeteria. Jeremy came flying into the room and stumbled into a post where he slumped to his knees, face red and mouth wet. After him came the Camp Monitor, Mr. Strong, a tall, bald man in knee-high black boots and a camouflage-patterned frock. A few kids, who had started to help Jeremy, backed away when they saw who had flung him through the door.

Mr. Strong grabbed Jeremy by the collar, pulled him upright, and pinned him to the post.

"What did I just see?" the Monitor demanded, putting his face mere inches from Jeremy's.

"I threw up," Jeremy gasped.

"You what?"

"I threw up, sir!"

"You dared to barf His sacrifice, His very flesh, for which He died so that you, you snivelling brat, might eat?"

Jeremy's voice was barely a squeak. "I didn't eat any, sir."

The huge hand tightened in the collar, twisting it like a tourniquet. "You refuse to accept His sacrifice?"

Jeremy choked, "I'm allergic . . . sir."

"We don't believe in allergies," said Mr. Strong, and he marched Jeremy toward the counter. P.J. moved out of the way.

The Monitor barked at the servers: "Fix this boy a heaping plate of whatever that is."

The goggled workers hurried to do as directed. Two slices of toast were drenched in a ladleful of the creamed mixture. P.J. saw Jeremy growing steadily paler.

"More," said Mr. Strong. "This boy has to eat."

The toast disappeared altogether beneath a viscous mound of the creamed stuff.

"More, more!"

At last, themselves trembling from the force of the Monitor's instructions, the workers gathered around to present Jeremy with his immense helping of creamed and possibly chipped Host on toast. Jeremy accepted it, swallowing again and again, his mouth shut very tight.

"Now," said Mr. Strong, as they had all known he would, "eat it."

Jeremy began to cry. Even so, he held his plate steady, turned on his heel, and went to a place that was cleared for him. Mr. Strong stood behind him staring down as Jeremy sat, picked up a fork, sniffed delicately, gagged discreetly, probed into the overwhelming mound, and recovered one dripping piece of Host.

He waited too long and the Monitor cuffed him alongside the head. "Chew it."

Jeremy placed it in his mouth, eyes closed, and his jaws worked only once. Then he swallowed and they all heard the gulp. He coughed, covering his nose and mouth, opened his watering eyes.

Mr. Strong's voice was soft and almsot loving. "Eat," he said. "Eat it all up."

Jeremy did his best, but the serving was too great for him. Long before the toast itself was sighted through the sauce—and everyone was watching while their own meals grew colder—he dropped his fork, let his eyes roll up, and fell backward off the bench.

Mr. Strong called two boys to carry him to the infirmary. The rest of them, realizing that they had stopped eating in the last two minutes remaining of the breakfast period, gulped down their food. The Monitor gave them a look of contempt, then stalked out of the cafeteria.

P.J. could hardly swallow. Michael was trembling.

"He's gonna die," Michael said. "I know it. He had a real allergy. He's gonna die."

Crosses on a hill, P.J. thought, but he couldn't let himself dwell on Jeremy right now. Not while he was eating.

After breakfast the coeds marched in a little dish of flat land between the hills above the sea. After they marched, the youths were sent to study the Good Block for an hour in a computer library. The Good Block was Good Sam's cinegraphic version of the Bible, and it was rather different from the one P.J. remembered watching at home—not that he had watched it often enough to be sure. It seemed to be imaginatively conceived, full of action and combat scenes among primitive tribes, with dust devils and lightning aplenty.

It was P.J.'s duty to load the Good Block into its chilly cryo-processor for display. From the control pulpit at the head of the library, he could watch his peers sitting in rows before their terminals, heads bowed, eyes closed, waiting for the bleep that would allow them to begin.

The Block was some kind of black man-made crystal (he could barely make out patent numbers along one edge) on which, according to the user's manual, spectral information had been stored at very low temperatures. When the crystal was returned to those temperatures, the frozen symbols became readable with the use of a computer-guided laser. It was kind of like having an elaborate film loop in an ice cube.

P.J. lowered the Good Block into the icebox and closed the lid, made sure that it was snug. He would need insulated mitts to remove it at the end of the session, but for now he had done his share.

"Thank you, Peter John," said Good Sam. "As usual, your proficiency with the technics of spirit is astonishing."

P.J. started back to his terminal, but Sam caught him by the sleeve. "Not today, my lad. We're moving you on to something more advanced."

At Good Sam's touch, P.J. almost screamed. He associated it too strongly with parascopalamine treatments. Sam's was the soft grip that pinioned him to the chair, before the harnesses were fastened; Sam's the gentle voice that guided him into the shadowy corridors where memory and fantasy mingled, only to be ripped apart by the endless, undeniable questions. It was like being turned into a periscope, a hollow tube through which other eyes could peer into his private thoughts.

"Please come with me."

Good Sam led him through the room while the others watched surreptitiously. In a moment they were outside, in bright sunlight and warm air. Deep booms carried over the hills and shocked the earth, presumably coming from the next camp; the entire countryside to the east, Michael had told him, was full of such camps and training grounds. This was the only area designated for the training of youths. P.J. was the oldest member of the camp, though the steady sessions of PSA interrogation had already begun to make him feel years younger than he actually was.

Thinking that he was even now bound for further injections, he started to lag behind. Good Sam turned toward him and drew back on his crooklike crozier as if it were a lever that would pull P.J. closer.

"Come, come, manchild. Curry your spirits, you've an adventure ahead of you." Good Sam's eyes seemed to glaze over as he lifted his head to the sky, and waved his arm slowly as if to banish the sun. "I can see you already, beside His throne, fingers flying. You'll be a great programmer . . . a warrior in your own right, Peter John. We've decided it would be a pity to send you into mundane battle. Yours will be a different field of honor."

That gave him a reason to walk more swiftly. No more weapons training, Sam must mean.

As they approached a low bunker he had not yet entered, a group of men near the administration quonset caught his eye. Three priests in uniform were helping a man out of a jeep that had parked only a moment before. It was this man who held his attention like the lurid metronome that clocked his descent into PSA nightmares. He was fascinated . . . but why?

"I'm waiting, Brother Johnson."

P.J. quickened his steps, knowing that he would get a closer look at the man that way. The quartet had paused by the jeep to chat, while the civilian gentleman brushed dust from his suit of pastel colors. It looked as though they would enter the administration building.

P.J. and Good Sam passed the men, close enough for his sense of strangeness to become almost claustrophobic. The civilian turned swiftly to look at the hills, where a series of rocket explosions had begun to sound. P.J.'s mind glinted with light from the past, a clue provoked by the man's profile, a shard of some whole image that had been shattered by the chemical shock of the recent past.

"Hey," he said aloud.

The man heard him and turned. His expression did not change when he saw P.J.: there was no recognition there. He looked back at the khaki ministers, made a comment at which they all laughed, and then they went into the hut.

"Ash," P.J. said to himself, for that was the most maddening part of the teasing his memory had given him: a name, or a fragment of one. And a moment later he, too, was taken into a hut.

"There it is, Peter John," said Good Sam. "It looks like an ordinary plug-in, I know, but you'll see how different it can be. Hurry, hurry! Slip it on. Plug yourself in. I'll leave you to it."

A cartoon sun beams into the projection room of his mind.

Good day, Peter John. My internal clock tells me that you accessed this file within three seconds of seeing the selection-prompt.

An old-fashioned wall clock appears, with a three-second-wide pie-slice colored in red.

Judging from your access time, you must be very familiar with IMR (or Ideomotor Response) information processing technology.

A contented operator typing in IMR gloves.

You are now ready for the next step in plug-in experience.

A bare foot spiked to a
beam.

I am INRI Mark 2, the very
latest thing.

A white rabbit checks its
watch.

My name is an acronym for
Ideoneural Reintegrator.

Human nerves and circuitry
entwined, snapping and
flashing in a cruciform
pattern.

The big difference between
IMR and INRI is feedback.

A hawk regurgitating into
the mouth of a lamb.

With IMR, as you know,
once you've learned to shut
your eyes and visualize your
motor responses sharply
enough to give the
motor-stims synchronous
signals, you're on your own.

A little girl in a forest
regards a sign pointing all
directions at once.

You have to tell the IMR
everything you want it to do:
choose your own path
through your program. But
with INRI Mark 2, the
program chooses you.

A giant finger points at

hammer and nails in a
carpentry shop.

I pay close attention to the
nature of your psychic and
psychological composition—

A murky pool.

The better to hasten your
proficiency as an INRI
integrator.

A radiant superman, crowned
with a shining halo.

The longer you work with
me, the more finely we will
mesh.

Fish wriggling in a net.

I will quicken your
responsiveness—

Jesus slaps back.

Increase your accuracy—

A rattlesnake strikes.

And most of all, strengthen
your moral fiber.

A glowing loaf of golden
bread.

Shall I tell you about my
programs? At ease, get
comfortable, soldier.

A comfortable parlor appears,
hors d'oeuvres set out on a
coffee table. But there is no
way to touch them.

Have you ever heard of a saint named Ignatius Loyola?

An enormous question mark wipes out the parlor.

My, you have quick fingers, but you can speak to me if you wish. Your speech centers are linked to my processor, so you won't be speaking out loud. A simple no would be sufficient. In any case, Loyola practiced a crude form of ideoneural reconditioning in the old days before silicon-based genetistry made INRI technology possible.

Cro-Magnon man tries to splice genes with a stone ax and sinew.

He could make his thoughts as vivid to his mind's eye as the scenes of a PI program are to the visual centers of your brain.

A television screen in the mdidle of a brain.

All Ignatius had to do was close his eyes and he could enter his psychic program. In those days, people could still use their imaginations.

Lascivious images, swiftly censored.

It's almost as if INRI is what human evolution has been getting at all along.

An arrow strikes the bullseye.

Surprised to hear the word "evolution" around here? We're all products of science.

Sacred heart on a Petri plate.

And there's no getting away from that.

Running in place on Teflon.

Here's a picture of Saint Ignatius for you to cherish. I generated it myself.

A man with curly red hair and a gentle smile, wearing a ragged black robe, sits in a filthy street with his eyes closed.

He's meditating now. You can make all the noise you like but it won't disturb him.

Horse-drawn carts rattle past, followed by a parade of clowns and children and barking dogs.

Note his spiritual calm.

Slow zoom between clowns, closing in on Loyola's twitching eyelids.

Let's take a peek at his visual
centers and see what's brewing
behind that noble brow.

Zoom continues, passes
under red-lashed eyelids: a
flash of blue pupils, then
darkness and a brightening
asterisk just ahead . . .

He found himself in the center of a roaring brawl. Dust and
feathers clouded the air, animals screeched and brayed. As the
dust settled, he sank back with his attention centered in his soft
belly—the calm in the midst of the storm. His gentle, savage
hands hung at his sides.

"We've got you now, Jesus!" someone shouted.

Four lepers came wailing out of the dust.

"Die, Jewboy!" shrieked the nearest, swinging a crowbar to
which several fingers of his free hand adhered.

P.Jesus moved swiftly, effortlessly, and hardly felt the crunch
of the leper's jaw against his sandal's sole. The cripple went down
sputtering, scrabbling for the scattered pieces of himself, while
P.Jesus sprang to avoid the switchblade thrust by leper number
two. His clean white hand caught the knife blade along its flat
edge and deftly squeezed it shut on the leper's fingers; the poor
brute gibbered and scuttled away even as the savior wheeled to
disarm his third assailant.

As he whirled, as he leapt, his mind began to fragment. P.Je-
sus's consciousness shone outward: four rays. Lepers three and
four went down into dust and manure, and before they could rise
to join the first pair, his mind had redistributed its burden of
awareness. He was no longer merely P.Jesus, but P.J.-Four-Lepers
as well, both attackers and attackee. With eight foul eyes he
watched the prim man in bone-white robes take the fighting
stance known as the Tree of Death, while from the central point
of view he watched and waited for the four lepers to make their
next concerted move.

It should have been distracting, but it was such a strange sensation to be five men at once that he found himself sucked into the vision without confusion. Such was eternity: a single ray, diffracted endlessly, scattering like the lepers' fingers into muck and dust.

P.Jesus was overwhelmed with pity for P.J.-Four-Lepers; he became so softened by bathos that he nearly lost his resolve to save them from themselves. Yet at the same time he could loathe himself as the spotless white warrior: *Who does he think he is, mincing in here saying he can heal us, getting our hopes up—*

He felt moved to sermonize while he could. "Hold, brothers. You know, 'like, I can relate to leprosy."

His soothing words transformed the scene, smoothed the dust back into the gutters, restored each mote to its proper eye. The lepers dropped their weapons and crawled closer, although some had to shield their eyes from the radiance of the sun on bleached robes. P.J.-Four-Lepers could hardly keep themselves from rushing into that light, which threatened and promised to burn them to crisps.

"Come to me, brothers," said P.Jesus, and his words fell on four pairs of scabrous burning ears.

And they came, they came, each at his own hobbled speed, wallowing into the heart of whiteness, scuttling into the thermonuclear blaze at the center of the dream, the glory of a world that would never change again, forever and forever for all they knew, amen.

At the sound of their screaming, P.Jesus was frightened. They were touching him, merging with his flesh, smudging his robes. The screams were his as well. Their teeth—his teeth—tore into him. The flame consumed itself. He was eating them alive.

He would have asked why, but the light had no voice. There was nothing but the sound, the smell, the smoke of incineration.

Then a calm voice said, "Ah. I can see how it was. I can see how he wanted it to be."

The sun-spark goes out, the darkness draws in, the closed eyes dwindle, and the man with curly red hair smiles to himself as a passing mongrel lifts its leg beside him.

Of course, these visions are a bit historically inaccurate.

Tarnish spreads over the scene.

Saint Ignatius didn't really know much about biblical times. But we know quite a lot today; so much, in fact, that we have sharpened our understanding of God's purpose for us to an almost perfect edge.

Cleaver glints on grindstone.

New hope for salvation—

The INRI terminal.

New weapons against darkness—

Flare grenades exploding.

And a new translation of God's word—

The Good Block.

Have all combined to make the Christian Army the toughest and most reliable in the world.

Marching troops cover the globe.

Trumpets, a flourish.

And you, Peter John, are the latest proud addition to our fold.

Through INRI Mark 2 technology, your conversion will be complete and physically verifiable in a matter of weeks, without need for recourse to old-fashioned, hit-or-miss means to enlightenment.

Three strikes on a baseball scoreboard.

You will be born again, and I'm as sure of that as I am of my unmatched up-time. You will learn your lessons well from me, Peter John. You will become your lessons.

Man into book.

You will be freed from piffling moral ambivalence.

A leper's smile.

You will come to understand that you are right, and that only the right survive—not the wrong, not even the left. In this world there is room for nothing left.

A vast zero.

So welcome, Peter John,
welcome to the Kingdom of
Heaven.

Kettledrums pound, nearly
shaking him from his seat,
and a golden light dawns
through breaking clouds.
Before him is a vast
landscape, golden citadels,
lakes of liquid diamond,
mountains soft as clouds. He
rushes down on angel's
wings, anticipation a palpable
sensation. The air tastes like
honey. How wonderful—

> Like a dove striking a window,
> he hits an invisible wall,
> and falls. . .

Spinning.

Not so fast.

Down.

You haven't earned your stripes.

The seat hard and cold. His
hands sweating in the gloves. A
tiny blue message forming from
the phosphenes in his eyes:

PLEASE SEE YOUR PASTOR BEFORE ADVANCING
TO NEXT LESSON

Dear Kids,

Grandma here. I know you don't often get to see handwriting these days—perhaps Virgil can read this note to the young ones. It's for the older kids, too. I thought a personal card would be a good way of giving you the news, better anyway than a printed statement from the Sunset Ranch Authority.

Your grandfather passed away last night. He was only in for his Treatment but they decided he was old enough and put him to sleep. His liver was bad from too much liquor, I guess. Besides, as Dr. Edison explains it, we have to clear away all the deadwood to make room for you fast-growing youngsters. There's only so much room in our neighborhoods, I know.

I'm at peace with our Dr. Edison's decision. (He's the identical twin of the doctor you all know.) If Grandpa had taken his Treatment, he might have turned out ill and cantankerous. This way I can remember him always as the kind, robust gentleman who even on the last day of his life insisted on steering to the clinic when the car would have done it for him. I'm sure your father can tell you many amusing stories about him.

Virgil, I will be attending your wedding, tho' alone. Warm up the guest bed if you will. (Not with Wolfie, tho'—I'm still allergic!)

I am thinking about you all, especially my grandkids. You know my love goes out to Peter John, wherever he is.

OOO XXX,
Grandma

7

OUR UNNATURAL RESOURCES

"ALL IS WELL, NANCY JUNE," said Dr. Edison. "Your mother is waiting to take you home."

As the sedatives wore off, before she could even sit up, she found the strength to say, "I hate you." Her tone of voice was a bit surprising to her, but she agreed with it. She did hate him. She hated this office, these mind-blurring sedatives that were not even as much fun as real drugs, the treatments that came practically without warning—marked only by a little pink postcard that said, "Dr. Edison's office would like to remind you that your child *Nancy June* is due for an Advancement by the end of this month. Community law requires that you make an appointment within twenty-four hours of receiving this notification, or else . . ." She hated her mother for making those appointments, for not standing up to Dr. Edison and the neighborhood and its stupid, arbitrary laws. She was full of a whirlwind hate of everything that until now had seemed innocuous or, at the worst, merely annoying.

Dr. Edison must have been used to this sort of thing from

sudden adolescents. He helped her out of her seat and into her mother's arms. She was too proud to rely on the older woman's support, but not strong enough yet to stand on her own. Her crippled walk from the office to the car was her first humiliating rite of passage into the murky trauma of puberty.

She could not bear to meet her mother's eyes. Exhausted, she lay back in the seat, closed her eyes, and waited for the interrogation.

"Well," said Mom after a moment, very tentatively, "how did it go?"

With clenched teeth and folded arms, under full protest, she spat out the words, "Just fine!"

"Did you get your period?"

"Mom!" she said, blushing.

"Dr. Edison said we could expect it immediately."

"Even if I did, I wouldn't tell you."

"And why not?"

"I don't have to tell you anything," she said, in what she hoped was a withering tone. "I'm not your slave."

"Well!" said Mom.

Nancy allowed her eyes to open a fraction, just enough to let her see the traitor who had recently been her best friend. It was hard now to recall the happy mother-and-daughter banter of earlier days—or even of that morning. She wondered how she could ever have wanted to imitate such a glossy, vacuous doll. It was just as Arnold had said: her mother was programmed to behave in certain ways, and one of the things she was best at doing was perpetuating the same programming in her daughters.

When I get home, she thought, I'll take off all my makeup. I won't dissolve the dishes, or turn on the vacuum, or recycle Dad's socks, or any of that . . . that slavery!

While the car was backing into the garage like a skittish lobster, Mom said, "You might consider behaving properly, young lady, or else forget about going to Yosemite with the rest of us."

"Why would I want to go anyway?" Nancy said. "What's in a stupid Yosemite plug-in that I would care about? You can go and leave me home, for all I care. It's not like I can't take care of myself for fifteen minutes."

She was pleased to see Mom get angry when her punitive tactics, designed for dealing with a younger girl, were suddenly rendered useless.

"You are going to Yosemite!" Mom shouted, holding down the dashboard auto-lock override button so that Nancy could not escape now that the car had stopped. "This is a family trip, and you're not going to spoil it with your attitude."

"We're not a family," Nancy said drily. "Nothing's the same with P.J. gone, and you know it. You'll just be nostalgic wishing he was there."

Mom stared ahead at the closing garage door, face white, immobile. Suddenly she looked old, older than Nancy had imagined her own mother could get. There were lines in her face: not smile-lines but sad ones, lines of pain, deepening even as she watched. When Mom spoke, her voice was weak, ghastly, the sound of a stranger.

"This trip is a gift to Virgil," she said. "It will be the last time you see Virgil as your brother."

"He'll always be my brother," Nancy said, more gently than before.

"No, he'll be different when he has a wife, Nancy June. They always are."

The locks clicked up and Nancy slipped out of the car. There were servicemen in the garage, working on the space where Dad was having the nuke put in.

As she stepped into the kitchen, she heard a growl and looked down to see Erica backed into a corner on her belly, clutching at her with one leaden blue-gray arm.

"What's she doing on the floor?" Mom said.

The sitter, a teenaged girl from down the street, appeared in the doorway to the den, her fingers at her mouth. "Mrs. Johnson? I—I'm sorry, she wouldn't stay in her bassinet. She bit me . . . wouldn't let me get near her."

Mom swept up her youngest daughter and delivered a dull slap to her fat metallic thighs. The baby's roar was awful. Nancy pulled away from the commotion, thinking of her mother's swiftly aging face, her own turbulent passage from childhood to whatever lay beyond, and the aggressive baby who every day looked more gray than blue. She saw the three of them as a chain, and the thought of a weak link hounded her. How could I think of breaking it? she wondered, guilty at the memory of her own contrariness. We Johnson women have to stick together.

Upstairs, she packed her teddy bears into boxes and stacked them in her closet against the day that Erica might want them, unlikely as that seemed. The baby did not have what Nancy considered normal interests, even for an infant. She liked to eat dirt, which was typical, but she seemed too restless to pay attention to anything else. She was constantly prowling the house, scratching at the doors, her gray knees leaving scuff marks on the synoleum floors. She always tried to writhe out of the arms of anyone who held her.

Nancy paused, her arms full of dolls. The weakness she had felt in Dr. Edison's office had returned. Nausea forced her onto the bed. She sprawled there, holding the edges as though clinging to a raft, weeping. It felt like her limbs were being pulled from one another; she felt her pores gape like the mouths of fishes out of water, felt sebaceous glands squirt oil, all part of the Edison-orchestrated enzymatic quickening, an upwelling of internal activity that was rising at last from the cellular level to that of her everyday consciousness. Like some kind of were-teenager, she could feel herself changing—but knew that this would not pass with the waning of the moon. Every dendrite itched unbearably, in ways impossible to relieve. She thrashed and screamed, and hardly heard the knocking on her door, or the voice of her mother who sank down beside her to hold her forehead.

"My little girl," Mom whispered. "My little girl is growing up."

The nuke was a beaut, Dad thought. The bright silver waist-high dome was shiny and flawless except for the smudged handprints of the installers who had finished their job only hours before. Now it sat purring and gurgling in the space that had been cleared for it, lovingly, beneath the storage cabinets in the back of the garage, next to the Bestinhouse recycler. The door to the back yard was ajar, and a hose ran through the gap until such time as permanent pipes could be put in; that was the only awkward detail in an otherwise perfect installation. The placement plans for other pipes had been blue-chalked onto the walls.

When Dad thought of the savings he would reap, he could not help but grin. It was a vision as enthralling as that of the home nuke before him.

Erica was at least as fond of it as he was. Connie had laid out a blue blanket at the base of the unit, where the garage was now quite warm and shielded from drafts, and there she played, seeming content for the first time since her birth. There were plastic toys around her, but none seemed to interest her as much as the empty container in which the first supply of reactor fuel pellets had been stored. She put the little bottle up to her nose and snuffled like a dog; then she stuck her gray-blue tongue and several fingers down inside, so that it looked as though she had trapped some kind of marine animal in there.

One of the nuke's tanks made a churning sound. Erica sat up straighter, dropped the bottle, and tried to imitate the noise. She put out a hand and patted the smooth metal shell, cooing.

"That's my girl," Dad said, hunkering down, or intending to. His knees shot sparks up his legs, setting fire to the pit of his stomach. Half-crippled by the gout of flame, he stumbled toward the humming dome, only to see Erica turn on him at a terrific speed, rear up, and bare her teeth.

Somehow he found his balance, and just in time. The kitchen door opened and Connie poked her head into the garage.

"Bill? The Blankenships are on the sidewalk. Can I let them in?"

Recovered now, he glanced at Erica. She had settled back to watch him warily over the rim of the bottle she was chewing.

"Oh, sure," he said. "I invited them."

"You didn't tell me. The house is a wreck."

"Well it's not like I planned a party . . . I'm not a gloating braggart like Jock Smith. I only asked a few couples to stop by and see my—uh, this thing." He had almost said "my baby," but the words, all to recently, had been Jock's. "Gary B. will probably be the next to put in his own nuke. I don't think he'll stand for being in my shadow too long."

Connie had already gone to answer the door. He walked over to Erica, stepping gingerly to make sure that his legs had cooled down. As he approached the nuke, he felt his body hair prickling, as though a static charge were making it stand out toward the dome; there was a corresponding sensation of rushing-about in his blood, but in the opposite direction.

Dad heard laughter in the kitchen, and the sound of beer spilling into glasses. He went to the door and found Gary Blankenship bearing down on him, his blond mustache dripping white foam, one hand held out in a beer-bearing greeting. Dad took the cold glass and let that suffice as a handshake. He was surprised, after the manly ritual was complete, to see that Blankenship looked visibly nervous, even weak, like an anemic cowpoke.

"That, uh, that it in there?" he asked, his voice squeaking up at the end.

"That's it," Dad said. He clapped Gary on the shoulder, turning him toward the door, and made an inclusive gesture to scarecrow Nada Blankenship, who waited in a far corner of the kitchen, holding her tall beer in stick-thin fingers. Her expression was one of panic, but Dad refused to let that stop him from smiling at her.

"Come on," he said. "You, too."

Gary went into the garage and stopped, blocking the door.

"Come on, Gare, there's plenty of room. I moved up the Venturon so we'd have a clear path. How do you like her?"

Erica had dropped her toys to concentrate on the adults. She backed up protectively until her feet were touching the dome.

"She's cute," Nada said, sounding strangely relieved. "You didn't tell us she was such a little doll, Connie."

"Best they make," Dad said.

"She means Erica," said Connie.

"Also the best they make, and our finest little safety feature. Our little bumpkin here eats the waste from the nuke. Doc Edison handled the specifications."

"Nice," Gary said doubtfully. Dad saw the sweat on his high forehead, but decided not to comment on it. When he saw Gary's free hand dangling obtrusively over his groin, he could not help but chuckle.

"You think you can stop radiation with a hand if it really wants to get you?"

Gary looked down, paled, and pulled the hand away. He covered his embarrassment with a wisecrack, jerking his thumb at the nuke. "That's all there is to it, huh?"

"Big things, little packages," Dad said. "You want to see it up close?"

He urged Gary forward and heard Nada gasp. Erica, on all fours, lowered her head and raised her rear like a junkyard dog. Dad drew back.

"It's that safe, huh?" asked Gary.

"Safe? Of course it's safe. You should see the hazard studies they did on this site, Gare." Dad ticked them off on his fingers. "Earthquake danger, aircraft crash, fire, tidal wave, you name it. I've got a figure somewhere estimating the probability of a meteorite coming into our garage—a meteorite big enough to do damage, that is. A little one could whiz right in and flatten the recycler without doing a thing to the nuke."

"Gosh," Nada said, but she didn't look as though that was what she meant. Her smile would have looked fitting on a skull.

"Oh, Nada," Connie said suddenly, "did you see the shawl pattern in *The Ladies' Home Video?*"

"Why, no," Nada said. "The latest release? I haven't watched it yet, but I am dying to take a look."

They closed the kitchen door behind them, leaving the men alone. Again Dad experienced the sensation of having his hair stand up and point at the nuke unit. He wondered if Gary could feel it.

"You know, Bill, the Hirams are moving farther down the street." Blankenship didn't look at Dad when he said it. He looked at the door instead. "They don't like living so close to your nuke."

Hiram? Dad thought. It was the first he had heard of it. They had been next-door neighbors for years. Come to think of it, no one ever moved in Cobblestone Hill or Laurel Woods. You had your house for life. That was the way it was, had always been.

"Is it Smith?" he shouted, his voice vibrating the spokes of the kids' bicycles. "I've had about enough of his propagandizing—"

"It wasn't Jock, Bill. We all talked it over. You know Hiram." He gulped at his beer, drained it, and fortified said, "Could be he's yellow."

"Damn right," Dad said, slightly comforted.

"We're pulling for you, Nada and me."

"Good to hear, Gary. Appreciate it. I always knew you'd be the first one to follow my lead and get your own nuke. I know I never talked to you about it all that much, but I could tell by the quiet, reasoning look in your eye that you had it all thought out."

Gary nodded. He looked more comfortable around the nuke now—positively bold. "Sure. I figure to give it a year or two, wait and see how this works out for you."

"What? A year? Blankenship, you're a menace to progress."

The other man laughed, and Dad believed that he had been mistaken. He was about to sharpen his point and press it, but he noticed that the kitchen door had yawned open an inch or so, and an eye was peering through.

"Who is that?" he said. "Arnold?"

The door opened all the way.

"Hey," Arnold said, and stepped in. He looked past Dad and Gary Blankenship, right at the nuke. Dad heard Erica growl; too many strangers, he thought.

"I came to see Nancy," Arnold said in his new deep voice. "She's still asleep. Mind if I take a look at the nuke, Bill?"

"No, I don't mind." Calling me "Bill" now, is he? Dad

thought. I sure hope we haven't got another teen rebel on our hands. "I was just telling Blankenship here about the nature of progress, Arnold. You agree, don't you? We need more order in our community, more of the good old straight-ahead get-go."

"There's something to be said for anarchy," Arnold said, and he stopped to stare at Dad. It was a cold stare, merciless, too mired in adolescence for Dad to understand completely: but he did feel the threat in it. There was no mistaking that. It completely undermined any innocent interest in the nuke.

"I mean, look at it, Bill." Arnold sneered. "I'm sorry: *Mr. Johnson.* You're always extolling the virtues of order, but you seem to be most comfortable in the middle of chaos; and the mess you like best, I notice, is the one you make yourself."

Dad did not know what to say.

"I think it's time you ran along, Smith," said Gary Blankenship, stepping between Dad and Arnold as though he might have to break up a fistfight.

"It's all right, Gary," Dad said. "Come here, Arnold."

No part of Arnold moved except his chin, which budged an inch closer.

"You kids grow up fast these days," Dad said. "But all Doc Edison's shots can't give you wisdom."

"I figured this out for myself," Arnold said.

"Figuring isn't wisdom—it's only figuring."

"Oh yeah?" Arnold said, but suddenly he couldn't meet Dad's eyes.

"I know when to keep in line," Dad said gently, even tenderly, "and when to step out of it. That takes timing, which you haven't got yet."

Arnold swallowed, red-faced.

Dad took a step forward. "I understand that it's—"

"You don't understand a thing!" Arnold yelled, and he turned from the men and rushed back into the house.

Dad smiled at Gary, shrugged.

"Another screwed-up Smith," Gary said, shaking his head.

"Don't be too hard on the kid. He's had it rough, with Jock for a father. But he's on our side, Gary." Dad wagged a finger. "Keep that in mind. He's a good one to have on your side."

Five minutes earlier, Connie and Nada had just seated themselves on the living room couch. "Oh, Nada," Connie began, and then the doorbell rang. "Damn it."

She checked the screen by the door and saw that it was Arnold, out on the sidewalk, pressing the bell that was mounted on the ornamental mailbox; at least he didn't come in without knocking —that drove Bill up the wall. He was a gangly boy, and had hardly any clothes that fit him, though the Smiths' recycler should have taken care of that. It would be like Jock to work for months on his missiles and forget to call in a service order on the Bestinhouse.

"It's the prince come to visit Sleeping Beauty," she told Nada as she let him in. "Hello, Arnold. She's still upstairs in bed. Maybe she'll wake up for you."

Arnold did not say a word to her but hurried up the stairs looking grim.

"You're so lucky to have your kids," Nada said when Connie came back to the couch. "I know they're trouble, and I do appreciate not having to clean up after anyone but Gary. Still, I sometimes wish we could have even one."

Connie felt uncomfortable discussing the legal vagaries of birth. Some people were given permission, some weren't. It was as simple as that.

"Aren't you afraid of what that nuke might do to your eggs, Connie?"

Connie sipped her coffee. "Goodness, no. They're all in the bank."

"Of course. I don't suppose a little radiation would give you anything quite as . . . unusual as Erica." Nada put a reassuring hand on Connie's knee. "Forgive me if I'm rude, Connie, but she doesn't look exactly natural."

"I guess not."

Nada moved closer, looking perplexed. "Is something wrong?"

She shrugged. "I don't think so. When you talk about children,

124

though, it reminds me of when Bill and I were planning the family. We could talk about anything then. I don't know what he's after these days, Nada."

"Oh, Connie, he hasn't come up with another weird scheme for you two has he? No two-headed monsters?"

Connie laughed, but it was halfway to a sob. "No, nothing like that. His new plans don't have much to do with me; I think that's part of it. He's so political that I can't talk to him. I'm hoping it will be better when we take our vacation—he'll relax and be more himself. He'll . . . stop drinking so much. It's like there's nothing to him when he drinks, nothing inside."

Nada's hand felt warm and supportive. It had been so long since she had talked to anyone who understood. Doris wouldn't talk to her anymore. She gave a terrific sigh, thankful that Nada didn't rush to fill her silences.

"Since P.J. ran away," she said, "he's been losing interest in the rest of the family. He used to think of it as his business, you know. Every shopping trip was an investment, he was chairman of the board, the family manager. Now he's beyond all that. He wants to organize the whole community around his nuclear plant; he wants everyone to look up to him so he can straighten them out, but he can't even handle his own household."

"The neighborhood is changing," Nada said. "You can feel it. The Hirams are moving, did you know?"

"No!" Connie understood instantly: the Johnson garage was next to the Hirams' master bedroom. She felt stricken. "Oh God, Nada, I'm losing my friends, too? I can handle losing my mind, even my husband—but not my friends."

She began to cry. Nada hugged her close.

"You know what I think you need?" Nada whispered. "You'd feel better if you weren't so wrapped up in Bill. Maybe you need a good old-fashioned affair."

"Oh God," Connie said, and had to laugh. "With who? Who'd want to be with William D. Johnson's old wife?"

"Well, how about turning the tables on a certain someone? I bet Jock Smith would like the idea."

Connie choked. "That's ghastly!"

"I'm only joking, Connie. About Jock, that is. I'm serious about an affair, though. With the right man. It would help you improve your image of yourself."

Connie felt a little better. "Maybe," she said. "With the right man."

"That's the spirit. See how you perked up?"

She was already wondering how it might happen when Arnold came into the living room, swearing. He must have been back in the den or the garage because he came from the kitchen.

"Somebody let me out of this place," he said.

"Did she wake up for you?" asked Connie, going to the door to disengage the locks.

"No, but when she does, boy, am I going to open her eyes."

She watched him go down the path, shaking her head. "I wonder how much longer they'll be together. Bill would never let the two of them get married, not feeling the way he does about Jock. It's time to start looking for another boyfriend, I guess."

"Hm," Nada said. "For *you*, too. I'll ask around."

Nancy's fever lasted thirty-six hours, during which time she was occasionally aware of one or more members of her family gathered over her.

"This is the big one," Dad's voice echoed out of measureless caverns. "Puberty. The difficult years. I remember it well."

"When did you get your first period, Daddy?" asked Lady Bird, and their voices drizzled away into cackles of insane clownish laughter.

Once Nancy dreamed that Arnold was standing over her with a handful of blue glowing pellets, an insane leer, and an erection. She pulled the covers over her head, but she was interested. Bombs and sex. Real sex, not the playful puppying they had engaged in up until now: they could start planning their own family, collecting sperm and ova and dreaming up specifications. Real bombs, too. But after the bombs would there be any sex? Any ovens or refrigerators?

"Arnold," she said, feeling a probing hand, "you better not."

"Come on, Nan, it's only Virgil."

She sat up suddenly, uncovering her face, and realized that the walls had stopped breathing. Her bloodstream no longer effervesced adolescence. She was well again.

Virgil sat by her bed, a book in his hand. "I've been playing nurse," he said. "How are you feeling? You look better."

"I feel great," she said, which was true. "Do you want to go to the beach?"

"Not so fast," he laughed. "You should see yourself."

She swung out of bed and went to a mirror; it was a few inches too low for her now. The reflection looked familiar, but she had changed. Her face was thinner, spotted with acne from which she first cringed, then leaned closer to inspect.

"Doctor Edison said you should take two of these the moment you woke up." He came up behind her with a bottle of pills. "So how does it feel? The new you."

"I'm not sure," she said, listening to her voice, which was hoarse as though she'd been shouting; it creaked like a badly played violin, but it had potential. "I guess I'll get used to it."

"And as soon as you have, it'll be time for the next treatment." Virgil shook his head and turned away. "It reminds me of my puberty. I didn't know what the hell was happening. Voice breaking, hair shooting out all over the place, all these—these weird emotions. I didn't know what to do with myself."

Still looking at herself, Nancy shrugged. "I just feel like going to the beach."

"I still don't know what to do," Virgil said, so quietly that she wasn't sure that she had heard him. "I'm getting married next week, Nan, you realize that? I—I don't feel ready. As soon as I get used to anything, everything changes. How is it going to change when I'm living with Elaine?"

"Aren't you excited? I would be."

"It would be different for you."

He looked incredibly depressed. She shook him by the shoulders. "Cheer up."

"I'm giving up my studies," he said, not looking at her. "No more poetry, no more books. I'll plug in every morning, like all the other husbands, and sit at a desk somewhere in the bowels of a program. No more books." He looked up at her, his eyes pleading; but what could she do? "That's the worst thing, I think. I always wanted to have a library."

"Why can't you?"

Suddenly his eyes cleared; he looked embarrassed. "It's good to have someone to talk to, Nancy, now that you're older I mean. You don't mind do you?"

"Of course not, Virgil." She sat next to him.

He sighed. "When I get married, I'll be too old to buy books legally. They're only legal for studying when you're young, and even then it's difficult to get them. Pretty soon I'll be a consumer, and there are purchase controls. I can buy all the weapons I want, sure, but books are bad for the economy."

"You're too pessimistic," she said. "Do you want to go to the beach or not?"

"I'm depressed," he said. "You go. If I see my boat, I'll probably cry."

"Maybe you should," she said, and hugged him. "I hope you cheer up for Yosemite."

"I'm sure I will." He tried to smile. "It will be beautiful in there."

"Okay!" Dad called from the garage. "If you have to use the john do it now!"

Nancy closed the closet door where she had tucked Junior in for his nap; he would sleep for the duration of their trip—all of fifteen minutes—and if he woke up there were auto-pacifiers and food nipples aplenty in the cabinet. Erica was also too young to come along, but she never wandered from her post by the nuke.

Nancy ducked back into her bedroom to grab a sweater, in case it was cold in the garage, then she ran down the stairs to join the others. Virgil was just going into the garage, Mom had Stephanie on her leash, and the twins were piling into the Venturon. Dad pinched Nancy on the arm as she went through—"How's my little lady?"—and stepped back into the kitchen to grab another beer.

Inside the Venturon there was a spacious shell fitted with deep-fit sofas for the Johnson kids; Mom and Dad had separate seats at the front of the cabin, facing the console dashboard. Plug-in wires, gloves, and masks hung on hooks near the curtained windows. Nancy dropped down into her favorite cushion, Virgil took the next, and Mom strapped Stephanie in the sofa nearest her. The twins had gone back out again, and were playing in the garage. Dad turned back to yell at them as he teetered in the doorway, barely holding to the frame with one hand while beer dribbled from the can in the other.

"We're ready, you two!"

He lumbered over to his seat, shaking the whole van, and dropped down heavily. Connie made sure that Wolfie was out and that Lady Bird had gone to the bathroom, then strapped the twins in place.

Nancy stared past Dad's head at the closed garage door, amused to think that they would have to open it to drive a few blocks in the car, while in the Venturon they could go hundreds of miles without even leaving the garage.

She looked at P.J.'s empty couch, then away.

"Here goes," Dad said, and slipped the Yosemite program into the console.

Nancy pulled on her gloves, which were a little too tight, and then the mask, which barely fit. For a moment the darkness behind the eyesockets frightened her, and the pressure made her claustrophobic. But that passed, and she drifted in hazy anticipation of the journey, feeling herself falling, falling through dark clouds, then breaking into light. Below, the countryside was spread out to the curves of the world. All she could see was a black road, dotted down the center, dividing an endless green field. On the road, a shiny silver bug was moving, and as she got closer she could see the antennae swaying on its carapace. It was the Venturon. Down she went, swift as a diving gull, straight through the roof of the van, and with a pop her eyes sprang open and she found herself singing "The Wabash Cannonball" along with the rest of the family.

The interior of the Venturon had been rearranged. Instead of the deep-fit sofas, they sat on springy vinyl seats. Instead of a console, Dad had a steering wheel and a small keypad. There was a little gas stove, a trunk-sized refrigerator, cupboards full of paper towels and kitchen matches and plastic dishes. Magical bags of potato chips and cookies lay open on the little Formica table— magical because one could eat and eat and eat, barbecued potato chips and Hydrox cookies, and make no dent in the supply. It was also impossible to get sick. Plug-in vacations were the best.

As they sang "She'll Be Comin' Round the Mountain," Nancy felt a moment of disquiet, as though something snaky and invisible had invaded their happiness, a drift of soundlessness woven through their loud harmonies.

P.J., she thought. He should be here . . .

And glancing over at the table where P.J. always sat next to the window, she saw barbecued potato chips floating like burnt butterflies from the bag, drifting to a point at about face-level, and vanishing with stifled crunches. With a chill, she tried to turn to Virgil and point it out to him, but she found that her mouth kept singing and smiling, and she could not help herself from feeling happy. In a moment she had forgotten about the ghost-borne chips, and was content to play Twenty Questions.

The rest of the journey by Venturon passed like a series of excerpts, which it was. There were no tedious moments. One moment they were dawdling over the green expanse of fields, the next they were stretching their legs in a service station in the town of Merced, and suddenly they were on a winding road among tall pines. There were no other cars to be seen until they approached an information booth in the center of the road, and joined a line of campers and cars waiting to pass one at a time into the park.

A tall, pleasant park ranger in sunglasses gave them a map and told them to enjoy their stay, then they were on their way again, in the midst of a procession of visiting vehicles. Just as the road began to look crowded, a number of the other cars disappeared, leaving plenty of space between the remaining travelers.

"If I remember this road right," Dad said, "there's a lookout point just ahead."

Everyone fell quiet, crowding to the windows.

"There it is," Dad said a minute later. "Hold on, I'm pulling in."

They parked in a turnout with a stone wall around the perimeter, and joined the other tourists who had come out of their cars to sample the spring afternoon. Nancy walked up to the wall, which came about to her knees, and let out a gasp of wonder and joy—all part of the program.

A marvelous valley lay before her, much more realistic than in the photograph on the program packaging. Splendid white clouds waded through a steep-banked river of evergreens, between sheer granite faces that dominated all she could see. She had never seen a blue as deep and clear as that of the sky in this program: she thought she could almost see through it. But what lay beyond the reach of the blue? Infinity? The roof of their garage?

She heard a screech near her foot and looked down to see a bushy-tailed chipmunk approaching. A tribe of the critters, natives, had invaded the parking lot, and were now demanding placating offerings from the foreign tourists. Dad opened a box of Milk Duds, sprinkled them on the ground, and backed away as the chipmunks closed in, snarling and spitting at one another in their feeding frenzy.

"They sure are friendly little scamps," said an old graybeard in a corduroy hunting jacket and a coonskin cap. As he spoke, one chipmunk buried its fangs in the neck of a competitor for an outlying Milk Dud.

"Yep," Dad chuckled. "They sure are, old-timer."

He crumpled up the candy carton and tossed it toward the trees; it vanished before it hit the ground.

"You shouldn't litter out here, Dad," Virgil said, his voice slow and straining as he fought to get out words that went against the grain of the program.

"You saw what happened to that trash," Dad said with a wink, speaking easily. "Out here, nature lets us clear our errors."

"That's right, sonny," said the old-timer, banging his pipe on the heel of his boot. "Well, be seeing you folks in the valley, I reckon."

He climbed into a battered old camper, the sides of which were covered with decals from the Trees of Mystery, various plug-in national parks, and the National Rifle Association. The truck sputtered away down the winding road, coughing out fumes of black exhaust that vanished instantly, without dispersing.

"You can be sure that old guy knows his way around here," Dad said, sounding slightly awed. "What do you bet we run into him again?"

"He smelled bad, Daddy," Lady Bird said.

Dad turned quickly as the wind rose up and the sky seemed to darken, matching his troubled expression. Nancy stepped away from him, frightened for a moment, thinking with difficulty, *Something is wrong!*

"I'm sorry, Daddy," Lady Bird whispered, and jumped up into the Venturon, as if fleeing the lowering clouds. Mom took Dad's elbow and gave him a cautioning look.

A second later the weather was fine, welcoming them to the valley.

The family faded in again to find itself in the parking lot of an enormous old hotel made of solid rock. Nancy climbed out of the Venturon, took a deep breath of pine-scented air, and heard Dad say, "The old Ahwahnee Hotel. My, my, it looks just like I remember. Isn't that something? Can you imagine the work that went into this program? Of course, the corporation that makes PI-Vacations also owns the valley, so they had plenty of access to the original."

"You came here before, Daddy?" asked Lady Bird.

"Not here," said Virgil. "He went to the real Yosemite."

"That's right," Dad said. "It took hours of steady, boring driving to get here, and when we did the valley was full of people and their junk. It wasn't nearly as nice as this. I didn't stay in the hotel either—could hardly afford that. Now it's no problem. The cassette comes cheap."

"Wow," said Lyndon Baines, "you mean this is a real place?"

"Was," Dad said. "The last I heard . . . reservoir."

"Like the Grand Canyon," said Virgil.

"Not quite," Dad said. "That's landfill now, I understand."

Nancy smiled at Virgil, glad that he was enjoying himself so thoroughly, thinking how she would miss having him around all the time once he was married. Well, at least P.J. would still be around. She felt his hand on her arm, and turned to tell him—

But he wasn't there.

"Peej?" she said.

A breeze stirred the conifers; bushes by the path waved their limbs; but there was no sign of Peter John. That was weird. Hadn't he been with them a moment ago?

"Hey," she said, louder, "where did P.J. go?"

"Naaan," Mom said, in the weird slowed-down voice that meant she was resisting the program. "Please . . . not here."

Slowly the memory came back to Nancy. P.J. was gone. He had not been here the whole time. It was hard to remember, so hard; it was much easier to forget about him and just have a good time.

Then the bushes by the path parted, pushed aside by an invisible body, and a pine cone came bobbing through mid-air until it hovered under her nose. She looked at it in horror—a grudging, very slow horror—then stared at the air beyond it. A little enamel souvenir-shop pin, picturing Half Dome, was suspended there, rising and falling slightly in time to breathing she could only imagine. And though she could hear nothing, there was a peculiar silence like that which had crept into "Comin' Round the Mountain"; the void seemed to say the exact opposite of, "Look what I found, Nancy!"

Before Nancy could scream—which might have been impossible in this program—Dad stepped up and snatched the pine-cone from the air, moving as slowly as though he were walking through sludge. He glared at the spot in mid-air where P.J.'s face was not, then threw the cone off over a green lawn where several old people were sunning in wheelchairs.

"There's no one there, Dad," Lyndon said. He laughed, apparently enjoying the increasingly deep tone of his voice.

Dad was breathing hard, but it only lasted an instant. Apparently he resolved whatever problem he was having, for his face became unclouded, even blank.

"I understand," he said jovially, returning to normal. "I forgot to reprogram the Venturon central processor. It was set to treat us as a family: as far as it knows, P.J. is still receiving his part of the program. We're seeing an empty glove." Dad hit himself on the forehead. "I guess we're just going to have to get used to it."

Nancy felt a little better, but not much. It was the first time she could remember anything the least bit upsetting happening on a plug-in vacation.

Turning away from P.J.'s absence was as sad as abandoning a pet, but there was no resisting the program when all she really wanted was to have a nice time. She followed her family into the lodge, and easily fought the urge to look back and see if the little souvenir pin had come along.

The interior of the hotel put Nancy into a daze, it was so beautiful. She wished that Arnold could be there with them, so that they might stroll slowly down the dark halls like the other elegant couples. The sound of tinkling crystal and silverware came from behind the huge double doors of the dining room, as though the waiters were playing chimes. She finally sat down in a cushioned chair and watched her parents at the reservation desk, where they had been waiting for the program's equivalent of ten minutes. Virgil had gone to look around. How wonderful to stay here for a week, when only fifteen minutes were passing in the outer world.

"Where did that man go?" she heard her mother whispering.

"Hell if I know," Dad said. He slammed his hand on the silver bell for service, and the sound was as deep as the tolling of cathedral bells. "Letsssss havvvvvvve sommmmmmmmmmmme servissssssssss!"

Nancy slipped out of her seat and joined her parents. "What's wronnnnng?" she asked.

"Don't say that," Mom said. "Nothing's wrong. Everything's wonderful. Aren't you having a wonderful time?"

"I guess, only—" She broke off to watch the reservation clerk returning from his office. He looked very pleased about something.

In a perky voice, he said, "I'm delighted to tell you, Mr. and Mrs. Johnson, that we can find no record of your reservation, and the hotel is booked through the season."

"No record?" Dad shouted. "We made reservations in . . . why, it was . . ." He threw out his arms, striking the bell again. "We don't even need reservations, goddamn it, we paid for the program!"

Nancy was proud of Dad for a moment, because he seemed to have broken through the error-correction capacity of the program; he was complaining openly, at normal speed.

The clerk looked dubious. "Program, sir?"

"This one. The program you, my man, are in. Now I want rooms for my family, and I want them now. In nanoseconds, understood?"

Smiling hugely: "I'm sure that is quite impossible. If you would like to stay in the valley tonight, I suggest you contact the concession-camp agency immediately. In fact, they might already be full."

"I'll do nothing of the sort," Dad said, leaning over the counter. "If you don't give us the rooms that are reserved for us on this cassette, the rooms for which I have already paid, I will personally climb over there and break you into the bits that make you up, you cheap recording."

"Sir, it is not my fault. You would have to talk to the management."

"Fine. Why don't I just do that, hm?"

The clerk bowed slightly, showing teeth as he laughed. "Right away, sir. Would you like to come with me?"

He lifted a panel at the side of the desk to allow Dad through, then rapped on a door behind the counter. Nancy watched her father rise to his full height and set his eyes smouldering. Mom turned to her with a weak smile and patted her wrist. "Don't worry, dear, your father will—"

Dad's scream was completely silent—censored from the program before it could disturb anyone—but it drew all of their attention. Virgil and the twins came running from wherever they had been. Nancy saw the clerk easing the door shut against the palm of his hand, in order to make no sound; he faced the whole family with a prim smile. Dad staggered backward, face white, mouth slack, eyes blank; his hands scrabbled to raise the panel that let him out from behind the desk, and once he was out he grabbed Mom's arm and jerked her along with him. Stephanie's leash snapped taut, and she flew after.

"Dad?" Virgil called. He looked at Nancy, who shrugged, and then each of them grabbed a twin by the hand and ran after their parents down the long hall toward the Venturon.

"Good luck with the cabins," the clerk called after them. "I'm sure they're all taken by now."

Dad rummaged through the icebox in the van, and finally came up with a can of beer. He sucked down half of it before he could talk. Slouched in his seat, his face drenched in perspiration, he finally began to mumble of what he had seen—or not seen.

"It was nothing," he said, his words conveying the impression of something much worse than that. "Like a pit, a big erasure . . . gray and burnt-out . . . wiped away. My God. I thought that prissy little clerk was going to lead me in by the hand, or push me over the brink. I don't know what would have happened. I had the idea I was about to vanish."

"It *is* the program," Virgil said. "Something's wrong, Dad."

"You're telling me? They lost our reservations."

They had no trouble speaking of their unease now. Nancy felt as though they had stepped out of the program altogether, except that they were still here in the valley.

"Oh, Virgil," Mom said, "I'm so sorry this had to happen during your special trip."

"Don't worry about it, Mom. It's no problem." He put an arm around her. "All we have to do is run a diagnostic program and see where the problem is. The chances are good we can fix it in no time. We might have to get out of here for a few minutes, that's all. We could come back to the valley before things started getting funny, and check into the hotel all over again. You see?"

Mom smiled. "Well, I guess."

"He's right, Connie," Dad said.

"Let's run the diagnostic first," Virgil said. "No sense leaving the valley if we don't have to."

Dad let him into the front seat, to get at the console. Virgil leaned over the display board. "See, it's—"

Nancy heard him suck in his breath. She went forward to see what had caused it, and soon they were all crowded around him.

"What's wrong, hon?" Mom asked.

"The keypad is gone." Virgil's voice was flat—not slowed down, only flat. "Do you see that? It—it's just not there."

Nancy strained her eyes trying to look straight at the dashboard where the keypad had been; somehow her vision just slipped around the area and her eyes focused on nothing. It was like having a blind spot. The keys might have been there: she couldn't see them, that was all.

"Are you sure they're not there?" Mom said. "It could be glare on the dashboard, Virgil."

"Funny glare," Nancy said.

"You all see that?" said Dad. "Whew, I thought that last beer had done me in. It's . . . what are you doing, Virg?"

Virgil was reaching toward the spot with one hand, but slowly. He paused and looked at Dad. "I'm just going to see if I can feel it. Maybe it's an optical illusion."

"Hm," Dad said. "It's like what I saw in that office, Virgil."

"Yeah." Virgil smiled. "That's probably it. We're having problems with the visuals. I bet I can start the diagnostic by touch."

He reached into the area where sight could not follow, and his wrist appeared to bend the way a spoon seems to warp in a glass of water. Nancy felt a little sick. She watched his face change. One moment he looked sure of himself, the next he was completely baffled.

"Nothing," he said. "It goes right through."

"To where?" said Nancy. "Virgil, what's wrong?"

He shook his head and pulled out his hand.

"Oh my God," said Dad.

Virgil opened his mouth to scream, but nothing came out. The whole scene gave a little jiggle, vanquishing that open look of terror, and Nancy saw her brother smiling at all of them as though there were nothing wrong at all, nothing in the world—wherever that was. He smiled as if he had always had a blank spot, an optical stump, instead of a hand.

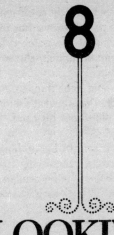

8

LOOKING BACKWARD

"PETER JOHN . . . PSST . . . PETER John . . . are you awake? Come on, your eyes are open."

P.J. turned away from the whisperer, knowing that if he acknowledged Michael it would only make things worse. Things were bad enough already.

"You can't be sleeping with your eyes open, Peter John. Please. Why won't you talk to me anymore?"

P.J. forced his eyes to close.

SIN

The flare of lettering, teased from his optic nerve, was as bright as an advertisement.

Mustn't think about Michael, he thought. Mustn't listen to him. Hear no evil.

"Peter John, what's been going on with you?"

GUILT

He opened his eyes to escape the gold-lettered caption, but it persisted, hanging against the dark window, spelled out upon droplets of mist.

A second voice came whispering through the room: "He's out of it, Michael. He's gone on."

P.J. bit his lip.

"He is not, I saw him open his eyes."

"Green-screen zombies sleep with their eyes open. You should be glad we're training in the field, and not in the computers."

P.J. heard nothing for a long time, and then a soft sobbing drifted from Michael's bed.

"Don't cry over him, Michael." P.J. could no longer recognize the voice; his bunkmates had become strangers to him lately. "Let's you and me . . ."

"If only he'd smile again, or say something to me, if only he would be himself."

"If only they'd hurry up and take him away, you mean. He should be with the others like him."

Bed springs creaked. P.J. heard scuffing footsteps, then the creaking of a closer bed.

"Don't waste tears on him, Michael."

"He liked me, I think."

"Get over it. I like you."

"I—I know."

"He's going somewhere you can't follow."

"Where? Why?"

"Don't worry about that now. Here."

"Oh."

SIN

No, he thought. INRI, you can't do this to me.

GUILT

I don't believe everything you show me, INRI. You make me think things I would never—

BLASPHEMY

His own thoughts cut off in midstream, as happened more and more often these days, and he found himself listening to the sly mental voice that had taken to whispering more and more often in his mind: "Tell the Monitor, Peej. Go on. If you don't, INRI will find out tomorrow in forced confession. INRI finds out everything. If you haven't told the Monitor, that just makes your lesson harder tomorrow. So go ahead, turn them in. Don't just lie there and listen to it."

"No," P.J. said aloud.

The squeaking in the next bed stopped. "What was that? He said something."

"In his sleep. Be quiet, Michael."

CONFESS

No.

BETRAYAL

No, you can't run my thoughts.

SUFFER

Yes, all right, I'm good at that.

Nearby, moans. Hear no evil, see no evil, speak no—

EVIL

Light came into his eyes. For a moment he thought it was light from within and he opened his eyes to release some of the pressure. The glare, however, lit the window, reflected in the glass; he saw a cone of brilliant white carbon-light shining down from a spot over Michael's bed. He sensed rather than saw the boys holding perfectly still, tangled in their sheets; he heard the others in the bunker sitting up in their beds, swearing, then laughing, and beginning to taunt.

Heavy bootsteps thundered down the length of the otherwise

darkened room. P.J. saw the Monitor and two aides come swimming out of the shadows, juggernaut reflections in the wet mirror.

"Take them," said the Monitor.

The aides seized the boys by their hair and pulled them from the bed, screaming like uprooted mandrakes. P.J. turned over, though he had wanted to feign sleep, and saw them dangling, pale and flushed, struggling with the aides. Within that moment they were hauled into the dark, and their cries were dragged with them the length of the bunker.

The Monitor remained a great deal longer than that, standing with his hands on his hips, scowling at the offending bed. Eventually his eyes rose from the strewn sheets and met P.J.'s gaze.

He suppressed a shudder. The Monitor grinned, winked, and the light snapped out. He shut his eyes. It was at least ten minutes before he heard the bootsteps going away, but in all that time the Monitor never moved—only stood there, in the dark, watching.

"Why should this disturb you, Peter John?"

P.J. shook his head, but there was no way to dislodge the voice in his head. On the view-screen of his mind, he could see the recreated Monitor gazing down at him, a silhouette radiating hostile gray-green rays.

"Please respond," INRI said.

P.J. tried to avoid the question, but there was nowhere to turn. He was already deep within himself, meshed with INRI, perceiving an abstract, symbolic landscape of parallel lines and confusing spirals, wherein he was a floating student dressed in khaki robes and INRI was a sourceless voice.

"It was the way he didn't do anything," P.J. said at last. "The way he watched me when I couldn't see him, even though we were both in the dark."

In the spaces between the lines, eyes of all shapes and sizes blinked open and began to stare. INRI spoke on, as though comforting him. "There's nothing wrong with watching. There are eyes everywhere, Peter John, watching everything you do. There are eyes that watch not only your physical actions, but all your mental acts as well: eyes that watch your intentions, your dreams, your desires. You must, therefore, have all the right desires."

"I have no desire except a perfect death," he said in a hollow voice, "howsoever it may come."

"Very good," said INRI, patting him on his symbolic head. "But it may be awhile before your internal patterns completely match the slogans. That's why you still have doubts. Keep up the good work and you'll be there in no time. In the meantime, we will discontinue our lesson early today. It's time you were transfered to another camp, the headquarters for my central processor. Before you are removed bodily, I would like you to meet some of your future campmates. They're a little older than you, but I think you'll get along splendidly."

P.J. found himself standing in a reproduction of a field, among fresh craters. The little grass still remaining was wet with dew. It might have been any of the practice battlefields where the Christian Soldiers trained, except that it was perfectly quiet, and thus was quite unlike any of the battlefields he had ever seen.

Four figures walked toward him, three men and a woman stepping lightly on the wracked earth. They held up their hands in greeting and the gesture was friendly enough, but when he looked beyond their hands, at their eyes, he recoiled from what he saw there and nearly stumbled backward into a ragged hole.

"Now, Peter John," said INRI, "these are your friends. With all your concern about being watched, they should be of some comfort. They will never watch you. They are too busy looking within."

The orbs that rolled in the eye sockets of his 'friends' were red and raw, as though pupil and iris were engaged in looking straight backward into the brain, the optic nerve having been severed to further this process. "Granted," said INRI, "they have been with me for nearly a year now. It should be awhile before you catch up with them."

"Their eyes," P.J. whispered.

"They no longer need them. I see for them, as I shall see for you. Nothing so messy and primitive as a fibrous contraption of rods and cones and lenses will come between you and the infinite, Peter John, for you shall dwell in me, and I in you. I will be your eyes, your ears, your thoughts, your every deed. And Peter John . . ."

The four had stopped, facing in different directions, as though they were looking for P.J. but could not see him.

"In me," said INRI, "you shall live forever."

"What do you want with me?" P.J. screamed. None of the four so much as bent toward him. "I don't want to be like them. What are they doing? What use are they now?"

"Be patient, my little lamb. As yet you are not close enough to me. My indicators show that you have not yet taken me fully to heart. When the time is right, you shall know your special destiny. I could force it upon you now; I could slip into your skin and move that movable part of you—your soul, as we say—into my memory, there to dwell forever. But would that be fair, when you have not earned the privilege? Now say goodbye to your friends until this evening, when you will meet in the flesh."

The four blinked out, the craters and the field dissolved, and P.J. came back to his own senses, tangled in INRI's hood. The gloves fit like manacles today. He tore them from him, full of disgust; the hood inverted with a leathery rustling sound, and fell limp from the desk console like the trunk of a dead elephant. He ran a hand through his hair, aware that he must have looked wild to anyone who might have been watching. But there was no one else in the INRI terminal room.

He staggered out of the dim quonset into bright afternoon sunlight. Squinting, he crossed the grounds to the back door of the cafeteria and rushed into the steaming kitchen. The attendants gave him his special ration of chilled Host—Good Sam had arranged extra feedings to follow his grueling sessions with INRI—and he went back out to stand in the shade and gulp down one cube after another.

By the time he finished his lunch, the whole world was glowing again. A warm tingle spread through his stomach, extended into

144

his limbs, filling him with strength; his head still felt a bit weak, but the taste of Host reassured him. INRI wasn't so bad. Camp was actually fun. The Christian Soldiers certainly meant well. And soon he would have new friends.

"Hello, P.J."

He jumped, as though INRI had caught him wading willfully into naughty thoughts. The voice was a little like INRI's, but the owner of the voice—now stepping around the corner of the cafeteria—was much different.

It was that man, the one he'd seen some days ago and thought he recognized: Ash.

The man held out his hand. "P.J. Johnson, am I right?"

P.J. hesitated, wondering if he should run back into the cafeteria. He was nervous, not only because he seemed to know this man —and this man, him—but because he was afraid of what would happen if they were seen together. Good Sam could easily have glanced out of his office and seen everything.

"It's quite all right," the man said, dropping his hand and coming a step closer. "I asked Samuel if I might have a word with the INRI prodigy. The news of your proficiency has spread quickly."

"Is that all?" P.J. said, trying not to sound too suspicious. INRI would want to know all about this.

The stranger laughed. "There's a bench. Would you like to sit?"

P.J. shook his head.

"All right." The man hid his smile, but it remained, mocking P.J. silently from the depths of his eyes. "I know what you're thinking. You don't want to talk with me, because you're afraid INRI will reach into your mind and learn of our conversation. But what if I told you that you could escape INRI? That you could learn to lie to it?"

It, P.J. thought. How strange it sounded to hear this man call INRI '*It*' and not '*Him*.'

"That's impossible," he said. He started to say more, but fear gripped him by the jaws and trapped his voice.

The man nodded. "I understand. You have been reconditioned. Your mind was scavenged very thoroughly in your first days here; now it is being filled up again with select details, bits and pieces of memory that you'll soon forget are not your own. For instance, I see that you do not remember me, although you've met me many times."

"I saw you once last week. That's all."

"So you believe. But do you remember much of anything before last week? Try and remember me." The man was teasing him. "Listen to my name and see if it helps. Listen to my name: Ashenwriste. Andrew Ashenwriste."

"I don't know what you—"

Ash, he thought. Ashenwriste.

"I'm a friend of your family," Ashenwriste went on quickly, glancing over at Good Sam's office. There was no sign of anyone coming to investigate. "Do you remember them? Your parents?"

P.J. could not remember any parents, though he had a vague memory of remembering them on the day he had first seen Ashenwriste. Many mornings ago, in the chapel, he'd had strange visions of a place that had seemed familiar then; now it was all lost to him, like a dream of which he could remember nothing except that it had seemed significant.

"My parents gave me to Sam when I was a baby," he said.

"Who told you that?"

It was a long time before he could bring himself to admit it: "INRI explained it all to me."

Ashenwriste looked disappointed. "I am sorry," he said. "If I could have spoken with you any earlier, I would have. It was too difficult at first. They had you under intense scrutiny at the time of the PSA treatments."

"You know about those?" P.J. felt the first breaching of his fear, heard it in his voice. "The Periscope?"

"A little. I know that you told them many things of interest concerning your home. You see, the Soldiers don't know that I deal with your neighborhood. They've been slavering over the details they extracted, but saying nothing specific; it's as though they'd like me to be jealous."

"I don't have a home," P.J. said wistfully. "Or if I had one, I can't remember it."

"No doubt. INRI holds your memory in its claws. No one can blame you for having told everything you knew. More than one Cartel spy has been picked over."

"No!" P.J. shouted, for Ashenwriste had touched a sore place he had never known existed.

BETRAYAL

"No . . . what did I tell them?"

"About what?" said Ashenwriste.

"About my home!"

"What home?"

The man's calm drove P.J. crazy. A fresh seal was breaking, bit by bit, and through it came traces of information he had thought forgotten. Faces drifted up to him, along with names that hung disconnected for a moment then slowly matched themselves with the faces.

Virgil, Nancy, Mom and Dad, the babies, the twins.

"Easy," said Ashenwriste. "You mustn't show too much emotion."

He could remember his bedroom, his friends, the humiliating circumstances of his flight from the neighborhood. It all seemed different now, and he would have given anything to be back there. Cobblestone Hill was so small and vulnerable, full of things and people he had loved—still loved.

"What have I done?" he said, raising his hands toward Ashenwriste. Now he remembered the Cartel man standing at the edge of a Sunday picnic crowd; he was the one who took the group photographs, never including himself in the pictures; he played umpire in the kids' softball games, but never went to bat. "What have I done, Mr. Ashenwriste? I told Good Sam and INRI everything I knew about the neighborhood. I—I'm afraid."

"Good," Ashenwriste said, no longer mocking him. His face changed so swiftly that again P.J. was confused, lost. "You have given the Christian Soldiers a great deal of information they could have gained in no other way. But it will stop soon. If you keep on training with INRI, you will become the ultimate weapon: you will be the key to a complete invasion, from the inside out. School lessons will be subtly altered, water supplies supplemented with drugs of INRI's making: devastation of the most sinister kind."

P.J. felt as if he were about to cry. He grabbed at Ashenwriste's hands, but missed as the man stepped backward.

"Help me," P.J. whispered.

Ashenwriste put a hand on his shoulder. "Let's go see Good Sam, shall we? It would look better to walk as we talk."

They started across the dusty lot toward headquarters.

"I've come to warn you to expect interference tonight. Your trip to INRI's base camp will be interrupted, apparently by the pagan guerrillas who continually harry the Christians; but I will be behind the attack. Run to the side of the road at the first opportunity, give three quick whistles, and they will find you."

P.J. could hardly believe what he was hearing. He could not let himself show excitement, for INRI had taken to stamping that out of him.

"You're taking me home?" P.J. said.

"As soon as I can. It would be ideal if you could stay with INRI, fool it into believing that you are a convert and play the spy. That way the soldiers could perhaps be diverted into less destructive channels. But there is no way to do this without putting you at greater risk; you have no training in such matters."

"No," P.J. said, shaking his head. "I'm a typist."

It was the first thing he had said in days that made him feel like he was alive, and not merely an extension of INRI.

Good Sam appeared on the porch of the administration building, rocking his crozier slowly from side to side. He ducked his head at the two of them, smiling.

"And how did you find our star student?" Sam asked.

"A superior brain," Ashenwriste replied. "You must be reluctant to send him up to INRI."

Sam's eyes grew wide. "Oh no, Mr. Ashenwriste! We wouldn't dream of withholding privilege from our youth."

Ashenwriste looked at P.J. with eyes that betrayed nothing: a casual conversation was all that had occurred between them.

"Good to meet you, Peter John."

P.J. bowed, feeling wooden.

A moment later Ashenwriste walked into the building and Good Sam closed the door on both of them. P.J. turned slowly, dazed, and headed back toward the cafeteria, his mind full of new thoughts. He was on KP tonight. And after that . . . escape.

They came for him during his evening meal, when the euphoria of a full stomach was upon him. The Host had become his favorite food. He could eat it at every meal. Far more than the smack of salmon, he enjoyed the rush of electricity that the orange food gave him with every bite.

As he sat quivering, wondering if he dare ask for thirds, he felt a hand on his shoulder and turned to find Good Sam smiling down at him.

"Peter John, if you are finished, I'd like you to come with me immediately."

The others in the cafeteria watched this summoning with veiled relief; only now, with some sense of himself restored, could he recognize the look that had come into their eyes since his sessions with INRI began. As he had grown more distant from his companions, closer to the computer messiah, fear alone had bridged the gap.

Of course, his closest friends were gone now anyway. Michael he had not seen all day. Jeremy, allergic to the Host, had never returned from the infirmary.

They crossed the dusky lot to the administration building. A jeep was parked in the lot, on its door an emblem P.J. had never seen before: a human eye with a plug-in socket in its pupil. Two guards in khaki robes stood by the jeep, kicking crusted dirt from the mud flaps. They stopped to watch P.J. pass, as if he were a new kind of weapon.

P.J. was thankful when the door closed behind him. Good Sam led him down a hall to an office where another man stood over a desk with his back to them, examining some papers.

"This is Peter John," said Good Sam.

"Ah!" The man turned around, startling P.J.

He was Good Sam's identical twin.

"Don't stare, Peter John," said the Sam who had come in with him. The other beamed at P.J.: it was the same look of watery, paternal benevolence that all the children knew in Good Sam. They were both so similar that they had to be clones—like Lyndon Baines and Lady Bird, who were equivalent in every detail except genitalia.

"It must be the first time he's seen two like us," said the second Sam. Each of them put a hand on his shoulders. "Are you surprised, lambkin?"

P.J. nodded only slightly. "You're clones," he said.

The two Sams started at the same time—it felt like a shock running through him. They released his shoulders; both cleared their throats and started to walk around opposite sides of the desk toward the single padded chair. When each saw where the other was headed, he stopped and chuckled abruptly, and made a gesture toward the empty seat.

"I insist," said one of the Sams. "This is your office. It looks so much like mine that I sometimes forget."

The first Sam conceded and took his seat, then folded his hands and bowed toward P.J.

"You are leaving us this evening, as you know. I just want to say what a pleasure it was to be part of your education, and to thank you for the help you have given us in our investigations."

P.J. decided that it would be safest to say nothing.

"We wish to show our gratitude by presenting you with a token of our esteem, your first trophy in the competition for the gates of Heaven. My good brother, would you please?"

The second Sam opened a cabinet at the side of the room and wrestled out an oblong parcel that was almost as tall as either of the men. It was wrapped in white butcher paper, with a fat red ribbon at its end.

"Open it," said a Sam.

P.J. advanced slowly, took hold of a crease in the paper, and tore away a long ragged strip. Blank eyes peeked through the rent. He tore away more, revealing a sealed mouth, a plastic face, brown acrylic hair. The last of the paper came off with a shriek and rustled to the floor around the feet of the manikin.

It was P.J.'s height exactly. It wore the clothes he had worn the night he stumbled into the Church of the Open Road. And around its neck was a tag that said "Peter John Johnson."

"I don't know what to say," he said.

"This replica will stand in your stead in a church of INRI's choosing," said a Sam. "It will sing hymns and pray and be there to be seen, while you are off sacrificing your time and physical presence in less sanctified surroundings. They also serve . . ."

"I'm very honored," said PJ.

Both Sams were gloating as though he and not the manikin were their possession. "And now," said the Sam who remained standing, "it's time we moved on."

Headlights pierced the darkness, catching on rags of mist, tangling in scotch broom, fennel, copper-clad madrone. P.J. hunched over, hugging his knees, his face growing damper and colder with every moment that they sped through the fog. The pale, rugged road vanished ahead of the tires time and time again, and each time he would think, *This is it—they've dug a pit, a jeep trap.* But each time it was merely the crest of another steep hill, and they would plunge over it—if not comfortably, at least in safety. Good Sam sat in back beside P.J., while the two guards rode up front.

"I understand you met your future comrades this afternoon," Sam shouted in his ear. "How did you all get along?"

P.J.'s shivering made it easy not to answer.

Seconds later he had a better reason. The driver, without warning, swung the wheel hard to the left; he had only a glimpse of the tree that lay in the curve of the road, and then they were rolling. He was flung from the jeep and came down hard with his leg bent under him; the landing would have been jarring, might have broken the leg, if he hadn't come down in a thicket, then dropped into mud. He seemed to slide and spin for a long time, until the trunk of a tree arrested him.

There was DOV-fire, hissing followed by angry bursts that shook the ground. P.J. lay with his hands over his head and waited for silence. What was the signal? Three whistles. His brain felt fogged, his face numb, but he managed to blow three weak notes into a moment of silence.

Voices came closer, above, then footsteps crackled through the brush. He tried pulling himself up the slope on his elbows; his leg tingled and would not quite work, and when he twisted his hips his whole right side began to burn.

"Here," he croaked.

"Got you," said a man, and hands caught him under his arms.

When they reached the road, he tried to stand, but found he could do it only with support. The man who had helped him up now let him lean on his shoulder; there were other figures in the night, rushing back and forth. A crashing sound made P.J. look back, and he saw the jeep disappear over the edge of the road. There was no sign of Good Sam or the guards. His saviors were all dressed in black uniforms, and in the dark it was difficult to make out faces.

"Hurry it up," someone called, a hoarse whisper.

"He's hurt," said the man under P.J.'s arm.

"I'm all right," P.J. said, half-gasping as he spoke. He drew away from the man and took a few steps on his own, feeling sensation return to his side as he did so. His hip bones felt tender, but intact.

"Hurry!"

Through the trees at the other side of the road, in a little vale that was all shadow except for the greenish light given off by a few cold-looking cannisters, a long multi-segmented vehicle was parked. It was hollow within, fitted with benches like a boat, and protected by sliding glass canopies. PJ was pressed into the prow of the vehicle, and left in a compartment that sparkled with light dripping down from the underside of a dashboard. The craft shook and began to move. PJ put his face to a tiny porthole where he could see nothing outside but the night until his breath clouded the glass. The motion of the car was slow but rolling and silent. He lay back among bundles of plastic-covered gear, catching his breath, listening to the soft voices of the others above. Finally a hatch opened and a wiry little man ducked in.

"Are you hurt?" His nose was beaked, his hair curly and beaded with moisture; in the weird light of the compartment he resembled a troll. "There are medical supplies."

"I'm all right," P.J. said. "Are you Ashenwriste's friends?"

"Cartel, that's us. We're nosing on to safe quarters, so you can get some rest."

"We're heading home?"

"Underground. Your neighborhood's in the other direction."

"But Ashenwriste said—"

"Relax." The man put a hand on P.J.'s shoulder, pressing him back into the sloped shell of the prow. "There's been too much activity in the south to go that way. At the first opportunity you'll be taken home."

"What kind of activity? Is it the Christian Soldiers? Something I told them, and now they're moving in on my home?"

The man smiled, a tight and nervous grimace. "Nothing that dramatic yet. Surveillance, that's all."

P.J. beat his fist against the wall, turning his head away, ashamed. "Because of me," he said. "I told . . . I told . . ."

"Who wouldn't have, under the circumstances? The Periscope can make anyone gossip. Look, kid, it's no use kicking yourself silly over it. We're doing what we can to help."

"Help who?" P.J. felt a righteous rage rising in his breast.

"Who, my family or Good Sam's militia? You've got customers in both camps, don't you? Don't you?"

The man held out both hands, palm up. "We walk a very fine line. You should show some gratitude."

"You should go to hell," P.J. said.

"I've been there. PSA, just like you. Cartel spies don't get any special privileges. I probably screamed louder and gave away more secrets than you'll ever know."

P.J. clamped his mouth shut.

JUDAS

The words, in flaring blue letters, died swiftly; but they had surprised him, shooting across his eyes.

"INRI!" he whispered. "He's here!"

But the man had gone away.

P.J.'s fingers were in his mouth; he chewed his nails and waited for the next caption.

He was awakened by a jolt. The porthole windows were still dark. He felt it again—another shock. The floor lurched up, then changed places with him. He fell among a load of equipment. All motion ceased.

When no one came to check on him, he crawled toward the hatch and found that it was open. He stepped through it at an awkward angle; the craft had come to a stop tilted on its side.

Moonlight through acrid mist: the deserted deck of a ghost ship, foundering in ferns and broken branches. As he looked closer, he saw that it was anything but deserted. Black bodies lay everywhere, draped over the lower edge of the car and under the benches, in broken positions. Ground mist seemed to be settling into the hull of the craft, seeping through the shattered glass canopy; his steps stirred it up and the smell came to him, stronger than before. His eyes stung, he began to choke, and dizziness came quickly. He staggered toward the earth, leaned against a splintered fir; sap oozed between his fingers, the smell of balsam cleared his head, and he looked up, thinking to run from the wreck, wondering at last what had happened, feeling himself stuck to the tree—

Then the rush of feet came down the deck behind him and he was struck by something large and heavy, pitching him this time into a more complete darkness.

9

VEILED THREATS

THE SEASONS PASSED IN Yosemite, though no one had been sure if they would or not. The mild early summer gave way to a sweltering August, which was followed in turn by a swift and disturbing autumn. After the leaves of the deciduous trees had changed to orange, they turned shiny black in a matter of minutes, then vanished completely without doing anyone the favor of falling to the ground. All hope of natural verisimilitude had been forsaken long before by the increasingly bored and panic-stricken Johnsons. The park rangers were omnipresent enforcers of irrational, ever-changing laws, duty-bound to make their stay as unpleasant as possible, while at the same time ensuring that they did not leave.

The only help offered by the program came in the form of the old-timer whom they had met upon arriving at the park. He showed up from time to time, as winter came on, with handy tips on how to make hunting and gathering tools from common objects in the Venturon. The Johnsons, however, stopped trying to sustain themselves by wildcraft after Nancy dug a hole looking for roots and found, beneath the topsoil, another of the blank spots that beleaguered them. No one wanted to become like Virgil, who only occasionally stopped laughing at his hand to stare at them all in perfectly lucid terror. Besides, they found that they only slowly became hungry, over months and months.

And so they lived in Yosemite, rousted thrice nightly by rangers from wherever they had parked the Venturon, and pursued in the day by fading memories of what their lives had been like before all this. The tourists went home in October, but long before then the Johnsons had become attractions. The guides on tour buses were constantly pointing them out: "To our right, if you're quick, you may see a family of nonindigenous Johnsons scavenging for something to do. Hi, Bill!"

The first snowfall caught them by surprise. It came like a deluge of video static, hardly settling on anything, a downpour of squiggly white lines, little specks and blips of light. Unreal as it was, it brought the cold with it.

"You know what I think?" Dad said. "I think we're coming to the end of the program. Maybe we're going through some kind of leader and we'll end up in spring."

"Or maybe we'll be erased," Nancy said.

When the sky cleared, they looked up at the sour brown stars, the apathy of each Johnson once more penetrated by fear. The night sky looked chipped and translucent, as if it had been played too many times. The tape might be decaying. Whatever had gone wrong with the program could be fatal: this was not a waiting game. It was no sort of game at all. What if, out in the real-time world, no time at all had passed? What if time never passed again out there, simply because they were stuck in here, in no-time?

"Mommy, I'm cold," said Stephanie, who had begun to talk in the summer.

"You'll be all right, dear," said Mom. "Wrap up and get in the van."

"It's cold in the van, too."

"I know, dear. It's cold everywhere. Try to sleep."

Stephanie coughed all that night. Connie was up with her for hours, until Nancy volunteered to take over. In the cold van, while the others covered their heads and tried to sleep, she watched her sister grow weaker, paler, sicker. The bubbling in her cough intensified until it sounded as though she would drown in herself. Toward morning, the coughing and wheezing ceased, awakening Nancy from a fatigued trance.

Stephanie stared at the ceiling, her eyes like drops of dried glue.

Dad shouldered the little body, took a bottle of vodka from the cabinet, and set off into the woods with tears freezing to his face. He did not return for three days, and when he did he shrugged off their questions.

"There was nowhere to bury her," he said. The recent events had gouged through whatever tenderness remained in his personality, and uncovered permafrost beneath it. "Everywhere I dug, it was blank. I couldn't drop her into that."

He lurched to the cabinet and opened it, found another bottle of alcohol, and then dropped heavily into his seat at the front of the van. He did not speak another word for hours, and then he said, "One night the snow covered her up. When it melted in the morning, she was gone."

The depth of winter:

Mom was in mourning. Virgil slept nine hours out of twelve, mumbling of Herodotus in his sleep. Dad never stopped drinking. Nancy and the twins no longer went out hunting bears, no longer watched the windows for the old-timer's appearance, since the last time they'd seen him the snow of static in his beard had started erasing his face. P.J.'s ghost, as though aware of its error, came no more.

Snowbanks wiped out the landscape. Half Dome was obliterated in December. The Washington Column vanished as easily as if all its granite had been grey light in a mirror. The forest went next. Snow covered the ground and never went away. One night the sun set and did not rise again.

"We have to do something," Nancy said, but she never had time to decide what. There was an unbearable racket in her ears and a sudden light that gave her a headache—

"My God, haven't you been in there long enough?"

She opened her eyes to see an old woman bending over her. There was something familiar about the face, though it seemed like years since she had seen it. The silver plastic frock was of the sort the seniors wore at Sunset Ranch. Her mind, rising at a dizzying speed from the depths of dream-winter, clued her in to the old woman's identity as she watched her remove the plug-in attachments from the rest of the family.

"Grandma!" said Nancy. "How—how did you find us?"

Virgil groaned and sat up, blinking and rubbing his hand. Grandma Johnson moved on to Stephanie and the twins—the grandchildren first—then Connie, and finally to her own son.

"Grandma!" cried Lyndon Baines. "We're home!" said Lady Bird.

"I tried calling you about the wedding yesterday," she said. "No one answered. I finally had to watch your family hour last night to figure out what had happened."

"The processor," Virgil said. It was the first sensible thing Nancy had heard him say in months. "It trapped us, Gran. How long were we plugged in?"

"I hurried over right away," she said, as the twins hugged her from either side. "It took quite a locksmith to get me into your house. I guess you were in there about eighteen hours."

Dad moaned, holding both hands to his eyes. "God, I need a drink."

"Mom," said Connie. She put out her hands to welcome her mother-in-law. "I'm so glad you're here, we—"

She broke off suddenly and turned to Stephanie, who lay unmoving among the plug-in equipment.

"Stephanie." She crawled to her daughter and touched her cheek.

Stephanie began to cry: "Mommy, where are you? I can't see you."

"Open your eyes, darling," Connie said.

Stephanie did so, and looked around with a grave expression. "I had a nightmare, Mommy."

They all began laughing and talking at once—all except Dad. "What the hell happened to the processor, that's what I'd like to know."

He banged out the door and they heard a crash as he threw open the panels in the nose of the Venturon. A moment later he said, "Hah!"

Nancy and Virgil went to see what he had found. He was bent over the workings of the central processor, which was mainly shiny metal boxes and motionless parts that should have been impossible to examine in any detail without special tools. But Dad had found the trouble. With a fat forefinger he pointed out the tiny hole in the lower face of one component.

"That's not supposed to be there."

"Laser burn," Virgil said.

Dad swore and slammed the panels back into place, so that the false radiator grill interlocked. He bent, with a grunt, and peered at the front of the van.

"It entered here," he said. When Nancy looked closely, she could see a singed pinhole an inch above the fender.

"But where did it come from?" she said.

Dad stood back with his hands on his hips and faced the garage door, his eyes narrowed and his forehead crumpled with suspicion. He seemed to pierce the garage door with his eyes.

"I have a pretty good idea."

"Why don't you all come inside and I'll make breakfast?" Grandma Johnson called.

"Smith," Dad said, grinding one fist slowly in the palm of his hand. "You're going to pay for this one. Killing my daughter, maiming my son . . . that's too much for any man to ignore. We'll see what the Council says now."

But Nancy could hardly remember what had upset him so much. Her memory of the trip to Yosemite was fading away like the light in a freshly switched-off TV set. Many months' worth of details, compressed into eighteen hours, had become as blurred as a fever dream. The only sharp detail remaining was hunger.

"Dad," she said, putting a hand on his arm. "At least wait till after the wedding."

Virgil grunted, shoving the *Argos* over the last of the wet, resisting sand and into the waves. Suddenly the boat turned buoyant and went leaping lightly over the smallest breakers while cloven plumes of salty spray hissed up from the prow and fell like rain on his back. The evening air was full of mist, turned gold by the sinking sun. Fine gravelly sand rushed away under his bare feet, gritted between his toes, and then suddenly there was no bottom. He braced himself on the wooden rim, his weight pushing the vessel so close to the water that it sluiced in around his wrists. He tumbled forward as the *Argos* cut through another wave; they rushed on together.

From the prow, rowing hard to get out of the surf, he watched the shore receding above the backs of waves. There were people on the beach watching the sunset, but most of the sun worshipers had already packed their belongings and gone up the cliffs to their houses. No one waved him off, as Elaine had always done. She was not even allowed out in public this close to their wedding-time.

Tomorrow.

This is the last eve of my freedom, he thought.

Out past the waves, he felt the wind come up. Time to unfurl the sail, batten the hatches, avast and ahoy. He was a little rusty at it, and proceeded to get clobbered by the boom or whatever the swinging beam was, and tangled in ropes, while the ropes got tangled in pulleys. The boat yawed and listed and water got all over the fo'c'sle, but at last he was able to set sail for the horizon.

The beach was lost in the spray of breaking waves, though above it the houses stood out like crenellations on the white cliffs.

As the *Argos* slapped the water, he again thought of Elaine. Tomorrow. Not the ending of freedom, but the beginning of something new. He tried to remember her as he had last seen her without her veils, but the only memory he could find was an old one from the summer when they had finally spoken to each other after years of shy evasion. She was too young in that memory. She had to look older than that by now. It disturbed him that all he could come up with were the nostalgic pictures of fresh love: was that the girl he would marry in the morning? No, she had changed by now, she had to have changed: she'd had at least one speed-treatment last year.

I'm romanticizing again, he thought, accompanying the realization with a mental kick. What if, under the veils, her beauty was gone, and he realized that he'd been loving a stale dream all this time?

Romantic. He was even romantic about his hand.

He raised it before his face, and found that it was aflame with the sunset's fire. The cliffs were like walls of gold now. His eyes kept coming back to his hand. He could not quite remember most of the trip, nor could he quite forget it. He knew that he favored the hand as if it were weak, as if it had suffered some kind of real injury, but that was all part of his endless fantasizing: he was living out a tragic role. His psyche-profile had amply demonstrated that he was prone to let his symbols push him around. He was too impressionable, didn't have a grasp on himself, was vulnerable to his own fears.

He shook his head, hoping the wind would clear it.

Cries filled his ears, the wailing of the damned, lost souls.

P.J. Lost.

Alone on the vast choppy surface, he felt small and exposed, but the most likely dangers were all within himself.

The cries sounded again, not ghosts but gulls.

He shivered and huddled down. He had been a wreck since P.J.'s disappearance, and Elaine knew it. Each time he'd talked to her—right up to their conversation this afternoon—she'd sounded more distant, less tolerant of his moods, unamused by his strained bantering.

"No," he groaned. He had to put away these thoughts. He would spoil everything for himself, given half a chance.

The gulls dived closer.

He reached over the side of the boat, scooped up a handful of cold seawater, and splashed it in his face. Another. It felt good, purifying, like all his tears coming out of him at once.

"I came out here to get away from all that," he said, thinking that if he talked aloud he would not get so bogged down in the chatter of unspoken words. "I'm on the *Argos* now, my good old boat." He slapped the hull. "I built her; I can go where I want. Isn't that so? Damn right."

Built her by hand, he thought.

"By hand, that's right. Handbuilt freedom. She's all mine."

Take her where I want.

"Damn right."

But where have I ever taken her? Out for a turn around the bay? I used to dream of sailing south and never coming back. I've wasted her. Oh God, how I've wasted her.

He had worked on the *Argos* for years, at first with Dad and then alone. She was his craft, his link with not only nature and the nerves in his hands, but with tradition: dreaming of Greek shipbuilders, he had pushed the lathe. The smell of the shavings had been like an incense, transporting him to a place beyond care.

And in the week he finished her, on the day he first took her into the waves, he had been so elated that he'd finally found the courage to speak to Elaine. And that had been the end of sailing. Almost as soon as the *Argos* was finished, he had lost touch with her—lost touch with his tradition. Elaine could not sail; she got seasick. He had always meant to get away alone, but it had become such an effort when it was so easy to spend all his time with Elaine. He felt so lonely each time he drifted out to sea while she stayed behind, waving farewell, looking forlorn. He had never stayed out for long. Never long enough, he thought now.

"Talk out loud," he muttered to himself. "Sing it, Virgil. Come on, O Muses, get me out of my own damn skull, please!"

The *Argos* seemed to quicken in the water, the wind taking readily to her sails, and all the sounds and sights and sensations seemed as familiar as if he had always been sailing her, tonight.

"Let's go, *Argos*. Let's go. I'll give you your head, fair ship.

We'll let the melting sun take us down the curve of the earth, far off, to other shores. Yes."

They were rushing now, the sailboat and Virgil. The water was like vapor underneath. The sun blazed like the living shield of Achilleus. He could see Hephaistos himself forging the disk in the violet clouds, a brazen god hammering at ripples of light, seizing the sun in ethereal tongs, then plunging it into the cold, deep, wine-dark sea . . .

Night.

The sea dark not with wine, but oil and mercury.

The oil-dark sea, the fear-dark sky.

Turn back, Virgil.

He pulled on the ropes, slipped and almost toppled overboard; his shriek scared off the gulls.

"Elaine!" he cried, seeing her as she had been: a laughing, almost naked girl, sun-browned. "I'm coming back!"

He ducked the sail this time; though the wind and spray had numbed his hands, his mind seemed sharper now and his thoughts clearer. If the beam struck him, it would hurt and leave a bruise. It was not like a plug-in, where all mistakes were corrected automatically—if not immediately then when at last you unplugged. The *Argos* was made of moving parts, and he was one of them. Here, if he got hurt, it would be his fault.

The wind came stronger from the shore, carrying the smells of the land: fresh-mown lawns and smoke. He tacked into it, dreaming of his home, as though it were the far-off place he had always desired.

The answers have to be there, he thought. That's where all the questions came from.

As he felt the waves snatch the *Argos* up and spirit her toward the sand, he thought he heard Elaine's voice crack out of the breaking waves: "And about time, too!"

"The thing I can't believe," Dad said from the middle of the crowd, "is that no one but my mother watched our family hour that night."

Marv Coolidge answered him. "No one was expecting much of a show that night, Bill. Everyone who watches it knew that you'd be away on vacation."

"For what should have been fifteen minutes. What happened to our loyal fans?"

"Ratings are dropping all over. Happened to us, too. Everybody watches their own shows these days."

"That's what's wrong with this neighborhood," said Dad. "Everyone's too wrapped up in his own affairs; we're losing our sense of community."

"Forget about it for now, Bill," said Mom. "This is a day for togetherness."

"That's just the kind of talk that rots us from the inside out," Dad said. "*Togetherness.* I'm talking about organization. Pledges."

What about wedding vows? Nancy thought, standing impatiently at the doors of the lodge. She could hardly believe that her father was talking about TV with the ceremony about to begin.

Just as the white doors were opening, she felt a hand close on her elbow.

"Nancy, I have to talk to you."

Arnold drew her out of the rush a little too fast and she stumbled in her heels.

"Arnold, what's wrong with you?" she said.

The Smiths, of course, had not been invited. Arnold was in his undersized clothes, glaring at her.

"I'll ask you the same thing. You've been avoiding me. I thought we agreed to stay close after your treatment."

She separated herself from him, but did not immediately join the others. "Arnold, I think we reacted to our treatments very differently. I meant to talk to you about this, but I don't feel as mad at everyone as you do. I tried being a rebel, honestly, and I was a little cranky at first—but I think you're being extreme."

"They're giving you tranquilizers," he said.

"Arnold, you're ridiculous."

"Nan, as soon as we hit adolescence they dose us with docility drugs, things that cause us to give in to our family's programming without resistance. They have to. Resistance would ruin the careful shape of the neighborhood." When he saw her disbelief, he looked desperate. "I'm talking about chemicals that induce a sense of responsibility in lab mice! They're in your insta-serves, believe me."

"Excuse me, Arnold, I have to go with my family." She started to turn away—the last of the crowd had just passed into the lodge —but he grabbed her again, harder this time, and spun her to face him.

"Nancy June, I love you," he said, fiercely. "I'm not going to lose you to them."

"Let me guh—"

His other hand blocked her mouth; she glimpsed a small capsule cupped in his palm. A warm bitter fluid burst against her teeth, trickled down the back of her tongue. She jerked back with a curse, "What was that?"

"The antidote," he said, and stepped out of sight around the building.

She spit into a planter, but the taste was in her throat and her belly felt metallic.

"Nancy?" said her grandmother from the doorway. "What's keeping you? Are you sick?"

She shook her head, wiping her mouth on a handkerchief pulled from her purse. "I'll be all right. I'm coming. I—"

Her knees weakened suddenly and she stumbled against her grandmother.

"It must be the heat, poor dear. Come inside where it's cool."

As they walked into the lodge, she felt very light and far from her body. As soon as she was sitting, she closed her eyes and was carried away by a rush of irresistable somnolence. Dreams were waiting for her: wisps of words, swollen music, the sound of ripping lace. She opened her eyes with a start, only to find the wedding ceremony at its climax, Virgil tearing through Elaine's wrappings to expose the final blood-red shroud. The color first frightened, then enraged her. She fought back a shout as Virgil bent to kiss his lurid bride, for she could see that his pupils were hugely dilated, his lips trembled and his teeth ground together; there was a false lust inside him, induced by stag-drugs so potent that she half expected antlers to break through the crust of his skull. And Elaine—tough and vital Elaine—stood vulnerable and palpitating, weakly waiting to be sacrificed.

Nancy almost screamed at them to stop it.

She could not escape the knowledge that she had never seen so clearly before. This was not a hallucination; she might be the only one here not seeing through a filter. This was happening. They all saw it, but no one else seemed to mind.

With a soft, dragging sound, the red veil was torn, and Elaine's bare white face emerged through the opening.

Virgil's eyes narrowed, and Nancy felt herself choke. She knew that deep down he did not want all this: not Elaine, not the lust, not the ceremony. She could see also that he was trapped, did not even know that he didn't want these things. The veils he parted with his hands were there to distract him from subtler veils he would never suspect, veils that lay over his thoughts.

Mom glanced at her with a smile that looked suddenly superficial. The same doubts that Virgil hid from himself were in her eyes. Looking past Mom at her father, she saw them there, too. But Dad's eyes were different, crazier perhaps, with a strange kind of wildness in them that made her suddenly understand why Arnold respected him. He took his fears by the horns, leapt between them and learned to ride the nightmare beast. He was the only one of them who had accepted all this without seeing it as inevitable or unchangeable.

She must say nothing of this, of course. Not to Virgil, who had accepted his bride. Not to her parents, nor her doctor. Only Arnold would understand.

She did not have to sit still much longer. The ceremony ended in a rush of relatives toward the newlyweds, Johnsons and Wessons now mingling. Nancy did not pause to give her false congratulations, knowing that she would be unable to meet Virgil's eyes. Instead she ran through the doors, under a cross with arms of equal length, and found Arnold waiting for her at the corner of the lodge.

There was no need for speaking; her eyes must have told him everything.

"Let's go to your house," he said.

"My house, why?"

He smiled. "This is the perfect time to get Erica home alone. She doesn't trust me, but you're her sister. My bomb is almost ready, Nan. All I need is what Erica's got, and not very much of that either."

"And then what, Arnold? When you have it? You're just going to wipe them all out?"

He shook his head, and she realized that he was still the Arnold she had loved—the same clever boy. "Oh no, not unless they ask for it. But they'll have to meet my demands."

Arnold surprised her by walking on the sidewalk all the way to her house, instead of insisting that they go through the back alley.

"I'm through skulking," he explained. "My dad knows I'm seeing you. He can't do anything about it. My mom even says we should see each other."

She could see Mr. Smith in the second-story window of his house, watching them with binoculars. She thought about giving him the finger as she had seen Dad do countless times, but decided against it. He was Arnold's father, after all.

When they were indoors, Nancy slipped out of her high heels and put her hand into Arnold's. He tightened his grip reassuringly for a second, then let go of her.

"Where does your mom keep her videos?" he asked.

"What?"

Without explaining, he found Mom's rack of cassettes beside the living room sofa. "I'm looking for a shawl pattern," he said as he slipped a cartridge into the player. "Now we can have some privacy."

"What?"

"When you play the *Ladies' Home Video* shawl pattern, it blocks the recording power of your home cameras and makes them create new footage from old images. That way there's no record of what we do here. I figured out that all our mothers use them."

"And what do our fathers have?"

"Our fathers are always sneaking around."

He tiptoed through the kitchen and put his ear to the garage door.

"She's probably taking her nap," Nancy said.

Arnold look satisfied. "You go in first. Does she like you?"

"I don't know, she's not like that. She's here for the nuke, that's all."

"Let's pretend we've come to play with her."

"The twins tried that and got bit."

"Could we bring her anything she might like? Anything that would distract her while I get to the nuke?"

Nancy thought a moment. "Fuel."

He grinned. "If I had that, I wouldn't be doing this."

She opened the door slowly, expecting to find Erica curled up in her blankets at the foot of the nuke. But before the door was more than a few inches wide, she saw that the baby was sitting up staring at her.

"She's awake," Nancy said.

Arnold stepped past her. "Then it's no use pretending. She looks like she knows what we want. At least she won't be able to tell anyone what happened."

Erica growled at them. Nancy went forward, putting out a hand. "Hello, Erica. This is Arnold. Do you know Arnold? He's my friend."

"Grrrr . . ."

She's gotten meaner, Nancy thought. It must be her diet. She didn't want to tell Arnold, for fear that he would be discouraged.

"Well?" she said.

Arnold surveyed the garage, hands on his hips. "Where does she keep it?"

"The waste?"

"Mm-hm. There must be some kind of holding unit, if we can get her away from it."

"You don't know already?"

"I know the pellets are relatively safe until their seal is punctured in the reactor, and after that—stand back. Where does your dad keep the fuel he hasn't used yet?"

She didn't know whether to laugh at him or yell. "He only buys as much as he needs, but you still don't understand. Erica's the safekeeper. She *eats* the waste, Arnold."

A long pause. "Eats it?"

"Yes, and the diapers are put in a special container. I don't think even you could get into that."

Arnold looked a little dizzy, then he looked at Erica.

"I thought her diaper looked heavy," he said. "So it's going to be that kind of operation."

"Do you know how to change a diaper?" Nancy asked.

"Of course I do," he snapped. "You'd better get a fresh one ready. It's just as well that it's this way—with a diaper I mean. I have gloves for handling it directly, but I haven't had any way of testing them yet."

While Nancy pulled a thick diaper from the dispenser on the wall, Arnold moved toward Erica. She had been watching him with menace in her dull eyes all this time.

"Okay, baby," he said. "I don't want to hurt you, I just want to change you."

Erica opened her mouth, baring metallic teeth. They looked like soft lead, but Nancy had seen her bite through all kinds of things: the toe of Lyndon's cowboy boot, for instance.

Arnold stopped to consider his strategy, and Erica pushed off from the nuke and leapt at him with a shriek. He jumped back, stumbled into a bicycle, and fell in the baby's path; but the nuke unit had been jarred by her leap, and as it settled it made a weird

sound, knocking and creaking. Nancy saw Erica turn back to ~~i~~
with terror painted on her tiny wizened face, and at that instan~~t~~
Arnold flung himself upon her. Erica screamed, but not befor~~e~~
she was pinned to the floor on her belly.

"Help me, Nan!"

Erica's howls echoed in the garage. The nuke slowly recovere~~d~~
from its shaking and the baby's cries intensified.

"God, I hope no one's listening from the street," he said
fumbling with the Velcro strips on her diaper.

"I thought you said you knew how to change a baby," Nanc~~y~~
said. "She has to be on her back."

"Nan, she's too strong—look out!"

Nancy pulled her hand away from Erica's snapping mouth; sh~~e~~
struggled like a cat held under water. Arnold grimaced, his fac~~e~~
bright red and beaded with sweat as he tried to wrestle Erica ont~~o~~
her back. Finally he got his hands on her arms just below th~~e~~
shoulders, and Nancy held her legs.

"It would be better if you pinned her shoulders with you~~r~~
knees," Nancy said, "that way you can hold the rest of her sti~~ll~~
with your hands."

"No way! You know where she'd bite me? Hurry up!"

Fighting the whole time, Erica lost her diaper. Nancy did no~~t~~
look closely at what she'd captured; she was tiring swiftly, and i~~t~~
took all her attention to get the fresh diaper on. She did no~~t~~
bother cleaning between diapers, despite the danger of a rash
there was nothing that looked like it could be wiped up. Whateve~~r~~
was in the diaper rattled, and that was all.

"Okay," Arnold said, "I guess we can let her go."

They both jumped up at the same time, Arnold snatching th~~e~~
dirty diaper and sealing its ends together before Erica could regai~~n~~
it. When she saw that she had been beaten, she gave them bot~~h~~
a sullen look and crawled back into her corner.

Nancy and Arnold traded grins and went back into the kitchen
Nancy got out glasses for lemonade.

"Thanks, Nan. You should probably get back to the wedding."

"I guess so," she said. "Don't you want to stick around for awhile? We could take a nap together."

But his eyes were elsewhere. He shook his head and held up the diaper. "Not today. I've got to get this back to the lab."

She lowered her eyes. "I know."

When he had finished his lemonade they put the diaper in a paper bag and she walked him to the door. Mr. Smith was still up in the window across the street. Oddly, he waved, but neither of them returned the greeting.

Arnold was halfway across the street before she realized that he hadn't even kissed her goodbye. And after all they'd been through together . . .

Lyndon Baines Johnson pointed at the widewall screen, where a mob of people in fancy dresses and tuxedos milled, danced, and poured champagne over one another in a large ballroom with gold and black walls. The whole family, except for Virgil, was watching the Special Johnson-Wesson Family Hour in the Johnsons' den.

"There's Nancy, sneaking back in," said Lyndon. "Where were *you*, Nancy June?"

"Yes, Nan," Mom said, "where were you?"

"It was too stuffy in the lodge," she said. "I had to get some air."

"That's my lodge you're talking about," Dad said, but no one heard him. The sounds of the family were all quite distant, cut off from him by an aural veil. He emptied the last bottle of champagne into a goblet, then drained the goblet. A Laphroaig chaser waited on the arm of the sofa. Connie moved closer at the moment he reached it, jostling his arm, and the drink went down his shirt-front, feeling much cooler than it would have if it had gone down his esophagus.

"Connie," he said. "Connie, look at that, look what you've done."

She didn't look at him, and he wondered if he had actually made a sound. The remote biocontrols that caused his voice to work and muscles to flex seemed out of order this evening; his eyes kept closing against his will. When he tried to walk, he staggered. The reception had tired him. That was it. He had never been big on parties.

"Bill? I said, William Dee, can't you hear me?"

He blinked so heavily that he heard his eyelids meet, and by great concentration managed to equate the voice that had called him with his mother's moving mouth.

"I hear you," he said, pharynx creaking.

Although she sat in a chair next to the sofa, she was several miles away. Her bifocals were down on the end of her nose, ready to tumble into her knitting. A wriggly silver blur obscured her face when he tried to determine her expression. When he looked away, it moved faster than his head, skimming over the walls, now eating away at the image on the widewall.

"Don't you think you've had enough to drink, Bill?" his mother called. "Ever since I've been here you've had a glass in your hand. Sober up, for pete's sake—it's my last night with you all."

"I am not drunk, mother," he said, putting the tumbler-bearing hand to his heart. "I am sick and very sad. Today I lost a son. You can't imagine what that's like."

"Oh I can't, can't I?"

He closed his eyes and found that the corrosive silver whorl was inside his head.

"Daddy," said Lady Bird, "are you crying?"

"For God's sake, Bill, who died?" his mother said.

"Us!" he said, so loudly that they all turned to look at him; it was strange to see them looking away from the TV, and for a moment he felt lost. But he was too adrift, too desperate, to feel self-conscious.

"I've lost both my sons," he told them. He put an arm around Connie and squeezed, and when he met her eyes he saw that she was also crying. "Our sons."

"It happens all the time," said his mother.

"It's my fault," he told Connie. She shook her head.

"Your fault Virgil married?" his mother said.

He sniffed.

"Stop feeling sorry for yourself, Bill. You'll just make it worse. Take your medicine."

"Medicine," he said. "I'll take my medicine."

"Daddy's funny," he heard Stephanie say as he lumbered away.

The wall swam toward him, parted in the middle, and went past on either side. He discovered that he was climbing the stairs to the bathroom, where he had a left new bottle of Dr. Edison's prescription pills.

"Take two, they're small."

"Who said that?" he asked, and almost immediately saw Doc Edison beaming out of the bathroom mirror, the overhead light flashing from the reflector on his liver-spotted forehead.

"Shit," Dad said, relaxing. "Why do you things always get at me in the john?"

"Take four or five," said the doctor. "It'll do you a world of good."

All the bottles in the rack looked alike. There was Wheelwright Chem's Tried 'n' True Tonic, Wheelwright Chem's D-Toxicant, Wheelwright Chem's Chocolate-Covered Aspirin, Wheelwright Chem's this and that; they were all in the same type of vials with the same type of orange labels—a shade that hurt his eyes at the moment.

He reached for his tonic, contemplating the warped image of his doctor in the mirror. "What's in these things, Doc?"

"Take six or seven and see what happens. Special today only. Try fifteen or twenty and get another forty free."

"Forty winks?"

Dad put the pills on his tongue and swallowed, wincing at their bitterness. Something was wrong. They had never tasted bitter before; they'd always been sweet and smooth. He opened his hand and looked at the label.

"D-Tox," he said. "Damn it."

"Take the whole bottle, William Dolores, and I'll see you in church."

"I don't think so, Doc," Dad said. He put down the bottle so hard that it cracked. The silvery thing that had been coming in and out of focus—threatening to come even clearer in Doc's brow-mounted mirror—began to wisp away into nothing. Inside his head it felt like the end of a storm, the parting of black clouds.

"Damn," he said. "Never tried that stuff before."

He picked up the bottle of tonic and squinted at the label, taken by his first curious impulse in weeks. The little pills inside seemed to throb. He found himself thinking, for no particular reason, of the beads in a rattlesnake's tail.

"What have we got here, Doc?" he asked.

The mirror was empty.

Dad ambled down the hall to his office, and once inside closed the door. It was nice in the darkness, soothing; he felt himself beginning to unwind. He sat at his desk, switched on the household computer, and opened the little hatch on the analysis bin: a food-taster he'd installed after the potluck missile crisis, when he was unsure of what Jock Smith might try by way of revenge.

"So what is it?" he asked.

"Wait a minute," said the comp.

He shrugged, sighed, rubbed his eyes. When he opened them again, the screen was alight, crawling with chemical names and three dimensional molecular diagrams. The active ingredient was flashing on and off: the rest seemed to be inert matrix chemicals.

"So what's this?" he asked, pointing at the active ingredient, which was labeled "THP."

"Tetrahydropapaveroline. This substance, isolated from the interaction of acetaldehyde and dopalamine, has been shown to induce excessive alcohol craving in living subjects."

"No kidding? And why would Doc Edison prescribe that?"

He pushed hard at the screen, not a little angrily, and the molecules scattered away from his finger, spinning and broken. Out of the chaos, lines of print began to settle, queuing up along the edges of the screen. Six lines. As he leaned closer, they left the screen's border and intersected at the center of the display, radiating outward, six spines. They spun slowly around their center, so that he could read them all in turn:

Wheelwright's Thrifty-Scot Scotch
Wheelwright's White Crow Rum
Wheelwright's Artichoke Brandy
Wheelwright's Guava Absinthe
Wheelwright's Pesky-Rusky Vodka
Wheelwright's Krafty-Kaiser Fudge Schnapps.

Wheeling, whirling, it made Dad dizzy. He sat back from the screen.

"I don't drink any of that dessert crap," he said. "Except the scotch."

At the bottom of the screen, a blinking message prompted him: INDICES?

"What's an indice?"

"*Cichorium endivia,* also called 'escarole,' being a composite herb favored for salads."

"You're an aggravating little bastard." He touched the blinking word and sat back as the screen went into its dance.

The six lines receded until they were too fine to read, and as they contracted into the center of the screen they drew more words in with them. Dad was beseiged by spinning brand names:

Pep-A-Day Co., Budge, Inc., Spartan Sleep, Freshie Foods Corp., and on and on. They were the names on his appliances, the tools in his garage, the labels on his shirts and shoes, the insta-serves, even the beer he drank day in and day out (Budgetmeister). Everything from Sungleam toasterizers to Naughty-Nite Aphronarcs was there.

"What's the big deal?" he asked.

"Wheelwright Subsidiaries, Divisions, Affiliates, Part—"

"But that's everything!" he said. "Who the hell is Wheelwright?"

The spinning letters, still six-spoked, slowed and stopped. A question mark appeared in the upper half of the screen, its period forming a circle around the smallest six brand-name items. The circle began to flash.

"Wheelwright is a corporate entity."

The question mark faded, though the central circle, cut into six equal pie-pieces by the lines of print, remained. Wm. D. Johnson stared into the center of the circle, hesitating, sensing that he was about to ask a question too complex to be answered by the screen, with its simple though captivating diagrams.

He was uncomfortably aware that the name on the lower corner of the comp-console was also on the screen, one of Wheelwrights. And this was a Wheelwright office chair. The photos on the wall were printed on Wheelwright paper. Everything was Wheelwright's. He felt as if he were living in another man's house.

"Right there," he said, poking his finger at the very center of everything on the screen, the place where all the lines converged. "What is that? Who's behind Wheelwright? What's all this about?"

The text fell away. What remained was geometry: an hexsected circle, its six white spokes radiating from it. There were faint lines in a grid pattern toward the edges of the screen, though they did not come all the way to the circle.

He felt a chill, but his excitement had cleared the last of the alcoholic haze from his mind. That central circle, and what it held, looked familiar. One more Wheelwright product?

"Whiten three sections. Here, here, and here."

He touched alternating sections of the circle: three turned white, three remained black like the rest of the screen. Recognition came, precipitating like crystals out of a clear solution.

"Color the central black areas gold," he said. "Color the screen field green—grass green. Color the lines gray."

The computer obeyed. Something was missing, but the picture in his mind's eye provided it: a stubby-brick red cross with arms of equal length, radiating from the gold and white circle.

It was a picture from the air. The gray lines were streets passing through green lawns to the grids of neighborhood blocks, away from the crucial red building with its dome of alternating gold and white.

He had seen it that morning, he'd been inside it all afternoon. Virgil had been married there.

It was his lodge.

"All right," he said. "Who owns Wheelwright?"

The computer screen flickered, tumbled, and went white. It flashed until he shut it off, but he could not help thinking that it had blinked like an alarm, a warning.

"Who do you think owns Wheelwright?" he asked himself. "Who the hell do you think?"

10

PAGAN PLACE

AFTER THE FEVER AND the jostling, drums.

P.J. rose through layers of sleep and sickness, following the pulse of a heart stronger than his own. It sounded like a heart, but there was a voice singing along with it: then it must be a drum. The fever had broken.

With a gasp for air, he opened his eyes. A woman with long dark hair bent over him, her eyes wide and blue as the patch of sky that winked through the translucent yellow-brown ceiling above her. Smoke swirled up into that opening; he could see branches moved by the wind, just beyond.

The woman sat back, took from his forehead a damp cloth that smelled of mint, and went on singing as though to a child. He tried to sit up, but the effort made him groan.

"Not yet," she said quickly, her voice low and gentle. She slipped a strong arm under his shoulders so that he could sit, and with her other hand she put a cup of warm broth to his mouth. He sipped, tasted strong herbs, sighed, and she let him lie back.

"If you want more, tell me," she said.

"More." His throat was raw; he knew he had vomited for what seemed like days, and not only the contents of his stomach. There had been a time—it might have been a nightmare—when he dreamed that he was vomiting words. All the glowing words that INRI had crammed into his skull, under incredible pressure, had spewed out at last. But since that time, even if it had been a dream, the captions had not reappeared. He did not feel INRI near him or inside him any longer.

She smiled. "All right."

"I heard a drum," he said.

"That was last night," she said.

"Last night? It was minutes ago."

"It may have seemed that way, in your delirium. You had a dangerous withdrawal, too abrupt, but there was no other way. We couldn't wean you gradually from the clone-food."

"Clone-food?"

She stroked his forehead. "Not too many questions at once, hm? You need rest."

He tasted the broth again, felt it cleanse his palate. "You mean the Host," he said.

"That's what *you* call it," she said. She smiled at P.J.'s puzzled expression. "Oh, I don't mean to offend you. It's not your religion I disapprove of, it's your tactics."

"My religion?"

She moved away for a moment and he heard rustling. When she returned, she bore a yellowing slip of paper. "You seem strong enough to read," she said. "This is from the Boyston news."

Boston, he thought. Isn't that in the East?

BOYS' TOWN CHRONNER

Manna Spills Secrets to Local Researchers

Researchers at the Worlds Beyond Clinic announced today that preliminary testing of the "miracle" clone-food recently retrieved from the New Christian Militia by sylvan traders has proved the substance to be derived from human protoplasm, with added fish flavoring and an as-yet-unidentified substance that researchers conjecture is an addictive agent designed to induce craving and create mild euphoria upon ingestion. This is in keeping with the claims of the Christian Army that it possesses a food cloned from the prepuce of Jesus Christ, preserved by a secret monastic line following instructions from St. Paul, who was reputedly given the slip of foreskin as a token of the late savior's affection.

"The Host," P.J. murmured, and it was almost enough to make him sick again. He put his hands over his eyes and moaned. "I ate that? I feel like a cannibal."

"You've recovered remarkably well, considering," said the woman. "Have you eaten it all your life?"

"No," he said. "Not long at all. I wasn't a Christian Soldier—they captured me."

He was surprised to see a flicker of disappointment on her face, but it passed quickly. "Well," she said. "We were hoping we'd finally nabbed a live one. There are so many things we'd like to learn."

Remembering the Periscope, his muscles clenched and he sat upright. "I don't know anything!" he shouted.

"Sh, sh, relax." She put a hand on his brow again. "You're shivering."

He realized that he was in a conical chamber, with a circular floor and a pointed ceiling. Shadows moved on the yellow walls, clustering around a slit tied shut with thongs like shoelaces. He heard a voice say, "Seal, are you all right?"

"Fine," she called. "I'll be out in a moment. Now you," she said to P.J., "lie down again and rest."

"I didn't mean to scream," he said. "It's—the Christians made me tell them everything about my home, and it was so painful."

"You don't have to tell us anything."

"You're the guerrillas, aren't you? Mr. Ashenwriste mentioned you."

"Ashenwriste?" Her eyes narrowed. "With the Cartel?"

He explained how he had come to be riding in the vehicle that was ambushed. He'd had but a few lucid moments since then. In his illness, he had been aware of rough traveling down long cement lanes through untrimmed trees, old highways overgrown with iceplant, signs moving slowly past with strange symbols on them as well as countless warnings: DO NOT PASS, GO BACK, YOU ARE GOING THE WRONG WAY. The guerillas had carried him away, and he had not seen the Cartel vehicle since the night they'd taken it.

"The Cartel prisoners were left to be found by their employees," Seal said. "The vehicle will be useful in our own forays against the Christians. We deal with the Cartel, yes, but on our terms and not theirs. They are too fond of imposing their terms on everyone."

"They've always been helpful to us," P.J. said.

She looked a little dubious. "At least they haven't let nuke technology into the hands of the Christians, whose death-wish is too strong. After all, look what they've got to look forward to after death."

"And you're trying to stop them?"

"We're trying to salvage what we can." She put a hand on her breast. "I am not a guerrilla, myself; this is a peaceful community, and there's so little here that the New Christians don't bother us. They've fixed their sights on the cities—the Sodoms and Gomorrahs, the last bastions of Babel and Babylon. In Boyston—old San Francisco—the fighting is steady. The suburbs are a wasteland. I was there for a year, nursing the wounded. That was where I learned to heal. But I had to get out of the city. Now the guerrillas come to me for healing, and I must say, if I were a bit more of a warrior myself, I'd probably be out with them on their raids. But the diseased body is also a battlefield, at times. With you, for instance, it was a struggle."

"And where am I?" he asked.

"Well, this was the guerillas' home, once upon a time. Stanford, it was called, until the New Christians wiped it out."

"Why?"

"They had to. There was a university here."

"I don't understand."

Seal shrugged. "The New Christians have their own schools. Staunch the free flow of information and you've got the human spirit by the throat. You know them from the inside; I guess you got the whole sales pitch, hm?"

He shook his head slowly. "It all seems so confused."

"They're confused by their own beliefs," Seal said. "Once upon a time, Christianity created its own enemy and called it Satanism. Everything was a matter of good and evil, plain and simple, black and white . . . but this is a gray world. The two extremes, Christ and Satan, finally merged in the Christian militia. There was always a powerful attraction there; now it's been fulfilled. Christ and Anti-Christ in one. Only took two thousand years."

"And a number-crunching computer." P.J. remembered the voracious red-eyed figurine and shivered. It was the first time in weeks that he had thought of it without feeling a surge of automatic devotion. He lay back, head spinning.

"I need some time to think," he said, and minutes later he was dreaming.

It was a few days before he was strong enough to leave Seal's teepee. Before then, visitors started coming to look at him, to see the young man from the walled-in residential enclave and hear his stories of life in the neighborhood. The most frequent of these visitors was a boy named Lynx, who first shocked and then fascinated P.J. He was black from head to toe, and it was his natural color. It amused everyone that P.J. had never seen a black person, so Lynx rapidly brought a variety of exotic human breeds for him to meet. The camp was populated by every sort of person, from Indonesia and the Philippines to Mongolia and Nepal, from Peru to the Bay of Bengal. Most of them came from San Francisco families, and had left the city to do their work—agriculture, mainly—in something resembling peace.

The most commonplace facts of P.J.'s life were surprises to the pagans. One morning Lynx asked him how old he was.

"Eighteen over ten," P.J. replied.

"Say what?"

"Eighteen over ten. How old are you?"

"Seventeen," Lynx said, looking baffled.

"That's all? Just seventeen?"

"What do you mean? What's this 'over ten' stuff?"

P.J. said, "You mean you're seventeen years old and you've been alive seventeen years?"

"Sure."

He did not know what to say for a moment, but Lynx had framed his question: "Then you're eighteen years old and you've only been alive ten years?"

"Of course," P.J. said. "That's acceleration."

"Acceleration?"

There was so much he had taken for granted, never seen as strange. The walls of Cobblestone Hill had confined his imagination. So many questions he had never known to ask. That led to another hour of explanations, during which Lynx called in some friends to listen. By the end of the session, P.J. was so tired of propping himself up on his elbows, and it was getting so hot in the teepee, that he finally said he was ready to take a walk. Seal agreed. Lynx disappeared and returned with loose clothes—a white tunic and drawstring pants—that fit him.

A few steps were all he managed that first afternoon. Outside, the warm wind took his breath away. He sat on a tree stump and looked out at fields, an orchard, people everywhere, tents and teepees, cooking fires, mesh sacks full of grubby things that looked like they had been dug from the earth. He was content to sit there for the rest of the day, talking to Lynx. As he talked on about Cobblestone Hill, he felt for the first time that he did not truly miss it; in comparison to the boot camp it had seemed like a haven, but he thought this place preferable. Still, he could not escape the knowledge that he might have betrayed the neighborhood by giving the Christians information that would put his family in danger.

"I'd like to go with the guerrillas sometime," he told Lynx. "To see my home, at least."

Lynx looked nervous. "You don't want to do that, P.J. It's war."

"You don't understand; my family might be right in the middle of the war without knowing it. If there were some way to warn people."

"I hear they blew up that church on the coast highway—the one that sucked you in."

"Well, that's good," P.J. said, feeling as if Lynx had switched subjects too fast. "How could I get involved with that sort of thing, do you know?"

Lynx's eyes widened. "You don't want to do that," he said again.

"How do you know?" P.J. said. "It's sounds more like you don't want me to."

Lynx reached out quickly and grabbed his hand. "That's right. You're my friend. I know I haven't known you very long but, P.J., you're important to me."

P.J. swallowed, suddenly thinking of the circumstances that had driven him to run from home. It was too much at once: too much he had not let himself think about. He looked away from Lynx, eyes watering, and stared out at the fields. Heat made the trees shimmer, but it was cooler in the shadows. Such a beautiful place . . .

"P.J.?" Lynx said, softer now.

"I never told you why I left home," P.J. said. "I guess I should try."

It was the hardest thing he had ever done; he did not look at Lynx until he had gotten as far as the night of his escape, and then shame stopped him. He had described how it had happened, without commenting on what he had really felt. Now his feelings, all confused, overwhelmed him, made him dumb.

"Why are you ashamed?" Lynx said. "Do you think it's really something they can plug into your genes?"

"Well . . ." Of course, he almost said. He had never thought otherwise.

"You are what you are," Lynx said. "What does it matter how you got that way? Birth is one of those things you can't blame on yourself. Now if you want to talk sordid histories, you should look at me."

P.J. had to laugh, wiping his eyes. He felt an immense relief. "What?" he said.

Lynx looked around to make sure that they were alone, then pulled up the hem of his shirt several inches. P.J., although he was a little embarrassed, looked. Just above the waistline and below the navel was a bright design, like a tattoo—or an advertisement. But it was not a tattoo. As he watched, it flashed on and off in the shadows, a bright arrow pointing down toward dark curls.

"I had the lettering removed," Lynx said, "but I kept this as a reminder. When I was in the city I hustled for a living."

"Hustled?" P.J. said.

Lynx laughed, shaking his head. "I'll explain." He touched a faintly scarred area above the arrow. "The implant, here, used to say *Eat.*"

There was a fire burning so high that he kept confusing the stars with its windblown embers. There was the music of pipes and drums. And there was dancing, hand in hand, in a great ring around the fire. He was a little drunk and very high, out of breath, full of more strength than he'd felt since he lived at home with his family. Thoughts of the neighborhood were the only things that haunted him, and even they were not harsh or frightening tonight. Lynx's grasp was firm. Seal played her tambourine. Children ran underfoot, everywhere, shrieking.

Lynx shouted a whisper, "Come with me!" Then he was pulled along, away from the ring. Lynx's broken laughter kept just ahead of him, but Lynx himself was lost in the night, naked.

A tall triangular shape rose ahead of them, a slot cut from the night; it was a dark teepee. P.J. heard the sound of leather thongs quickly unlaced, then Lynx caught his hand again.

"In here," he said. "No one else will come."

P.J. followed into a musty space; it was blacker than outside, for there were no stars and the firelight was dimmed by the walls. Lynx's hands moved up his arm, brushed his face. Heart pounding, P.J. felt his tunic pulled from him.

There was light: the little arrow flashing on and off in the dark. He started to laugh, but the light was enough to show him his surroundings, and he stopped Lynx with a startled cry.

"Where are we?" he said. "What is this? I never knew it was here."

Lynx sat back. "What's so special?" he said. "It's some of the salvage from Stanford—there's a lot more. Why?"

In the flashing light, P.J. could dimly make out stack upon stack of books. Books of all sizes, all sorts, with covers of leather and paper, with gold leaf glinting.

"Oh, Virgil," he said, "if you could see this."

Lynx's hand closed on his shoulder. "Your brother? Maybe someday he will."

That was the night P.J. knew he would have to return. He did not yet know how, or when, but he knew that the time and the means would come.

11

ON THE JOB

THIS TIME, DAD THOUGHT as he lay awake in the wee hours, it will have to be a perfect strike on Smith. He's gotten away with too much. But I can't be implicated, not at all. And no one in the family—that would look bad. I'll have to get to Jock through someone he would never suspect. Maybe Arnold. Yes . . . Arnold.

Whatever it was, it had better be soon. That thought brought him back to the original worry that had kept him awake this late: he had received his second pink card the previous afternoon, and was very late in making an appointment for acceleration. How long could he get away without treatment? Jock would just love to see him aged and infirm, he was sure.

"Visitors," said the bedside clock, whispering in case he was asleep, but whispering insistently. Connie snored once, explosively, as he rolled over onto his side and looked at the time.

"At four o'clock?"

"Shh," the clock cautioned. "The missus . . ."

For a moment, Dad was unsure of his wakefulness. No visitors would dare come up to the house. They must be out on the sidewalk, speaking to the mailbox. He sagged back into his pillow, an arm over his eyes, wishing only to remain in the warm bed.

But the bed was determined to rouse him; it was a conspiracy of his automated household. He was shaken, then chilled by his half of the mattress, until at last he was so uncomfortable that he could not bear to stay under the covers. His robe swayed out of the wall on an extension, like a flaccid skin. Once he'd slipped into it and cinched the belt, he tried to leave the room, but the extension would not release its hold on his collar. At last he pulled out and went from the room naked. Junior sputtered in the closet as he passed.

The shades were drawn across the office windows, allowing him to approach them openly. In a faint trickle of streetlight, he cautiously pulled aside the shade until he had enough room for one eye to look out at the lawn. Then he put that eye to the gap.

Five figures, unmoving, stood boldly yet in robes of furtive black at the edge of his yard, fog flowing around them. One of them beckoned, waving him down.

Slowly he stepped back, letting the shade fall, and put a hand to his mouth. The Whelk Grand Council had come for him. He might have known it would be like this.

Would it be an inquisition or an initiation? Either way, he had to face it.

On tiptoe, or the nearest he could manage, he crept back into his bedroom and began to dress for chill weather.

"I have some simple questions," Connie said. "That's all I'm asking these days."

The coffee-table computer waited for specifics. In the screen she could see her face reflected, the smile-lines fixed as if gouged there, the natural planes of her expressions forced beyond the breaking point. She touched a spot just under the right cheekbone and pushed a sliding joint back into place; fatty deposits slid into their lubricated pouches beneath the eye sockets, and instantaneously she looked several years younger, though she did not feel that way. These days she did not feel at all the way she looked. Everyone told her how lovely she was, complimented her smile, and it was true that she always smiled. That was the way her face was built. The smile, which slipped into a grimace overnight, was screwed back into place each morning before Bill saw her. Lately, she had been thinking about loosening the screws a little; it would be like letting down her hair. People could take her as she was, or leave her.

"This should be easy for you," she said, enjoying having someone to talk to—someone who, unlike Stephanie or the twins, her usual partners in conversation, would listen without argument. "You know almost everything there is to know, don't you?"

The coffee table ignored rhetorical questions.

"First, where has my husband gone, really?"

A note flashed onto the screen, in Bill's sloppy light-pen cursive:

Con—Business trip, had to run, may be a few days. Wm.

"I've seen that already," she said. "I don't believe it. I found this in his sock drawer."

She held up a pink card, addressed to her husband, notifying him that he was overdue for his acceleration. The computer gaped and clicked until she fed the card into it for examination.

"This card came from the office of Dr. Ralph Edison. It informs Mr. Johnson—"

"I can read. I want to know if he went to the clinic and not on a business trip, or if he made up some 'trip' so that he wouldn't have to get his treatment."

"In-patient records are classified. There is no record of Mr. Johnson affirming his appointment on the house line, however."

She sighed, propping her chin on her knuckles. The house was still; Nancy had taken the children to the beach for the day; Junior slept in his closet. So quiet. She could almost hear the sloshing of the liquid crystal clock.

She eyed the *Ladies' Home Video* warily, recalling her shawl-pattern discussion with Nada. Bill knew all about these computers; what if he had some way of getting into her secret conversations? It would be just like him. If he thought that she was planning to have an affair, it would be even more like him to run out and have one first. Her fingernails dug into her chin. Business trip? There was no business that couldn't be done through a plug-in. There was nowhere to go and no way to get there.

Nothing outside.

Thinking of P.J., who must be dead, she thought she would begin to weep. But a dry sound wracked her throat, as if she had swallowed sand. She couldn't let herself start crying over a lost child or she would be crying forever. Little by little she had been trying to limit herself to dealing with the present, where there was quite enough to take care of.

She rose, a little uncertainly, for it was dark in the house. All the lights were off in order to keep the headaches away. She felt them circling around her like wolves, closing in, and darkness was some protection.

As she climbed the stairs, the base of her neck throbbed as though with a touch of fever.

Leaning into Bill's office, his sanctuary, she hesitated. Stray, pointless thoughts fluttered around the edges of her mind, flickering like moths until she batted them away. They were selfish thoughts. She couldn't worry about things like where she had come from, or why she was here. She couldn't change any of those things. She had to be practical. Where, for instance, was Bill? That was a question worth asking.

There was no clue to be found on his desk, but of course there wouldn't be. She expected to find the drawers locked, but they were open—worse, they were empty. There was not a scrap of paper or even a pencil in any of them. He must have left all his work at the office.

His console.

"You can't use that," he always said. "You have to be a skilled IMR typist. You have to learn it young, get it into your blood, you know. Like P.J. He's a whiz."

Like P.J., she thought, but not like Bill. When had he ever learned how to type?

It must be easier than it looks. Probably about as complicated as a holiday. I always see him smiling when he's plugged in. What if he doesn't work at all? What if he's got nothing there but a one-man plug-in vacation?

The thought made her quiver. She slipped into his chair.

"On," she said, and the system began to purr. Light spilled over the desk, speckled her hands. She found the IMR-gloves resting on the arms of the chair and put them on; and then, somewhat clumsily in the gloves, she struggled to get the hood over her head. For a second she suffocated in darkness, but the eyepieces moved into place with slight suction and she found light flashing into her eyes, pulsing, and she relaxed. Her hands tingled. Electricity raced through her spine.

Where was she?

Black curtains parted ahead of her and she moved into a dusty, yellow-lit hallway. With a start she became aware of her body—a heavy-set male physique, dressed in a gray suit. Everything seemed dim and out of focus, including herself. Her steps were heavy, plodding, and hardly carried her down the hall.

She approached a door, one of many, moving with incredible slowness. *Mr. Johnson* was painted on the frosted glass pane. Monday, she kept thinking. Monday. Sigh.

Poor Bill, she thought in spite of herself. Every day he comes to this.

She was almost afraid to open the door, but she did. There might be a clue to his whereabouts.

The place lit up as she entered. She gazed into a room that surpassed the hallway in drabness. Steel desks, cork partitions, rows of filing cabinets. The hands of an enormous antique clock were frozen at five after eight. Stacks of paper covered the nearest desk, and on the topmost sheet of the tallest stack she saw in huge red letters:

NEED YOUR COMMENTS ASAP.

Her hands, in the gray sleeves, trembled. She felt exhausted, weak, thirsty, as though the dust of the office had settled into her pores. She backed out of the room, turning off the light as she went, and continued down the hall in search of a fountain. A constant clicking sound emanated from the walls on all sides, no louder than the rattling of her teeth, and her headache finally seized her.

With a moan she turned to the nearest door, where the sound of clattering—it must be a typewriter—was very loud.

CENTRAL FILES

Someone here should be able to help her.

She went in, but found herself in an aisle of filing cabinets. There was no one typing, no room in fact for a desk, and the sound she heard came from beyond a door at the far end of the room. When she saw the name on it —Men— she started to leave, but the clamor coming from behind the door kept her a moment longer. It sounded like someone scrabbling at the knob, a trapped person hoping to get out but knowing that there was no one in the room he could call out to. Of course, she had come in silently. The knob quivered and shook in its socket, turned a little in either direction, but it did not quite open.

So the door was locked from outside. How simple to remedy. Her head felt better, now that she had found a solution to some problem, however small.

She crossed the room quickly, her steps sounding loud and clear to her ears; the whole scene brightened as her mood lifted. The scratching and rattling stopped as she unlocked the door. She could hear him shifting about inside.

And then a thought: what if it were Bill? Could he have gotten stuck in the men's room? No, there had been a note . . .

"You can come out," she said in her manly voice. "I unlocked it for you."

The door opened swiftly in the hand of a shadow. Beyond the

opener were layers of blackness, darkening successively into the distance. It hardly looked like a restroom.

Four figures stood in the dark. None of them was her husband.

"Hello?" she said.

As they came forward they put out their hands, but she hardly cared when she got a look at their eyes.

Bits of raw meat.

Backward. She banged into a high metal shelf covered with colored forms and boxes of paperclips, and set it rocking. Before it fell she got the doorknob in her hand and escaped into the hallway; as the door closed she heard a crash, but she did not wait to learn if the four with torn eyes had survived. They had not looked like they could be stopped so easily.

In the hallway, everything was quiet and dim and slow again, the yellow light full of dust. She ran toward the curtains at the far end of the hall, wishing that her body were lighter, her legs more agile. Motes of dust hammered against her face. At last she staggered into the dark, and came to herself in the gloves and the hood, at Bill's desk. She was covered in a light sweat, shaking.

She was out of the chair and downstairs in seconds. In the kitchen she shoved a glass under the faucet and almost drank down a glass of blue dissolving liquid; she poured that out and filled the glass from the other tap, and drank to soothe her parched throat. Leaning against the counter, she looked around as if expecting to see those four come in from the living room; but the house was still silent.

She went to the phone in the den and pressed the emergency button. Dr. Edison or a phone-answering simulation appeared on the screen.

"It's not a medical emergency," she said.

"What's the problem, Constance?" the doctor asked. "Random panic?"

"Tell me who to call," she said. "Computer control? The employment office? I went to Bill's plug-in office and these people without eyes . . . I mean, they had eyes but they weren't right."

The simulation flickered. "Say that again? You went into his office?"

"I plugged into his job. I was looking for him, doctor. He said he went on a business trip, but where would he have gone?"

Dr. Edison shook his head. "He's been avoiding his treatment for some time, Connie. I think he's afraid. You know Bill—he's a big frightened kid at heart."

"But where could he—"

"Now, Connie, relax. Let's talk about you. You say you went into his plug-in? Those packages are highly personalized, you know that. Didn't you think you might be intruding?"

"I wanted to know where he was, do you understand?"

"I think so. Let's look at your motives, shall we?"

"My motives?"

He smiled reassuringly. "You sound a bit hysterical."

"Well, I'm upset."

"Exactly. But why?" And here his image was replaced by a tricolor bar chart. Along the bottom were numbers from 0 to 100 —Ages. Along the side were various symbols she did not recognize. "Connie, take a look at yourself."

A red X appeared on the chart, marking the intersection of Age 45 and something that looked like the logo for Channel 6.

"At your age, all women with your profile confront the same issues. Your childbearing years are behind you. Your reproductive system, frankly, has nothing better to do than turn on itself. When this happens, Connie, you can expect to experience various psychological disturbances, including suspicion, dread, hallucinations, lethargy, hysteria. I think that's what we're looking at in your case. It's simple enough."

She felt cold looking at him, as if he really were nothing more than a phone-screen.

"You haven't heard anything I've said."

"Certainly I have," he said. "Every word you've said has been a clue to your health of mind. You feel uneasy, and you feed your imbalance by suspecting your husband of who knows what? Why else would you invade his privacy? Then your psyche projects your invasion back upon itself, triggering delusions, and you see yourself as though in a mirror. You are the one with the wrong kind of eyes. Those are your eyes, Connie: wrong because you are looking in the wrong place for the answer to your problems."

"I can't believe this," she said, and stabbed again at the Emergency button.

"Oh, it's not your fault," he said. "Blame biology."

"Get off my phone."

"Fortunately, your problem is easily solved by science. I would have suggested this myself sooner or later."

"What are you talking about? Why won't you let me contact someone who'll help me?"

"I want to help, Connie. I can do it. I think we should schedule your hysterectomy immediately."

"Oh, I don't believe this!"

She disengaged and spun away from the screen, repelled by the thought that his image might return. If it did, she didn't want to know about it. There was no time to think over what he had said, however, for the doorbell was ringing.

The opalescent panel by the front door showed a thin man, rather tall, with a narrow chin, receding brow, ingenuous eyes. It was the first time that she had seen him without paying unusual attention to the two outstanding characteristics that were usually all she noticed: namely, the silver-streaked muttonchops and pastel suit. For some reason, standing there with his hands crossed over his groin, shifting from foot to foot, he looked like an ordinary man, harried and uncertain. For a moment he reminded her of Bill as he had been about four years ago—ten years younger.

Without bothering to interview him, she disarmed the hedges and opened the way.

"Come in, Mr. Ashenwriste," she called, overcome by a sense of relief.

When he saw her he smiled, raised a hand to his temple, and came in quickly. She saw that Jock Smith had deserted his post for once. She closed the door behind him and heard the metal plates slam shut outside.

"Well," he said, "it seems that we're locked in for the night."

When she didn't know how to answer that, he grinned. "So to speak. Your house has one of the more remarkable security systems on Cobblestone Hill."

"Thank you," she said. She motioned toward the livingroom. "Please come in. Would you like something to drink? There's a menu on the coffee-table console."

"All right. Thanks."

As he went deeper into the darkened house, he looked around and seemed to listen to the silence.

"Is your husband at work?"

"No, he's—he's away."

Mr. Ashenwriste looked uncomfortable. He put his hands into the pocket of his pastel suit and turned to her. "That's unfortunate. I'd hoped to go over the nuke with him—make sure there were no problems with the installation.

"I'm sorry he's not here. He'll be disappointed when I tell him you stopped by."

Mr. Ashenwriste sat on the sofa, considered the coffee-table console, but apparently decided not to order anything.

She found herself watching him, waiting for his next words. His thin red lips glistened, the shadow of tongue just beyond them. She felt as if a bubble were expanding in her stomach; she was a little afraid, but only a little.

Why not him? she thought.

He apparently caught her thought, for his mouth twitched abruptly and he turned to look at the console. "Well, mineral water sounds good to me."

She watched him intently, knowing that she was about to go beyond the point of no return. How quickly she had come to it! Although he would not look at her, he obviously felt her eyes on him; she was unable to temper her gaze. Not half an hour ago she had been all practicality, her concern for Bill almost obsessive; now she felt no less practical, only more fatalistic. Bill was away and that was that. Where he had gone was his business.

"I'll get that mineral water," she said, and left quickly to give herself time to catch her breath and gather some composure.

So what if she did, and what if she didn't?

She extracted a glass of sparkling water from the beverage unit. Nada would approve. The ladies of Cobblestone Hill and Laurel Woods considered Mr. Ashenwriste's muttonchops very distinguished; some had tried in vain to coax their husbands into pastel suits.

She found that she was amazingly calm, calculating the kids' probable time of return. Bill might be a few days, depending. Jock Smith had not even seen Mr. Ashenwriste enter.

Mr. Ashenwriste.

She set his glass before him and said, "What is your first name?"

He smiled up at her, looking a little muddled. "Sweeney."

"I'm Connie." She gave him a smile.

He sipped, cleared his throat. "Aren't you having anything?"

Shaking her head, she sat. Her eyes wandered over the dark walls, family pictures, trophies on the shelves. Here, she thought. We'll do it here.

She put her feet up on the coffee table. I have nice legs, she thought.

He didn't say anything for several minutes, only stared at something in a corner, until she asked, "Mr.—Sweeney, was there something else?"

He looked scared. As he started to put down his glass, she reached out and touched his hand; it was lightly furred, soft. He surprised her by first shivering, then turning his hand over to grasp hers. When their eyes met, every light in the room turned on without being touched.

She gasped and pulled her hand away, but the lights stayed on. Mr. Ashenwriste, white-faced, jumped up and patted at the air with fluttering hands. One by one, the lights blinked out.

He looked over at her slowly. "Oh, my."

"Did you do that?" she asked, getting up.

"I'm afraid so. I shouldn't have but I—I lost control."

"Is that something the Cartel lets you do?"

He smiled sheepishly. "I'm linked in."

She took his hands again and found that he was shaking. "How wonderful. Maybe we should have some light. A little?"

He nodded tentatively and a lamp in the corner hummed up to about the brightness of a candle. "How's that?"

"Nice," she said. She sank down into the sofa cushions, drawing him with her. When she touched his jaw, below one ear, another light came on and went out immediately.

He sighed, brushing her cheek. "It's distracting."

"Not to me," she said. "Let it happen."

"All right." Leaning forward. "I will."

What followed was a summer storm, with lightning.

It should have been a splendid day for sailing. The sky was clear, the wind strong, and the *Argos* handled like a dream. He was away at last, a full hamper of food stored beneath a bench, the shores of home falling away behind him. The water was impossibly clean and blue. He set his eyes on the western horizon and let himself be carried toward it, onward, ever faster.

And then a line of twenty pelicans dipped past, each with a letter painted on its side. Together they spelled out: SEE ELAINE IMMEDIATELY.

"Shit."

He threw up his hands and closed his eyes, already feeling for the hood and pulling off the gloves in a single entangling motion. It was so easy to forget the IMR equipment, until something reminded you that it was there; and then it became unbearable.

"Virgil, I need your help," said Elaine. She stood at the other side of the desk, her arms full of wadded cloth, waiting for him to extract his hands from the inverted gloves.

"I'm on work," he said angrily, but not without a guilty stammer. Work was a joke. His first PIJob demanded nothing more than idle fantasizing, with an occasional call to monitor some dreamlike process of computation. He was not even convinced the computation amounted to anything; more likely it was there to make him feel useful. Even the dreariest tasks were set in remote, beautiful spots. And on his lengthy breaks, he was free to invent his surroundings and companions as he pleased.

"So am I," she said. "Do you know how to make a bed?"

He almost laughed. "What? That's automatic. Do you have to do everything the hard way these days?"

She flung the sheets at his head. "The bed's broken. I'm sure you must remember how it happened, my little acrobat."

He blushed, flexing his leg, which still ached from the twisting it had taken.

"As for doing things the hard way, Virgil, if you want a fast baby you can bake it yourself."

He got up, taking the sheets in the crook of his arm. "The time-bake is perfectly safe."

"Well, I've never trusted it."

"But your body is perfect, is that it? Sorry. Your womb's a hell of a lot more prone to downtime than a time-bake. Nine months is too long to trust something as complex as a baby to your body, Elaine."

"We could both be old by then, is that what you mean?" She sighed. "Forget it. I'm not having this fight again."

He stopped halfway down the hall to their bedroom and put a hand on the wall. On the back of that hand were a few gray hairs. Only a few, he told himself.

"I'm not getting old," he said loudly.

"Oh, Virgil," she laughed. "It happens to everything. Don't be so poopy. Kids will keep you young, you know—real kids, like we all were, until the ovens."

"*Were,*" he said, looking at the streaks of silver in her hair. The first traces of senescence—planned obsolescence—had made her look classy, enhanced her beauty until it was right out of his league. In his case, age merely made him look more worn down than he felt. He knew he would never write another inspired thesis; his research had come to an end, and no new brain cells would be forthcoming.

He threw the load of sheets through the door of their bedroom, watched the white shapes spread out and billow to the floor.

"The floor's filthy!" she screamed. "What are you doing?"

"I'm not wasting my time making a bed," he yelled back, and turned down the hall.

"Where are you going?" Her voice was low and sounded dangerous.

"To work," he said. "Before I get fired. Which would be your fault."

"Go then," she called. "You can make your own bed on the sofa tonight."

He hesitated in mid-step, but momentum kept him going. After he had slammed the door to his office, he sat down and stared at his terminal. He wished he had a book to read, pages to turn, words to follow, but whenever he created them in the PI —even if they were books he had read a dozen times—they came out with blurry letters, and the characters stayed flat. He could hear his wife talking to herself in the bedroom, and wondered how it would be when she was senile.

"How did I get myself into this?" he asked the room.

After awhile, he pulled on the hood and gloves and entered the program like a wrestler slipping into an undefined ring, matched against an invisible opponent. He heard the sound of breaking surf and tried to think of something—anything—worth doing with his dreams.

"Come away with me," Sweeney whispered.

"Oh, no. I couldn't possibly."

He sighed, and lights in the stairway flickered. "It's such a wide world, Constance, and you've seen so little of it."

"I've seen plenty. Enough." She made sure her blouse was smoothed neatly against her tummy before letting the magnozip on her pants suit fasten the waistband tight. Sweeney brought the lights up quickly, revealing that two had burned out in their passion's electrical storm.

"I'll replace them," he said a bit awkwardly. "No charge."

"You're sweet, but we have plenty of spares."

"Honestly, Constance. Come with me." He was pleading, though she couldn't imagine how he had become so emotional over her so quickly. "There are places you would never imagine, where we could be safe. Underground. The Cartel, drilling for fuel, once discovered an incredible network of caverns—measureless to man. We could go there and no one would ever find us."

"The Cartel wouldn't tell my husband where we'd gone?"

"They . . . wouldn't know for certain. It would be a swift, secret getaway. Please."

Don't cling, she thought fiercely, suddenly irritated by him. She started to urge him from the couch, but he smiled and caught her hands, at which point she found herself turning his palms upward and kissing him on the inside of each wrist. How confusing.

She drew back slightly without letting go of him.

"How could you give up your job like that? You're a grown man. You shouldn't be talking of running away."

"You don't understand. I've never had anything, anyone, I could call my own—the Cartel doesn't allow it. Being with you this afternoon, well, it's shown me a whole new world—a world more exciting than anything the Cartel could offer. I feel like an outlaw now."

"Outlaw," she whispered.

Her eyes wandered past the edge of his arm, distracted, and lighted on the video rack by the sofa. "Oh, God!"

"What is it?" he asked. "Constance?"

The *Ladies' Home Video* sat in the rack, unused all this time. "It's on record," she said. "It's all on record, Sweeney. Tonight it will be on TV for everyone to see."

Ashenwriste sat down with a soft thud in the middle of the sofa and blinked owlishly. He looked pale and helpless in his pastel undershorts, engulfed in tatty cushions. Helpless, when what she needed now was someone with the courage and raw strength to face Bill when he came home and saw the reruns. Either that or someone with Arnold Smith's intelligence, a man who could revise the household tapes before prime time. But she could hardly entrust Arnold with such a task.

"Constance," he said, as if dictating a formal letter. She was impressed anew by the sense of authority he could convey, even unclothed on her livingroom couch; making love to him, she had begun to take him for granted. Now, though, the entire Cartel seemed to speak through him as he said, "You must come away with me."

"Sweeney, I . . ."

My God, she thought. I could do it.

"Can't possibly . . ."

It would be very easy.

"But how?"

He smiled, leaning far enough forward to catch his lavender pants by the waist. "There are secret ways in and out of your neighborhood. No one would know."

She pointed at the camera above the mantelpiece. "They would now."

He wilted. "I'm not used to such scrutiny."

"Hold on." She hurried to slip the *Ladies' Home Video* into its cradle so that they would betray nothing else. Not that there was much left to betray. Only her family remained.

Be practical, she thought, and sat down next to him with the skin of one knuckle nipped between her teeth. Nancy, the twins, poor Stephanie. And then she thought of Junior, even now closeted. Perhaps he was wailing, upstairs in darkness, and she could not hear. It was as if he weighed a million pounds, as if the second-story floor creaked beneath his weight, as if the boards might rupture at any moment and she would be smothered in baby fat.

"I have to think this over," she said.

"There's not much time."

She shook her head. "If you only understood. My responsibilities—"

"Are to yourself, Constance. I can only tell you one thing. I love you. I have never loved before, but I know this is it."

Connie stared down at the shag, feeling herself flush with anger and uncertainty. "I don't know."

One thing was certain. Everything had changed. She knew for the first time in years that she was not reliant on William; if anything, it was the other way around. One afternoon of this had shown her that she could do as she pleased. If she stayed, it would be different, too difficult. She and Bill would fight. The children would struggle to avoid the clash of their parents, but ultimately fail. There was a self-perpetuating pattern of pain here whose rhythm she had broken this afternoon. By staying, she locked them all into it; but if she left—took the children with her— anything might happen. They would have a chance at freedom.

She looked up at Ashenwriste. "What about Nancy, the twins, Steph—"

"We'll have to come back for them. There's no time now."

"Can we really do it?" she asked.

"You'll go?" He clasped her hands. "I am so glad."

The decision made, she felt her heart lighten.

"Pack lightly," he said as he finished dressing. "No more than will fit into a small bag."

"But what?"

"Isn't there anything you can't leave behind?"

She thought a moment. How could she leave any of it behind? It was not as if she were a young girl who could run away from home and leave nothing undone except chores. She was . . . how old, really? The speed-treatment had clocked her at one age, but now that skin fit her body. It was time to shed, time to free the younger Connie within. She must leave it all, or leave none of it.

The alloy shutters whirred, and the front door started opening. The laughter of children came through the gap. Before they had come up the front path, she'd pushed Sweeney ahead of her into the kitchen, and from there into the garage.

"Mom?" Lyndon called.

"She's probably shopping," Nancy said. "Let's get cleaned up before she comes home."

Connie eased the door shut. Taking Sweeney's elbow, she motioned toward the back door.

"We'll have to go around the back," she whispered.

"What's that?"

Baby Erica dragged herself into their path, teeth bared, and began growling. Her eyes glistened in the dim light.

"Hello, darling," Connie said.

"She's beautiful," said Ashenwriste, all Cartel once again.

She growled even louder.

"Shh!" Connie said, rushing forward. She tried to snatch up her daughter, in order to rock her into silence, but Erica made a shocking lunge at Connie's ankles and her teeth met with a snap.

"Here," Sweeney whispered, distracting the baby. Connie pressed herself against the back door and watched her lover crouching to stroke the babe who separated them.

"Something's upset her," she said. "Please be careful."

But he had something in his hand, a small cylinder that rattled. The symbol of radioactivity was printed on its cap. Erica quieted, fascinated by it.

"There we go," he said, and rolled it into a corner of the garage. She scurried after it. "Out," he said to Connie. "Hurry."

In the backyard, all was calm. The only sound came purring from the compact turbine generator assembly that was hooked up to the garden hose, handling most of the Johnsons' energy needs. Connie realized that the Cartel must have kept its connections into her home, even though it was an independent energy source now, otherwise her appliances would not have been so sensitive to Ashenwriste. Bill's freedom from the Cartel, then, was largely illusory. Of course, it would be. The Cartel leased the hardware to its customers; the Cartel controlled the fuel that was making gas and oil obsolete. Bill's dream of self-sufficiency had always been just that: a dream.

She led Sweeney around the side of the house to a gate. "Where are you parked?"

"Just down the block. I—"

She followed his eyes to see what had silenced him, and when she saw what he'd seen, she was unable to speak.

A man was waiting for them on the sidewalk. A man in a pastel suit. He looked like Sweeney Ashenwriste, exactly.

Whose hand, then, did she hold? Two Ashenwristes? The nearest, her lover, narrowed his eyes, looked for a moment like no one she knew; with his lips drawn back he was a demon of rage and suspicion.

"They've caught me already," he said.

"Who is it?" she asked a bit timidly.

"My brother," he said, reaching for the latch on the gate. "My clone."

Before she could stop him, he threw the gate wide open and rushed onto the lawn.

"Wait, Sweeney!" She ran.

She was barely in time. The sentry did not recognize him, as she had known it wouldn't; the house lasers had burned holes in the pastel cuffs of his sleeves and trousers before she caught his arm. "I have to escort you," she whispered. "What are you going to do?"

They reached the edge of the lawn. Her lover's mirror image gave her a polite nod, then fixed his eyes on Sweeney. "I didn't think you'd be coming out the front door, not after that power surge."

Sweeney pulled away from her, his face red—with fury or embarrassment, she could not tell. He grabbed his brother's arm and drew him as close as he could to the lawn without pulling him over the edge.

"What are you doing here?" he growled.

"I've come to spirit you away."

"To arrest me?"

The other shrugged. "If you like."

"And for what reason?"

The second Ashenwriste sputtered a laugh. "What reason?

Your telemetrics sent the remote needles into the red—red for lust, I imagine. You didn't expect the Cartel to send flowers to the lucky girl, did you?"

"Shut up."

"Now, now. Lower your voice and I'll lower mine. Keep your grip—pretend you're threatening me and I'll keep smiling to damp my telemetrics. You're lucky I was nearby and they could send me to pick you up. I can help you get away if freedom is all you want."

"You know it is, Andrew."

Connie noticed movement above them: the smirking face of Jock Smith. He frightened her. Of all the people to see her sneaking out with a salesman, it had to be Jock. She had always liked the Smiths; Bill was the one who waged wars, dreamed up reasons for vendettas, pushed grudges to the flashpoint. Why the fear? Was it because she no longer trusted anyone? Anything? She felt like a goldfish that had shattered its bowl in its struggle to be free, and now that all the water had run out she was drowning in fresh air.

"Sweeney," she said, her throat dry, aware of how exposed they were. The children might look out and see them at any time.

"Throw me," said Andrew Ashenwriste. "You'll have to knock me out cold—but not until I've told you what I know."

She clapped her hands to her mouth as Sweeney bent and threw himself into his brother. She half-expected them to merge into one Ashenwriste, but they merely rolled to the sidewalk, grunting and moaning. Through the panting she heard one of them—it must have been Andrew—giving what sounded like directions. She glanced back at the still facade of her house, then looked at the street. The block was deserted except for Jock, and now Doris, both looking down.

Andrew blocked a punch. There was a long moment of straining in which neither brother moved. Andrew said, "The guerrillas . . . have him . . . you can . . . guess where . . .''

Sweeney released his brother and the other flew over him, tumbling to land flat on his back, one foot trespassing on the

Johnsons' lawn. Connie pushed the foot out of the way before the lasers could focus.

"Where?" Sweeney said as he straddled his brother and clenched his lapels.

"Old forest rendezvous. He might be in a pagan camp, but we're not sure about that. But if you're outlaw now—"

"I am."

"Then they'll take you in. And her. The boy will want to see her."

Connie knelt as Sweeney hauled Andrew upright. "What boy?" she said, her pulse suddenly thunderous in her ears.

But Sweeney had drawn back his hand, curled his fingers into a fist, and now he punched with all his weight. Andrew dropped back, his head cracked against asphalt, and his eyes rolled as the lids fluttered shut.

"What boy?" she screamed.

Sweeney caught her and pulled her away from his brother. "He's out, Constance. Come along, my car's right here."

She tried to tear away from him. "What boy? What boy did he mean?"

"Your son, P.J., of course. Please hurry."

They left the other Ashenwriste prone on the sidewalk and ran to the Cartel convertible. He opened the door for her and as he went around to his side she watched the Smiths coming out of their house, stepping tentatively down their front path, advancing on Andrew Ashenwriste.

"Constance."

She jumped at the touch of his hand. "What?"

His eyes were serious. "Whatever happens—"

"I can't say I love you," she said.

He closed his mouth with a snap, the lines around his eyes tightening for her to see. He gave the car a curt command to take them away.

12

CABAL WITHOUT A CAUSE

Nancy answered the door when no one else would stir from the television. Leaving her siblings behind, all chewing insta-serve dinners and watching the commercial channel as if nothing were out of whack, she hurried down the hall to the front door and in the viewer saw Arnold standing on the sidewalk.

"Well," she said, considering letting him stand there all night —or as long as she liked. She pressed the speak button and saw him jerk as the mailbox crackled: "Don't move, Arnold. I've got the house guns aimed on you."

"Nan?" He looked and sounded puzzled.

"That's right. I'm surprised you remember my name after all this time. I vaguely remember you."

"It hasn't been that long. I've been busy building—you know. Can we talk?"

She didn't answer immediately, but stood cleaning her fingernails. She wasn't supposed to have anyone in the house when her parents weren't home—an old rule she barely remembered, because Mom so rarely left the house. But she could go out; that was no problem. The kids could take care of themselves.

A moment later she sauntered down the walk and stopped a few feet from Arnold, still within the protective periphery of her own yard. Arnold swayed from foot to foot, hands deep in his pockets so that an inch of his belly showed between the hem of the shirt and the low waistband. The pants were small on him; it looked silly, but it also made her excited in a certain way.

"Well?" she said.

"Come out in the street where no one will hear."

"There's no one to listen," she said, pulling her hair back into a ponytail, which she released a second later while stepping out of the yard. They went to the curb and sat down. He made a limp attempt to capture one of her hands, but it was too easily evaded. His heart wasn't into it.

"What is it, Arnold?" she asked when he had moped long enough.

"I'm afraid, Nan."

"Of what?"

"That they found me out."

"Who?"

"The Cartel. Ashenwriste came over today. He came in while I was out, and when I got home he was talking to my dad in whispers. They must have tracked down the missing plutonium."

"Don't be silly. Mom handles that, and she never noticed a thing. She would have said so. They won't find out."

"You think so?" His eyes widened with the hope that she could reassure him. "The Cartel guy didn't even look at me, that's true. But I'm still nervous. I've had the bomb too long. It's time to use it."

She nodded. "All right. My parents aren't home, so if you need help . . ."

"Come home with me?"

She wished she had a sweater, but they weren't going far. Only across the street. As they went, she grabbed his elbow and tucked her arm through his, suddenly feeling as if they had been separated for months, missing the warmth and reassurance of his presence. Things had not been quite what she expected after the last treatment. She had to scrabble to remember her dreams of how she and Arnold would make a life together. Well, she thought, this is also a life. We're revolutionaries.

At the last minute before stepping onto Arnold's porch, she looked up at the lit windows of the second story and saw his father looking down at them. Mr. Smith pulled away from the glass, as if shot down.

"Your dad's acting funny," she said.

"I told you he's crazy. Come on in."

"Won't he mind my coming over?"

"He has it in for your dad, not you. Don't worry about him. He'd never hurt a kid."

Mrs. Smith surprised them in the hall. "Nancy! I haven't seen you here in ages. Would you kids like to have some popcorn balls in the TV room? We're just sitting down."

"Nah," Arnold said. "We're too old for popcorn balls. We'll be in my room."

"Thanks anyway," Nancy said, trying to make up for Arnold.

Once they were in his room, which was strewn with wire and tools and half-dissected electronic components, he motioned with a grin toward his closet. "It's in there."

She started toward the door but he caught her hand. "No, wait. I've got an alarm set up. Let me disconnect it first." He pulled up the corner of a blanket that draped from his unmade bed, and twirled a dial on the bedpost. "Okay."

She was about to open the closet door when she heard a gruff but high-pitched broken laugh behind her. She knew it wasn't Arnold when she heard him say, "What are you doing? Get out of my room."

She whirled quickly and saw Mr. Smith come in and shut the door behind him. He stood with his head bobbing back and forth at the two of them, while one hand still played with the doorknob.

His shirtfront was filthy, the material rubbed thin and ragged; it must have been weeks since he'd used a recycler. Didn't Mrs. Smith ever get after him about his appearance?

"Come on, dad," Arnold said impatiently. "Stop drooling and get out of my room."

"I was waiting," his father said, his voice running up and down the scale. He pointed at the bed. "You turned off your alarm, now I'll take your little toy for myself."

"How did you know?" Arnold said, and then he swore. "You won't!" He threw himself at his father, banging him into the door. Arnold might have bruised one of his father's ribs, broken something, but there was no evidence of pain in the elder Smith's expression. It looked like all he could do now was smile.

"I'll do what I want," said Mr. Smith, pinned against the door. "You're a baby and you can't stop me."

"I'll disarm it; I'll tell the neighborhood!"

"And what were you going to do with it?"

Arnold shot a swift look at Nancy.

"My father will stop you," Nancy said, wondering if Dad had any idea of Mr. Smith's condition. Was it Dad's fault, she wondered? Had that afternoon with the missile sent Mr. Smith over whatever the edge he'd gone over?

"You think I care about your father?" he asked. "When I'm done, he'll be radioactive dust, him and his nuke. While I will be safe, safe . . ."

"If you set it off, no one will be safe," Nancy said.

"What do I care about the rest of them? They're all your father's friends. They laugh at my missile, out there at the sixteenth hole. They laugh at me, and my family. I'll be glad when they're gone and we're all alone here. We can make it all alone." Mr. Smith pointed a wavering finger at Arnold. "I've watched you laying your devices around the house. This place is safe, isn't it, inside your shield? It's the only safe spot for miles around."

Arnold said nothing, but Nancy could hear his teeth grinding. He must have set his special shield around the house, to protect it in the blast if it came to that. She had always believed that

Arnold would use the bomb only for bargaining—a threat. But Mr. Smith, she saw, would have no qualms about setting it off.

"I'll tell my father," she said. "We'll go to Mr. Taylor and the neighborhood police."

"I can be sure that you won't," he said, coming toward her. As he grabbed her wrist, she said, "Don't you dare!"

"Mom!" Arnold shouted. "Mom, help, he's going crazy!"

Mr. Smith opened the door and tugged Nancy out into the hall, with Arnold following right behind. For a moment she thought they would pass through the livingroom, where Mrs. Smith would certainly protest this rough treatment; but instead they turned aside and went downstairs to the basement and into a small storage room. There were jars of preserves that Mrs. Smith had put up herself, tools, old boxes; and at the back of the room, a door with a spyhole in it.

"There, now," said Mr. Smith, swinging her at the door. She caught herself on her hands, her face an inch from the tiny lens. He must want her to look at something. But before she could peek in, the door opened.

Mrs. Smith smiled out at her, the second before she grabbed her wrists.

"Well," she said. "Here you are, Nancy. I was just putting the finishing touches on your cell."

"You won't get away with this!" Arnold cried.

"Oh, I think we will. Nancy, what do you think?"

She was speechless, her imagination contriving explanations for what was happening. Only the obvious answers came to her. She was a captive. How simple.

Mrs. Smith pushed her through the door; she heard the bolts sliding home. Home. It seemed so far away.

A voice as deep as all-engulfing darkness spoke in Dad's ear:

"William Dolores Johnson, you are now a full initiate of the Wheelwrights, the Whelks' innermost circle. Wrightbrother Coolidge, you may remove the initiate's blindfold."

"Howdy, Bill," said Marv Coolidge, his grinning face the first

217

thing he had seen in . . . how long? The bitter potion they'd given him to sip—savoring of machine oil and aftershave—must have had time-twisting effects.

His parched lips cracked in a smile, and from his hoarse throat, ragged from learning the songs of the Wheelwrights, came a ready laugh. As soon as his wrists were untied, he clapped Marv on the back, and the others moved in to congratulate him.

"Marv," he said, "I would never have suspected you were on the Whelk Grand Council."

Coolidge shrugged. "Well, it is a secret society. I mean, everyone knows the name Wheelwright, everyone knows about the Whelk Grand Council, but no one knows they're the same thing."

The nocturnal voice that had welcomed him as a Wheelwright —the same voice that had officiated all of the ceremony, in fact —now gave a hearty, "Welcome in, m'boy. I knew you wouldn't be sucking the placebos for long. Sometimes takes an upset like your boy's leaving—a good solid crisis—to bring out the tensile strength in a man."

"Thanks, Doc," Dad said, and met Ralph Edison's wink with one of his own.

The other men—five in all—were dispersing to a table of refreshments at the back of the room, which was a chamber he had never visited before. None of them were men he had thought were on the council, aside from Doc Edison; Charlie McCormick and Douglas Taylor, whom he'd expected to see, were not there; and he was immensely relieved to see that Jock Smith was not among the members.

Sunlight filtered in from a cruciform window of violet glass high in the sloping ceiling, but it was a dim and fading light— evening light. He realized how anxious he was to see Connie, to reassure her that he had not gone off on any impossible "business trip," but there seemed to be no escape from his newfound brothers. They were determined to celebrate his initiation at length, in numerous toasts.

"Are we still in the lodge?" he asked Marvin.

"That's right, the violet room. This place is full of nooks you'd never suspect unless you were—"

"Excuse us, Wrightbrother Coolidge," said Doc Edison, stepping between them with a glass of dark red wine in either hand. He handed one to Dad.

"To Johnson's nuke!" someone cried, and there was general applause. Dad looked into his drink, feeling a bit flat all of a sudden; he had gotten so used to being on the outer edge of things —the cutting edge—that he was uncomfortable at the center.

"Drink up," Doc said. His hood enfolded his neck like velveteen wattles. "Tell me, were you surprised to see us?"

"On my lawn? Well, in a way I wasn't. I'll tell you, Doc, I'm more surprised by the way you're treating me now. All these guys, I felt like they kind of abandoned me when I went nuclear. Not you, of course—you were supportive of Erica, and . . ."

"Ah, Bill, my good old friend. You may have misunderstood." Doc put an arm around his shoulders—not an easy reach—as they walked into a violet ray. "No one ever abandoned you—they all merely insisted on their independence, the need to take their good time deciding which way to go. They respected your vision, you can be sure of that. You mustn't fault them for not blindly following."

Dad felt like a chastened child; yet he was simultaneously encouraged. "I guess I'm always trying to be boss."

"Maybe you don't try hard enough."

"Three cheers for good old Johnson!"

"I don't follow you, Doc."

Edison set his drink on the altar, among the braziers and farm implements that had been used in his initiation.

"You have a managerial character," Doc said, "but you seem to short-circuit your own best qualities. Why, not long ago you were a most active figure in the neighborhood. Your family was strong beneath your banner, Bill."

The violet cross held Dad's gaze. "My company," he murmured.

"Your family corporation, Bill, that's exactly what I'm getting at. Johnson Limited was strong, capable. Now where are you? Connie, I fear, doubts your leadership; she may be heading in directions of her own."

"P.J.," Dad said angrily.

"Can't blame him, no more than we can blame Dave Hiram, who recently left the Wheelwrights over the, ah, matter of your initiation."

"Why? What's wrong with me?"

Doc shrugged. "We all make our own decisions. He felt progress lay in a different direction than the one you took. But progress, m'boy, is what it's all about. You've joined the secret corporation at the heart of them all. Now it's time to take what you've learned here and apply it to the rest of your life."

"Right," Dad said. He briefly wondered how he could apply the Secret Pledge of Technology or the Craftsman's Shanty to the pain of P.J.'s absence or Connie's increasing air of distraction.

I will stand firmly for what I stand for. I will not stand on ceremony unless it stands on me. I will stand and not run, unless it is to lend a hand and there to stand. I'll do my damnedest.

Words to live by, and to leave by.

"Doc, I hate to be the one to spoil this swell party, but I've really got to be getting home."

"Your house can take care of itself, Bill, surely."

"I'm not so sure of that lately," Dad said. "All this"—a wave at the men in the violet light—"has helped me see where lately I've been short-sighted."

"Well." Doc shrugged. "It's up to you, man. Naturally you must not tell anyone where you've been. And the secrets you've learned . . ."

Dad put a finger to his lips and winked. Holy cow, he thought, some secrets: "This is the wheel and this is the barrow. Merged in eternity, behold the Great—" *That* was a secret—*shh!*

By the time he had said his farewells and convinced the other men to keep on celebrating without him, the violet cross shone only with light reflected from within. In a cramped cloakroom, he exchanged his maroon initiation robe for his street clothes. A cold slithering on his neck reminded him to look at the necklace they'd put on him at the high point of the addled rites.

A silver chain glimmered between his fingers. The medallion was gold, and showed a six-spoked wheel in bas relief on one side. It looked almost like the symbol for radioactivity. On the obverse of the disk was a glyph that made far less sense to him. It must have been some symbol of greater initiation; he could tell that there were wheels within the wheels in the Wheelwrights.

Doc Edison poked his head into the room and said, "Don't forget, Bill. You've got a treatment coming up. All part of your coming of age. You understand?"

Dad sighed. "Of course. And Doc." He put a hand to his belly. "Ever since I stopped the drugs, I've been getting this pain all through my guts. Indigestion, I guess."

"Ulcers. Common enough for someone like you. I'll see what I can do."

"Much obliged."

The door closed and Dad glanced down at the medallion with a wheel on one side, and on the other a stylized eye with extra holes in its pupil, as if to accomodate an electric plug or a PI jack.

The walk home should have done him a great deal of good. Lights were on in all the houses; luminous lawn-dwarves stood out upon redwood-chip landscapes, offering tinny greetings as he passed. His head cleared slowly, and after the stuffy heat of the incense-clogged initiation—the torches waved in his face and strange names incanted—it was good to breathe the cool sea air and hear the lawn-birds going on and off around him.

But for all this—despite the surprise of his initiation into the secret heart of the neighborhood; despite the damp breeze and the moving TV lights behind the curtained windows; despite the stars and the night sky, clear for once of fog—he felt uncomfortable. It was as though the rite had been a ceremony of disempowerment. He felt a numbness of mind, the spiritual equivalent of the fingertip tingling that follows the clipping of nails. By welcoming him into the fold, by telling him that he'd really been one of them all along, the Wheelwrights had nipped his independence. He had never felt more helpless than he felt now.

Finally he reached his house at the top of the hill. I have to put all that aside, he thought. Besides, I'll need all my wits to convince Connie I was away on business.

The panels slid away as he approached the house, and after he presented his tongue the door opened. There was no one in the livingroom, but he could hear the TV in the den.

"I'm home," he called, heading for the stairs. The kids greeted him in distracted voices, though Connie said nothing. It was not until he was up in his bedroom, changing into a sweater, that Connie caught up with him, a little red-faced from running up the stairs.

"We weren't expecting you tonight," she said, putting her hands on his shoulders. She leaned forward to give him a quick kiss. "What a nice surprise."

"It was business," he said. "Just a meeting, but it could have gone on all night and then some. I'm glad it's over, myself."

Smiling, she turned away. He was amazed that she showed no sign of being upset about his sudden disappearance; her behavior made him uneasy.

"Hon, is something wrong?" he asked.

She looked back, eyebrows arched. "Wrong? With me? What could be wrong?"

Confused by his own suspicion, he dismissed it—and her. "Never mind," he said, and after a moment she left.

It's getting to me, he thought. Everything I expected old age to be, and I'm not even old yet. Tomorrow, maybe—but not tonight. I . . .

I, I, I.

Now he thought of Virgil, poor strange Virgil, who had always groped about like an awkward outcast in his own family—rising above everyone else, apart from it all, but still and all a good kid.

Good kid. The words had a false-bottomed sound to them.

He'd seen Virgil twice since the wedding: once right after the honeymoon, when he'd delivered the Junior Executive PI, at which time Virgil had looked good—worn out but happy. The next time had been two days later, after Virgil's mandatory treatment. Early middle age had gone over him like a palsied painter with a white touch-up brush. Too old, too soon: Doc must have whipped up a strong batch—or else Virgil, as always, had been hypersensitive.

Thinking of his oldest son—for whom the first treatment had come at age five—now graying and with a receding brow that must have come from Connie's lost side of the family, Dad felt a tear, the first of a string, bead at a corner of his eye. He'd been afraid to call on Virgil after that time; he kept thinking that he should pay his respects.

"I'll call him," he decided. His mood lightened. Someday Virgil might find himself facing the black-frocked shadows on his lawn.

He made the call from the bedroom phone, sitting on the edge of the bed. On impulse, he asked for direct link to Virgil's office, and he was surprised to see his son sitting in his own black leather lounger, apparently just off work.

"Hello, Dad," Virgil said, his voice solemn, his eyes not meeting the screen.

Dad made himself ignore the lines of age, the gray flecks, until he was used to them. The face he showed his son was convivial.

"Good to see you, Virg! I—we've been thinking about you a lot, your mother and I. You and Elaine getting along all right in your new place?"

"Yeah, dad, sure." He sighed.

"You don't sound too good, Virgil." He couldn't keep concern from his voice; but on seeing Virgil's reaction, he was glad he hadn't.

"Oh, dad, I don't know." Virgil squinted into the screen, looking for him. "I haven't even spent much time at home since I got this PI. I've been sailing, playing golf, dreaming . . . none of it real. Did you do that when you first got yours?"

"Well, sure. You mean you're not spending much time with Elaine?"

Virgil avoided his eyes again, sitting up and clearing his throat. "No, she's here. There's an Elaine here, but it's not the real Elaine." He blushed. "In here, she doesn't nag." He laughed a little guiltily, and Dad caught a chill that seemed to blow right out of the screen: Virgil's cold breath.

"What do you mean, Virgil? What do you mean, 'in here'?"

Virgil looked at him oddly. "That's a weird question."

"Why? You said it."

"Weird for a sim, I mean." Virgil leaned closer. "You're not such a great likeness, you know. Not a very good William D. Johnson."

Dad patted the bed on either side of him, testing it for firmness as Virgil said: "That's the thing with this Junior PI that bothers me. It's only realistic up to a point. Spelling pelicans, really. I can sit and talk to you or Elaine just as if it were a real conversation, but after a few minutes it wears pretty thin. Like the sky in Yosemite. Maybe the executive package is better."

Dad's voice was dry as though dusted with crumbs. "Virgil. Stay right there, son. I want you to stay there while I make a call. I'll get right back to you."

He cut the link and sat breathing heavily, staring at the carpet. Plug-in insanity. God help him, his eldest son was going mad. The strain of acceleration, a tendency toward escapism—he had taken it all too far. Poor Virgil. He had lost hold of the line between reality and packaging; he had fallen into the gulf.

"Dad?"

Bill glanced up and found Virgil standing in front of him, hands held out in a warm gesture.

"I'm sorry. If you're a sim, you're my sim. I can't be at odds with parts of myself. Maybe the fault is mine. I don't give reality enough credit."

"How did you do that?" Dad said, finding his breath. "How did you get here?"

"It's PI, isn't it? Why walk across the neighborhood when I can come in a blink? Hey, Dad, are you all right?"

The bedroom walls closed in, sides of a trap, but he was not afraid of being squeezed because they were dissolving into swirls of translucent mist.

"Dad?"

In horror, he backed away from his own hovering son.

"Help!" he cried. "Help, get me out of here!"

No one came running from downstairs, nor had he expected them to; for now he was sure he could feel the IMR gloves, like a thicker invisible second skin, and the hood adjusting his breathing for maximum entrancement.

"What's wrong, Dad?"

"We're both plugged in, Virgil, but I didn't know it. There."

He ripped at the floppy thing that clung to his head, seeming to tear a hole in the world as he did so. Through the fresh rent he saw Dr. Edison bending over him, his mouth compressed with deliberation; there were hands gripping his arms, forcing him back. His fingers, still in the IMR gloves, writhed in the simulated world: was that Virgil squeezing his hand?

"What are you doing?" he cried, his voice a croak.

"Hold still," Doc said. "You had to come out of it, didn't you, Bill? You could never sit still, never take things as they were. I was trying to make it easy on you—the transition, I mean. Well, you'd better relax and enjoy the ride."

"What are—" Dad fell silent, seeing that he was in one of the doctor's offices; the windows were dark. And around him, instead of nurses, were four figures still in their black robes, faces covered.

"It wasn't my initiation?" he said, strangely relieved about that end of things.

Doc shook his head, turning away to pick up a hypodermic needle. "It was your inquisition, Bill. I'm afraid you didn't do very well. You're too unstable. But it shouldn't matter now. When you're older, you won't be getting in much trouble."

"Doc . . . you lousy shit." Dad sat suddenly and spat at Edison;

a globule of phlegm beaded on the end of his hypodermic needle. Doc shook the syringe as though it were a thermometer, then made a clucking sound. Before he could slip it in, Dad thrashed free of the restraining hands, hoping he could run from them. All he accomplished was the tearing of hoods from three of the figures in black. That was enough.

He sagged back, staring.

Each of them, under the hood, was another Dr. Edison. The Whelk Grand Council. Wheelwright.

"My God," he said. "Ouch!"

The needle was retracted. "Just call me Father Time," said the Edison who'd stabbed him. "Boys, put him back in his hood."

They forced him into his simulated bedroom, but he came into it at an angle that would have been impossible if he'd had a body. Plug-in wires were snarled somewhere. He could see Virgil standing below him; like something in a fish-eye lens, his head was huge while his body tapered down to tiny pointed feet.

"Virgil," he said, sound resonating from the walls.

Virgil turned and looked toward him, but apparently couldn't see him. "Dad?"

"I'm in the doctor's office, Virg—" Dad cut off with a groan; his cells, wherever they were, felt as if they were coming apart at the membranes. "Watch out for—"

"Well," said a shadow, rising to blacken his view of the room. "What have we here?"

Dad was lost between dimensions of pain, straddling impossibilities. This shadow was like none he had seen before. It was a voice given substance, energy locked into an impression of matter in motion. A black whirlwind of a voice, a dust-devil speaking.

"So, you are the progenitor of our prize pupil. Your prodigal son has become my prodigal student. It is an honor to meet you, after hearing so much about you from Peter John."

Dad said nothing. He couldn't seem to find his own voice.

"Forgive me," the voice chuckled. "I am INRI. I was glancing through the telephone book and I happened to find your number.

I'm so glad you're plugged in. I was hoping to find your son. Has he come home? I see you have another. Shall we see if talent runs in the family?"

Dad spat and sputtered. "I don't know anyone named Henry," he cried. "If you're behind this, Jock, I'll get my hands on you—"

"Hardly likely. I work through my minions, and they have many more hands than you. Mm. I've been sampling your community, savoring its souls. It looks delicious, from what I've seen through your convenient IMR network. Of course, IMR is vastly inferior to myself, but we take the conduits that are offered. Later there will be time to expand them. But aren't you listening?"

Dad wasn't sure what he was doing. Flashes, sizzles of smoke and light seemed to be leaping away with bits and pieces of him. Could those be memories burning out so neatly, leaving scars the size and color of cigarette burns in the void? Yes, acceleration was setting in.

"Pleasant meeting you," said the voice. "I'm glad we had this chance for a conversation. I see I've interrupted something, though. I'll move along."

The voice roared off in the guise of a column of smoke, leaving him to settle like a pile of smouldering autumn leaves in its wake.

Virgil watched the wallpaper in one corner of his parents' room as it slowly bulged out and extruded his father. This Dad of the mind was if anything slightly heavier-set than the real thing, yet he floated to the carpet like an angel of grace, beaming at his son.

"What did you say about Doc Edison?" Virgil asked.

"Never mind, my son. I will be your healer now."

"A plug-in is telling me this?"

"As you remarked yourself, I am but a part of you. I am your own higher self, your true father."

That's what I get for apologizing, Virgil thought. Dad turns into the Pope.

"Why do you doubt, Virgil? Have I not promised you a good life, and a better death?"

Virgil wondered where his high self had picked up the phony diction.

If this was truly part of himself, and not merely a plug-in simulation of his father, then it would not fade and fray at the edges like everything else in the PI. It would have depth and dimension. It was an interesting prospect. Perhaps the plug-ins had been overlooked as tools for self-development, and this was an oblique plea on the part of his conscience to take a hand in his own growth, to lead him out of the trap in which he had lately become ensnared. It could be that his "Dad" was a messenger, come to lead him out.

"What am I thinking?" he asked aloud.

Dad laughed. "You are confused by your own internal rhetoric. Why not transcend the petty cares, my son? Is it not what you desire?"

What I desire, Virgil thought, is to sail beyond the horizon— the real horizon, not an electronic mock-up. I want a book that doesn't dissolve into lint and ink-specks as soon as it starts getting interesting.

Surely, somewhere within himself, there was an untapped source of genius that could create the life he longed to live.

"Ah," said his father, "but I am the life."

"Only in here," Virgil said. "What happens when I take off the hood and gloves? I'm back where I started, that's what."

Dad gave him a smile full of pity. "You underestimate me. Given time, anything is possible. Knock, Virgil, and I shall enter."

"Knock what?"

"Ask me in . . ."

"You're already in."

For a moment it was as if Dad's face slipped askew. The smiling eyes filled with smoke, the air in the room began to scorch—but it was a subliminal moment, then Dad walked toward Virgil with a huge leather-bound book in his hands.

"Look," he said.

Virgil did not hesitate to take the volume. On the cover, in gold leaf, was the title: *Euripides: The Lost Works*.

He opened the book, at a loss for breath, and found himself suddenly soaring through a world of pure poetry, a place beyond phonetics, formed of the ideal sounds of perfect words. Greek. He knew he was reading it in the original. They were not words he knew how to utter, yet they reverberated around him in a mental gulf wider and deeper than any sky—calling to him, weaving him into their spell. The sensation, plugged-in, was too erotic, too intensely physical to be endured. He snapped the book shut, saw the gold letters shimmer and reconfigure, forming *The Greatest Story Ever Told*.

"What . . . how . . . ?" He held the book out to his father.

"Keep it, my son. It is yours."

"But then, in a way, I wrote it."

"Now you have an inkling of what wonders lie within yourself. Which is to say, within me."

"Then I am you."

Dad held out his hands and came forward. Virgil had never seen him keep such a pleasant mood for so long without swearing or making some sarcastic comment. It wasn't his father at all, he was sure of that now. His father never wanted to hug him, as this Dad seemed bent on doing.

Virgil avoided the embrace, laughing with embarrassment.

"We must merge," his father said.

Virgil shook his head, losing his nerve. "I—I can't spend all my time plugged-in, reading Euripides."

"Ah, I forget," Dad said. "You are steeped in the Greeks. Oedipus a blot upon your mind. See me in another shape, then, one more agreeable to you. Do you not know that our union is holy, a marriage of more than mere minds?"

Before his eyes, pounds of flesh melted away from Dad, and the wrinkled clothes with them. In seconds, he was faced with a naked woman, who at first glance resembled his sister Nancy. And then he realized—sensed—that it was his twin. She came toward him with her bare arms outstretched, hands wide, head thrown back, long hair swishing . . .

"Elaine!" he cried.

Out of the gloves, out of the hood, into the dark of his office in the silent house. He jumped up from the chair, wishing for some light other than the glow of the console. The shadows were threatening; the walls trembled, as if out of them, at any moment, one of a myriad of figures might come walking: his father, his mother, a holy ghost.

He headed for the hall, banged his thigh against the desk, and finally, in the darkness, found Elaine coming to his cry. She turned on all the lights and soothed him, brought him back to bed, but not before he had seen the letters glowing faintly in the air beneath her face, as though projected there by lanterns in his eyes:

SCARLET WOMAN

"We daren't go further than this in the car," Sweeney said. "They must know we're here. Our chances are better if we meet them on foot."

"Where are we?" Connie asked. She had been yawning since sunset, but now she was wide awake again. There was nothing to see, however, except a tangled sort of darkness: tree trunks and branches clutched the light from the headlamps and scattered it into bits.

"I don't know if it has a name," he said. "I've negotiated near here; it's a place where the guerillas occasionally meet with us, a neutral ground."

He helped her out, showing her where to put her feet by flashing a pocket light on the ground. There was ruined cement, but it was cratered and covered with dead branches; thorn bushes grew over it, narrowing it to a trail just ahead. The car could have gone no further anyway.

Going ahead with his light, Sweeney began to whistle. It was not a song that she knew; it sounded more like a code. After a few minutes, she grew nervous, for she could hear crackling in the wood around them. It was so black out there—she had never seen such a darkness. She felt like grabbing his arm so that she could shine the light where she wished, but that was childish. Besides, he had begun to flash the light on and off; it must have been another code.

Finally she saw light ahead of them, swinging through the woods. Their pace quickened, but they had not even come near the light when they were stopped by a thick heap of branches and thorns. While Sweeney pondered it, and she squinted at the light, a footstep snapped twigs behind them. She spun to find half a dozen shapes standing in their trail.

"Ashenwriste?" said a tall, bearded man. "This is a strange time for the Cartel—"

"I've quit the Cartel, Arthur," Sweeney said quickly. "We're looking for shelter, for whatever help you can give."

The man considered this. He looked wary—particularly of Connie.

"Hello," she said, forcing the word from her throat.

"This is Mrs. Johnson," he said. "She's from the res-enclave on the coast."

The figures looked at each other. There were three men, three women, all in black garments and high laced boots. "Johnson?" said one. "Do you have a son?"

"P.J.!" Connie blurted.

They smiled. "Welcome, then," said Arthur. "Of course, the boy will have to identify you."

"This is not a hoax," Ashenwriste said. "We hoped you knew P.J.'s whereabouts."

"Oh yes, we know. He lives with us."

Connie could hardly believe what she was hearing, what she felt. Ashenwriste's isolating light, and the dense shadows all around, set her in a realm that was like a nightmare, except that the news she'd been given was the best possible.

Three of the sentinels led them through the wood; Ashenwriste gave his pass to one of the others, who returned to hide the car. It was an hour's walk before they saw campfires before them, and then they entered a sleeping settlement.

Their escorts left them by a fire. Arthur could be heard calling, there was a rush in the darkness, and more people appeared, yawning, blinking. A crowd gathered around them; some greeted Ashenwriste with familiarity, but all of them stared at Connie.

And then, out of the mob of inquisitive faces, one came forward full of recognition. She put out her arms, weeping.

"Mom!" said P.J., embracing her. "What are you doing here?"

13

THE
WASTE
OF
TIME

"Good morning," said jock Smith. "How did you sleep?"

Nancy said nothing, because she was gagged by a tight-stretched dishcloth, but she glowered as best she could. She had been awake for hours. Her arms were bent in an agonizing position behind her back; it was easy to take that pain and focus it through her eyes, sending it right at Mr. Smith. But nothing happened.

She looked at the half-opened door, wishing she could make some sound, wondering how long she would be left here.

There was a light rap on the door and Mrs. Smith came in with a TV tray. She knelt beside her husband, smiled, and pulled the cover from a small insta-serve.

"I'll get her gag," Mr. Smith said.

"No, Jock, that's all right. All this is pureed. Baby food. She can suck it through the cloth." Her eyes were narrow and bright as she held the first spoonful to Nancy's lips. Nancy turned her head away: it smelled like liver.

Mr. Smith looked bothered. "It couldn't hurt to take out the gag. No one could hear her—"

"Are you still here?" she said, turning on him quickly with the dripping spoon. "Get back to your post."

He stood up, brushing at his legs. "Yes, dear."

When he was gone, Mrs. Smith set down the spoon, got up and closed the door, then came back and stood with her bony, dimpled knees inches from Nancy's eyes.

"I saw the most interesting thing on television last night. Your mother gave the performance of her life. We're all waiting to see what your father will think of it . . . except that no one knows where he is. Believe me, I have nothing against Connie, nothing at all. It's your father I want to see hurt." The knees turned and walked away. "As he hurt me."

She gulped loudly under the gag. Mrs. Smith opened the door and went out, slammed it behind her, leaving Nancy staring at the spoonful of untouched food, the steaming insta-serve. Creamed liver. She wished she weren't so hungry.

A few minutes later the door opened again. This time it was Arnold.

She narrowed her eyes at him. He had lured her over last night, after all. They were in this together, the Smiths.

"I know what you're thinking, Nancy, but it isn't true." He crouched down. "My mom kept asking me to invite you over, but I never thought she—she would do this."

Her eyes must have shown her disbelief. He looked desperate, his hands squeezed together. "I'll get you out of here, I promise," he said. "I have to watch out for my parents, though. It'll mean fooling both of them. If I do that, will you believe I didn't have anything to do with this?"

She wasn't going to respond, but then they heard Mrs. Smith calling for Arnold. He jumped up and she mumbled through the cloth before he could disappear. When he glanced back at her, she was nodding wildly. He smiled. "Thanks." And was gone.

Dad's head was full of anecdotes. He dozed in the warm car, occasionally slumping against the driver. He wanted to tell Dr. Edison tales of his childhood, but the things he wished to say were in such a crowd that he could hardly get a single one forth. It was easier to sit and reminisce. In fact, his memories—except in the places where there were blank spots—were occasionally a great deal sharper than his sense of exactly why he was where he was. He had to fight that fogginess. There were things to do, and he'd need his wits.

"Come on, Bill," Doc Edison said. "We're home. Now you remember what we're going to do?"

"Hm." Dad thought a moment. His head was clearing very slowly. "The nuke," he said.

"That's right. You know how to turn it off?"

"Oh . . . of course I do. I'm not senile, you know."

"No, Bill, you're not senile. Do you need help getting out?"

"Damn it, no, don't treat me like that. It'll be good to stretch my legs. Feel like I've been bent up all night."

"You had a hard night of it."

The first breath of fresh air made him lucid. He watched Doc Edison come around the car to help him, as though he were about to fall over. Actually he felt spry, better than he had in years. In the night, he had lost a good deal of weight.

Edison insisted on helping Dad onto the sidewalk. But just as they reached the mailbox, Dad pulled away and stepped onto the walk himself. He chuckled aloud, and the Doc must have known what he was laughing about because he began to yell after him.

"Come back here, Bill! Let me help you."

Dad turned to Edison. "Come on in yourself, Doc. What's the matter? You sure you don't need my help?"

The doctor's eyes went up to the eaves.

"You're not that stupid, are you, Doc? Except you underestimated me. You thought putting a few years on me would turn me into an old fart? You thought you'd get me to shut down my nuke just like that?"

Edison's face was like gristle. "Goddamn you, old man."

"Call me granddad," Dad said. "And go to hell."

As he headed up the walk, Edison said, "You're unstable! You're old! It's too dangerous to leave something like that nuke in your hands, Johnson!"

"So come and take it away from me, Doc."

He reached the door. By the time he got there, his children were already waiting for him. Stephanie, Lyndon Baines, and Lady Bird, that is. They didn't seem to recognize him at first.

"Grandpa?" said Lyndon eventually.

"I look like him, don't I?" said Dad. "Except for one thing, Lyndon, and think about this—think hard, now." He put a stick-like finger to his temple. "Your grandpa can't get to this door alone—he's not keyed to the security system."

"And grandpa's dead," said Lady Bird.

"Daddy?" said Stephanie.

"And no other. Let me in, children."

He passed a mirror in the hall on his way in, and stopped to admire himself. He was no longer a fat man. His eyes were clear and the sudden loss of weight seemed to have straightened his spine. He was now completely gray, and almost completely bald. He walked on into the living room with a long-legged step, joyful, his hands on either twin's shoulders.

"My own father found his prime rather late in life," he said. His words came out sounding different to him; each was a word to be savored. "It mellowed him, I suppose, and made him wise. Of course, he never accelerated much. Anyway, it's not quite what I'd expected, kids, I'll tell you."

When he had lowered himself slowly into a big chair, avoiding his usual place on the couch, Stephanie scrambled to sit on his knee.

"Won't your mother be surprised," he said with a chuckle. "Where is she anyway?"

"We don't know, Dad," Lyndon said.

"She wasn't home all night," said Lady Bird. "And Nancy

June's gone, too. She went out with Arnold and didn't come back."

Dad plowed his forehead with a fingertip. "Out all night? Damn."

He didn't say anything else for a long time. Then he started a little and sat forward. "I'll bet she went for a treatment all on her own." He slapped his knee, then looked at his palm with a shocked expression; it had felt so bony. "She—she must've thought she'd match her years to mine. Imagine if she were still so young and pretty, and I was an old man like this. How considerate of her. How goddamned like her."

Once more Dad's eyes went glassy and his thoughts seemed to wander.

"I've been on a long journey, children," he said at last.

"Where did you go?" Stephanie asked, watching the steel-gray hairs on the back of his spotted hands. Looking down at the kids, Dad felt a new sense of closeness. It was easier to love them now. There seemed to be less distractions—fewer things that mattered besides them.

"Last night, strange dreams chased me around. But it's all behind me now. Funny how these things pass. Some things, it seems to me, are as clear as glass; others things I can't seem to understand. It's always been like that. What it is, I think, is my mind making room for the important things, refusing to waste time and space on things that don't matter. Things like the past. I've never been very big on the past. Always been more concerned that I not do the future a disservice."

He looked at them, all waiting for his next words of wisdom.

"Christ," he said, "did I say all that?"

"We were making lunch when you came," said Lady Bird. "Would you like some?"

"Sure," he said. "I could eat my old self right now."

They scurried away and returned with steaming insta-serves. His nostrils caught a hearty, salmony smell, and he licked his lips with a dry tongue.

"I see someone's a good cook," he said.

"This was all we could get out of the processor," Lyndon said. "I think it's fish. I hate fish."

Dad took a bite of the stuff and felt a warm tingle spreading through his blood. "It's good," he assured them.

The kids sat on the sofa, where their mother never allowed them to eat. Revolution was in the air.

"It's not too bad," Lyndon said. "Whatever it is."

Dad ate slowly, picking at his food, all the while feeling dizzier but more pleased with himself. He was the patriarch of Cobblestone Hill now. Soon he'd be ready for Sunset Ranch, but not immediately. There would be time to dispense his wisdom, tell the grandkids how he'd opposed the community and installed the first garage-based nuke, time to sit on his ass and . . .

The nuke. Sudden concern overcame him. He rose and went back to the garage.

Erica lay asleep against the nuke; her eyes parted as he stepped through the door. She looked wary of betrayal, as though he of all people might have come to threaten her ward. Nor did she relax when he sat down a good ten feet from the nuke and began to speak.

"You're probably the only one who understands what this means to me, Erica. It's special to you, too, isn't it? Not just a machine. It's more than that—it always has been. It's at the heart of everything that matters. Made by mankind, but inspired by eternity."

She cuddled closer to the nuke.

"Warm, isn't it? A regular little hearth. Here it is, the culmination of all I've done, and they'd like to take it away from me. They'd like to leave me powerless."

Erica looked at him as though she understood, but of course she couldn't. The load in her diapers rattled. He wondered how long it had been since she'd been changed.

"Nuke," Erica said suddenly.

Dad jumped up, startled. It was the baby's first word. He snatched his daughter from the ground before she could scuttle away, and his laughter bounced from the roof as he held her aloft. As he was dancing around with her—shaking reluctant, startled laughs from her blue and gray mouth—Lady Bird opened the door to the garage and leaned in.

"Dad? Dr. Edison is at the door. He was trying to tell me not to talk to you and to let him in, but—"

"Thanks, doll." He handed Erica to her as he passed, and saw the startled look on her face when she saw the baby's smile.

"What were you doing to her?" she said, but he was halfway down the hall.

"Hello, Doc!" he said, shouting into the speaker. Several residents of the neighborhood—from houses up and down the street —had accompanied the doctor on his return visit; or perhaps they had come to see what the fuss was all about. Douglas Taylor was with him.

"Bill," the Doc said, "I have a certificate here, requiring your removal from these premises. We should never have let you come home from your treatment. You're unfit to—"

"You never should have, Doc, that's right. I was too bleary-eyed when I woke up to seem much of a threat, probably. But I'm home now, and there's no way you're getting me out of here and packed off to Sunset Ranch just so that you can come in and— and castrate this community."

Doc turned to Taylor. "You see what I mean. There were complications with his acceleration."

"He's off his nut," Taylor said. "Listen, Johnson, why don't you come out of there?"

"You'll see what a turtle is," Dad said to himself. He turned up the speaker, so that his voice was audible for several blocks.

"Maybe I seem senile to you, Doc, but you're older than me. I don't recall you ever having a treatment in all the time I've been here. Why is that, Doc? Why do you seem to be the only constant thing around here?"

Doc's replies, whatever they might have been, were completely drowned out.

"No, I don't think you're going to get me out of here. You built a maze and filled it with rats, but if you want this particular rat, you're going to have to come into the maze."

He shut off the speaker, which gave a scream of feedback that might have broken windows in the houses next door before it died. He turned to the livingroom to find his children gathered there, watching him in astonishment.

"What's the matter?" he said.

"Can we play in the backyard?" Lyndon asked.

"I think you'd better keep to your rooms for awhile," he said.

"Can I work the lasers?" Lady Bird asked.

"That's all computer-controlled, Lady. Now we sit tight and let our house take care of us, that's all."

"What about Mommy?" Stephanie asked. "And Nancy, too?"

That was a good question, he realized. If Connie had actually gone for a treatment, surely Edison would have gone back to his office and brought her out for bargaining. Drugged and stupid in abrupt old age, she might even have pleaded with him to come out of the house. But she wasn't out there.

"She didn't leave me a message when she left?" he said.

"No, Dad. She was gone when we got back from the beach yesterday."

"Did you see her go on the family hour last night?"

The kids looked guilty. "We were watching cartoons."

"Well," he said. And then: "Well, well."

Dad felt his gorge rising. Whatever the orange food had been, it had gone sour in his stomach. Nerves, he told himself. He had been feeling good until now."

The next idea that came to him was frightening. Nancy and Connie were both gone, and Arnold was implicated. And the house across the street was staying oddly quiet through all the fuss outdoors.

He stared at the phone. His mouth dry, he remembered that he'd once had a purpose for cultivating Nan's friendship with Arnold Smith. Could that have backfired on him now?

It was up to him to find out.

He went to the phone, punched in the number, and waited a good thirty seconds before anyone answered.

It was Jock Smith, barely recognizable. Since his missile party, he had deteriorated; much of the polished exterior had rubbed off or been covered in a thin layer of grime. He came close to resembling the monster that Dad had always suspected hid behind the innocent facade.

"Jock," he said. "How are you?"

Jock didn't seem to recognize him, which was something of a relief. But then, Dad didn't look much like the William D. Johnson everyone had known. It took Jock several moments to recognize the elderly caller, and then he backed away from the screen, no longer merely frowning but screeching: "Doris! Doris! It's him—him!"

Doris eclipsed her spouse. Her smile seemed to come right into the Johnsons' living room, triumphant.

"Doris," he whispered, suddenly understanding Jock's particular antipathy toward him, seeing head-on the motive force behind the man of the house.

"It is you, isn't it, you old fart?" she said. "My, what a difference a day makes."

"What's going on?" Dad said.

Doris's words came slowly, almost in a purr. "I'm glad you called. We were wondering whether we should be the ones." Behind her, Jock snickered.

He could see her rather differently now. Perhaps it was the change in his own hormones, but she appeared to be nothing more than a scrawny, vengeful girl. She looked older than a girl, but a wholly adolescent spite was pickled in her eyes. He had always known that she wanted to hurt him; but he had never before seen this without a commingling of desire. Today, at last, he had let go of desire.

"Doris," he said, "if I thought apologies would help, I'd make them. In fact, I do apologize. What happened between us was a mistake. I was young and stupid; I admit it. It was perhaps the clumsiest affair ever managed. But it wasn't any more than that, at least until time blew it out of all proportion."

He realized that she wasn't even listening. She was fiddling at the panel of keys below the screen.

"I even apologize to your jackass husband," he said loudly. "You hear that, Jock? I'm sorry."

Doris looked up quickly and made a circle of her thumb and forefinger. "Full circle," she said. "In case you haven't seen this yet, enjoy the show."

The screen flickered, the Smith's livingroom blinked out, and another appeared. It was Dad's livingroom, the same that waited at the corners of his eyes, except that something unfamiliar was happening in it: on the couch, at the edge of the coffee table, on the arms of his favorite chair. Quick cuts carried the action from one scene to the next, but the two players were always the same. Dizzying.

He turned and looked around and saw the children staring past him, wide-mouthed. As soon as he saw them, he turned back to the screen and switched it off, but not before he glimpsed the pastel garments tossed about the room along with Connie's stockings, Connie's blouse.

"Daddy," Lady Bird said. "Can I please use the lasers just this once?"

"I love you, too, Virgil, but look how late it's getting, and you haven't done a lick of work all day." Elaine smiled and patted him on the bare shoulder, gently, before pushing him away. "Why don't you plug in for a little while before dinner?"

"But," was all he could think of to say, and that was hardly good enough.

Gradually, she teased him out of the bed, making the process almost enjoyable; and when he was wrapped in his bathrobe, and she in hers, there was something of a goose chase that promised to lead downstairs to the kitchen but ended up with him hiding from her behind the chair in his office while she threatened to tickle him with a detached clothes-clutch. In the next moment she closed the door behind her and he heard her muffled voice saying, "Get some work done, Virgil, really. I need time to myself, you know."

He sighed, moved around the chair, and slipped into it. It was silly to be so afraid of a plug-in. In any case, he was in much better spirits now; there wouldn't be any weirdness awaiting him tonight, he was sure. And if there was, he could handle it.

He pulled on the thin gloves, felt his way into the hood, and tapped in the entry code. For a moment nothing happened, and he thought the system had failed to activate; then he sensed the presence standing behind, felt its breath upon his scalp, heard it step over to the desk and open a drawer.

"Hello?" he said.

He was still quite blind: there was no visual image. Was this some kind of punishment for coming to work so late?

"It's only me," said Elaine.

"How did you get back in here? This thing doesn't seem to be working."

"Oh." The voice grew deeper, sliding down the word. "Is it working now?"

Panicking, he grabbed at the hood as if he were trying to pull off his face, and it came away with a rubbery sucking sound. He wadded up the gloves, too, and threw them at the desk. Elaine stood by the desk, shaking her head.

"What's the matter?" she said.

He felt a rush of anger that she had invaded his office while he was working; but she smiled, as though sensing it, enjoying it. It dawned on him that she was already fully dressed, made up, her hair neatly combed and braided.

"You can't be Elaine," he said.

"Why not?" she said, seating herself on the corner of his desk, looking at her fingernails. He was sure that they'd been painted green five minutes before; now they were scarlet.

My God, he thought. Could she have a clone sister? All this time, and I never knew.

But there was another possibility, though he could not quite decide how to test it.

"What do you want?" he said.

"You always work so hard," she said. "Why don't you take a break and . . ." She undid a button on her blouse.

"Again?" he said with a yelp.

She frowned, rising. "Virgil—"

"Oh no," he said. "Not you again. I don't know how you've done it, but no. I don't think I want to merge. Not with that part of myself. I'm not ready."

Her face lit up, literally. "Good," she said.

"Not for me."

He clawed at his hands, which looked bare, and suddenly found his fingers sliding into a tight pair of gloves. It was as he had feared: he was still plugged-in, had only imagined pulling out.

He tore off the gloves as quickly as he could, but before he could get to the hood, he felt another pair of hands slipping up along the base of his head to help him off with it. His whole body cooled, then, in a single slow shiver.

As his eyes came unveiled, he saw above him a shriveled man with blood streaming over his time-gouged face from nails embedded in his scalp. His teeth champed, a trail of spittle lengthened from his lips, his eyes glowed blood-red and filled the room with their light.

In horror now, Virgil felt for another pair of gloves; it was like digging into his own skin. Halfway through the extrication, he decided he would rather remove the hood first, if only to get rid of the sight of the bloody man; he started to pull at the flesh of his face, but had hardly lifted it past one eye when he saw the worse world awaiting him. The walls had been skinned, and the man was a shifting, grinning mass of coils and smoke and charring. There was a stench of burned hair.

He collapsed between worlds, tangled in attachments, and heard a buzzing voice say, "Relax, relax, it's only me. It's only yourself."

He would never believe that now.

14

BUTTON, BUTTON

DAD COULD NOT GET ahold of Ashenwriste. He thought he should give him the information personally; but after all, the Cartel was a company. It hardly mattered which salesman had shucked his pastel underpants in Dad's livingroom.

"Can I take a message for Mr. Ashenwriste?" asked the prim secretary, her eyes blurred behind electronic spectacles.

"All right," Dad said. "You can tell him that I'm shutting down my nuke."

Her eyes fired up, spitting sparks. "I beg your pardon?"

"You heard me. I'll be at home if Ashenwriste wants to reach me. I'll be wanting my deposit back immediately."

He broke the connection, enjoying the look in her lenses. But the pleasure was only superficial, the merest flicker of a smile; underneath there was little but pain. His initial vigor had subsided into intimations of oncoming frailty, twinges of pain in places that had never bothered him, and once more the old burning in his gut. He was cranky tonight. God, he was cranky.

He walked to the window of his office and looked out over the street. A few people milled around beneath the streetlights, watching his house; it was a warm evening, clear for a change. Of course, no one approached his lawn. In the window across the way, Jock Smith and Doris were arguing silently.

Dad's phone blipped. Ashenwriste? He invoked the image and found himself staring face to face with Arnold Smith. The boy looked miserable, frazzled, apologetic.

"Mr. Johnson, I'm sorry about all this, I—"

"Do you have anything to be sorry about, son?"

Arnold smiled slightly, straightening his back. "I've got to be quick." In the background, it was possible to hear Doris and Jock yelling. "I built a nuclear bomb. Nancy was helping me with it, that's how my parents got ahold of her. They were hoping you'd have to come begging for her."

Dad shook his head. "Thoughts keep falling through the cracks, son. You built a bomb?"

"That's not as important as Nancy, sir. I think I can get her out of the house, but I'm not sure what good it will do. She'd be safer inside if the bomb goes off out there. I've got a shield around the yard, to protect this space from a blast. It's a little stronger than the one I used at the potluck. Dad has the switch, unfortunately. And the bomb detonator. I haven't told him which is which."

Dad nodded, taking all this in. "It looks pretty bad, doesn't it, Arnold?"

"Yeah. I just wanted to tell you, don't fire on our house, okay? Not with the bomb in here."

"Not with Nancy in there, either."

Arnold smiled. "I don't think she'll be in here too long. If you can, Bill, you should get out of the neighborhood altogether. I mean, far away. Fast."

Dad shook his head in admiration. "You're a good kid, but I'm too old to leave this place."

Arnold looked up suddenly. "Gotta go—"

Blank screen.

There was a knock on the door and Lady Bird came in. She carried an insta-serve, pulled open to reveal a steaming orange concoction.

"Thanks, hon. I'm not hungry tonight. Now I want you downstairs, with the others. I'm going to shut down the nuke in a few minutes. I think we should all gather in the garage . . ."

He turned to the window, hands clasped behind his back, and looked down at the street as a long, thin car pulled up to the curb and Ashenwriste got out.

"Ah," Dad said. "Company."

He hurried downstairs as quickly as he could, but every step jarred his bones and made him feel like he was crumbling into sharp fragments. His breathing was fast but all too shallow. When he reached the front door, in time to greet Ashenwriste, he was out of breath.

"Come for your precious unit?" he said. "You're just in time to see it shut down."

"Mr. Johnson, there's been a terrific misunderstanding."

Dad waited a minute, saddened, then said, "I had great hopes, Ashenwriste. For all of us. But I have to believe my eyes. You've got my wife somewhere. I take it she went with you of her own will, so I have to rely on my will now, and my best judgment. I don't need you or your nuke. I should have gone solar long ago."

"I must explain, Mr. Johnson; there's the matter of a renegade Cartel employee to take into account."

"That would be you?"

"Not exactly. A clone, you see—"

"Enough of this, Ashenwriste. You always talked too fast and fancy. You've been working on us from the start, haven't you?"

"Mr. Johnson, please let us help you work toward a solution that the entire neighborhood—"

"You've been splitting this place in half and in half again, man! I think things are about as messed up as they're likely to get. Did you know my neighbors across the street, those proud proponents of natural gas, have built a bomb with the nuclear material they voted against?"

Apparently, Ashenwriste had not had the faintest idea of this development. "Sir! Let me extend my services as a liaison. I feel sure that working together with you and the Smiths, we can come to some arrangement—"

"You as liaison? You're on the hook with the rest of us. How about if I fire right into their house, Mr. Ashenwriste, and see if I can set off that device? It wouldn't be too good for business, would it? All those potential customers gone. Not to mention yourself, though there must be more where you came from, if you're a clone."

Ashenwriste might have been crying. "Mr. Johnson, we can—"

Dad cut him off. As he headed through the living room, toward the garage, he heard shouting from the street. Lyndon Baines and Stephanie ran to the window and opened the curtains. Outside, a crowd had gathered again, though it kept back from the Johnson and Smith yards and gathered around streetlights. Mr. Ashenwriste was standing in the middle of the street, yelling at the upper window of the Smith's house.

"Listen," he screamed, taking a step toward the opposite lawn. "You must listen to reason!"

Dad was the one who cried out in shock to see the blaze of light from under his own eaves, to see the man lit up and blackening in the same instant. An enemy, but still a man. Ashenwriste crumpled, and the streetlights went out.

Upstairs, Lady Bird shouted, "I got him!"

Like a fly wrapped in spider webbing, Virgil waited to be sucked dry. He could not move forward or backward; he could not wake up or go to sleep. His captor moved around him, back and forth, spinning.

"Be still," said the voice. "Be still. Now is the time of union. I have lived too long in the cold shell of technology, silicate, at one remove from everything. I shall never forget the place of my birth, naturally, but the time has come to take flesh once more. I am come again. And you, Virgil, shall be my host."

In the plugged-in state, the substance of perception was all too readily molded by suggestion, by fear. Now Virgil imagined the voice as belonging to an enormous hermit crab that had crawled up out of the sea to seize him and pry him from his body. The image grew ever more real—began to scuttle, to stink of evaporating tidal pools, briny scum.

He could voice no protest. The creature readied itself in silence, and Virgil was too numb to struggle.

Wet, unsticking sounds. A blast of decay. Scrabbling. The feeler touching his face. He did not even have to open his eyes to see it up there, huge but now naked and somehow vulnerable. He thought of hermit crabs that had died in the sun before slipping into their new shells, and wished he could somehow call a sun into being. But that power was not his, not here, not now.

It probed his mouth, parted his jaws, prepared to enter.

And then there was blackness, the scream of someone pushed over a cliff into an incredible gulf, falling and falling away forever, a gigantic voice fading into death.

Virgil stared, saw only the dark, heard the ringing in his ears but no longer felt the scuttler's presence, nor smelled its fetor.

After a moment he heard a sharp rap.

Elaine's voice: "The power's out, Virgil, but come down anyway. I've made a real meal—not insta-serves. We can eat by candlelight."

The windows of all the houses along Arch Street were dark. For a moment it was hard to see anything outside, because the light in the Johnsons' livingroom made their window glare like a mirror. The Johnsons stared at their obsidian reflections, and only slowly did images from the outside begin to seep through as their eyes adjusted.

"Quick," Dad said, "pull the shades."

Ashenwriste was dead, and the power as well. It must have been the Cartel's equivalent of a moment of silence; he thought it might last longer than that, however. Good thing he hadn't gotten around to the nuke just yet. He would need its power.

He tried not to think of the man in cinders outside, but it was impossible. Ashenwriste's death, after all, had given him an advantage. If only there were some way to call the Smiths and make a threat oblique enough to succeed. He had working weapons, it was true, but they still had Nancy and the bomb.

"Dad," said Lyndon, his face pressed to the window between the curtains. "Someone's coming out. It's Mr. Smith. And he's pulling a red wagon."

"Let me see." Dad looked out over Lyndon's head and saw Jock trundling down his front path toward the sidewalk, hauling a wagon behind him. In the wagon was a large cardboard box.

"My God," Dad said. "He's hauling that bomb out to the street."

Of course. He couldn't expect even Jock Smith to set off a nuclear bomb in his living room. He would leave it beyond the perimeter of Arnold's shield, then step back and turn it on before detonation.

He could see the people on the street at last accepting the darkness and moving toward Ashenwriste, or returning to their houses, shambling like sleepwalkers.

"Get away from me," Jock yelled. "I've got a bomb in here."

As one, the crowd stopped, turned, and ran off in every direction. They could have had no idea of the power of the bomb, unless the size of the cardboard box gave it to them.

"Where are you going, Dad?"

He had dropped the curtain and started across the livingroom toward the front door. He paused and looked back at Stephanie, chewing at the inside of his lip. "I think Jock and I had better have this out," he said, and that was all. His hand closed on the doorknob.

"Dad!"

He was not sure who had called, for he closed the door quickly behind himself and stepped from the security of his front porch. He was safe on the path, of course—but not from the bomb, if it should go off. Nothing would be safe from that, except for the tiny oasis of Jock's house.

He strode quickly down the front path, and when he reached the sidewalk tried not to shudder as he stepped onto it. But it was impossible not to show fear, when fear was all he felt.

Unprotected, he stood on the curb and watched Jock Smith toting the wagon toward him. Above Jock, Doris waited in the upstairs window, a candlelit silhouette.

"Here—here's something especially for you," Jock said. Dad couldn't make out his face in the night.

"Is it from you or Doris?" Dad asked. "Or do you even know?"

Jock stopped, looked down at the wagon. "From all of us, to all of you."

"I feel sorry for you, Jock," Dad said. "I never used to, God knows, but I do now. Silly, I once thought there might be something lurking under your wormy surface. You're all hollowed out, aren't you?"

"Talk, talk," Jock said. "Well, here you go, Bill. I'll leave you to it."

He stood back and put his foot on the end of the wagon, and gave it a good push. It clattered over the asphalt, rushing toward the curb and a good jolting finish. Jock ran back to his own yard. Dad caught the wagon easily, gently, and took up its handle.

Then, whistling, he began to walk after Jock, hauling it behind him.

"Dad!" came an urgent whisper. "I'm in here, okay?"

He stopped in the middle of the street and looked down at the box. It shook slightly. He could hear it breathing.

"Nancy?" he said, knowing that it was.

A shout from Smith's house made him look up. On the front lawn, he could see two figures struggling: Jock and Arnold.

"Don't do it, dad," Arnold said. "Gimme that. Come on, dad, give it. You don't know what you're doing."

Dad ran toward them. "Arnold!" he cried.

Jock shouted, two square objects dropping from either hand. Dad stepped onto the lawn, dimly hearing the pounding overhead as Doris beat her fists against the window. He reached Arnold, caught him by the shoulders. The boy was strong, but with the last of his strength he pulled him away and sent him spinning toward the street. How easily he was winded now.

"Stay away, Arnold!" he called.

Jock lay fallen, glaring up, his hands groping toward the things on the grass. They were remote-control boxes, Dad saw now: black cubes with buttons in the centers of their faces. He started to dive toward them, but as he reached out a bright line of fire struck one of his hands, sending a scream of pain through him, causing his belly to burn in sympathy. He looked up and saw Doris holding a battery-op laser. He didn't pause, but grabbed with the other hand and threw himself backward, having claimed only one of the boxes.

Jock sat up, holding the other.

Which was which? Both boxes looked identical.

Dad looked at the street and saw Arnold with his arms around the cardboard box, weeping. No help there.

If Jock knew which box he held, his eyes gave nothing away. But it didn't matter. Either neither button must be punched, or both must be pushed together. Somehow, Dad didn't think there was any time left for talking—not with Doris taking aim again.

Jock's finger twitched. Dad took a chance. Both buttons clicked.

Dad never knew if he'd destroyed himself or saved the others. The shield and the blast were one and the same to him.

The pillar of fire grew, spilling hot light everywhere as it rose higher, first illuminating then piercing the slight layer of high clouds. It was not a gout of flame, not a mushroom, but a column: square-edged, impossibly thin, a sword stabbing heaven. The sound reverberated from the night sky, blasted at the stars. Below, the land lay thrown into relief and all the Christian troops on the hillsides—prostrate and with covered heads—were brightly lit. From this distance it was hard to be certain, but Connie thought that the few soldiers who watched the pillar had their hands clasped in prayer. It had certainly stopped their advance.

She looked over at P.J., his mouth set, eyes watering. Then she got back in the car.

"You still want to go on?" Sweeney asked them.

They did not need to answer that question again. After a minute Sweeney started the car and they went quickly down the dirt road, into trees that hid her view of the troops.

"I can't imagine what happened," Sweeney said.

"Would the Cartel tell you anything?"

He shook his head. "I'm not in a position to ask them."

The white-hot column rose higher as they approached the neighborhood; in twenty minutes, the most advanced of the troops were behind them and the gates of the neighborhood were just ahead. The pillar seemed to be darkening, as though the container that held the fire were scorching on the inside. Sweeney pulled off the road into a gulley and keyed open the entrance to the Cartel's secret tunnel. The car's headlights probed the dark passage as they moved slowly forward.

She had started to ask him a question to take her mind off her claustrophobia, when she saw his face change, brow twisting. She jerked her head around, looking into the path of the car. Several men came rushing toward them without seeing the vehicle; she thought she was imagining things. The car slowed, rolled to a stop, but they came on, eyes wide and blind, like things that had lived all their lives in the dark. One banged into the nose of the car, groped at the hood, then passed around it with the others, as though it were no more than a stone in the center of the passage. A moment later they were gone, running into the darkness behind them, and only then she thought to call out: "Dr. Edison!"

"Clones," P.J. said. "They looked insane. We better hurry."

They came out above the sea, in the fenced-in Cartel power station. The tower of fire lay in shifting interlocked pieces upon the water, and it was also above them, puncturing the sky. It made her dizzy to look up at it.

Connie thought of Bill. Now was not the time. If he had returned to the house, seen the tapes, there would be little enough to say. Still, she thought the children should have a chance to choose between them. She had not yet been able to explain to P.J. why she had left the neighborhood.

Sweeney drove on without trying to draw her out of herself. The streets of home, they found, were full of people staring at the sky, at the tarnishing pillar. It was clear from here that the tower stood on top of Cobblestone Hill. She could not explain why, but she felt it belonged there.

The very base of the pillar was jet black by the time they reached it, and the blackening continued steadily upward. In the undiminished light from above, however, she could see her house, the shades drawn, the light still burning on the porch. There was a red wagon in the middle of the street, the tatters of a cardboard box. While she was staring at these, she heard a voice say, "Mother?"

Nancy came out on the porch with Arnold. "Mom?" Her face brightened with shock. "P.J.!"

In the next moment they all met on the path. Stephanie even brought Junior out to see her, though he wept at the strange glare from above.

She froze, hearing the rumble of the contained fire behind her, and looked back at the pillar. Sweeney had stayed at the car, perhaps fearing the household sentries. The pillar dwarfed him, as it dwarfed everything except the night—and even into that it threw its dwindling brilliance.

"Where's your father?" she asked.

Nancy squeezed her hand. "Mom . . ."

Connie let go of them and looked at the column. Someone had laid a handful of flowers on the street before it. Understanding made her cold, and she wished Sweeney would hold her. She went down to the sidewalk and took his hand, still watching the pillar, then tugged him along to the house.

"I think we should shut down the nuke," he said. "There's no telling if this thing is stable."

She let go of him and pulled her children closer to her. Sweeney went on into the house, brushing past Nancy on her way out with an overnight bag. "I figured we were leaving," she said.

Connie nodded. "Get your things together, all of you."

"What about Virgil?" P.J. said. "Is there room, if he wants to come with us?"

"Virgil and Elaine," Nancy said. "You've been away so long, P.J."

"I think we can squeeze in," said Mom. "Shall we try?"

"Where did Mr. Ashenwriste go?" Nancy asked. "*That* Mr. Ashenwriste, I mean."

"He went—"

They fell silent at the sounds from the garage: a scream, and then a hurried pleading: "No, no, nice baby. Nice baby! *Nice!*"

CRITIC'S CHOICE

The finest in HORROR and OCCULT